NEXUS

NEXUS

VAMPIRE

NEXUS TRILOGY
BOOK ONE

ROSALIE LYNE

INTRODUCTION

Nexus: Vampire is the first in the Nexus trilogy. In Nexus: Vampire Gemma finds herself while trying to adjust to life's many changes and finding a killer bent on ruling the supernatural world.

Gemma Sheard and her brother move in with their aunt, uncle, and two cousins after their parents die. Adjusting to a new place, environment, school, and family, Gemma never gave thought to meeting someone; one she cannot explain her attraction to. Errol Leigh has a dark and mysterious secret, one he hopes to keep, that is, until he sees her in town and then in school. His family's secret is dangerous as they are targets of someone they don't know, who will stop at nothing to get what he came for. He struggles with his desire for her company as well as keeping his secret. The vampire world is not the place for a human, especially now. Will they make it, or will death visit them once again?

CHAPTER I

I never thought a trip away from home could change my life forever.

I watched the scenery go by below me as I looked out the plane's window. My own reflection showed me my lack of enthusiasm in my blue eyes and heart-shaped face. My light brown hair was pulled back into a ponytail for this trip, as I knew I didn't want to deal with the tangles or frizz later. I looked over at my twin brother, Agento, to find that he was passing the time with his laptop and earbuds. His green eyes reflected our mother's, but we both shared our father's light brown hair. Agento kept it short as he is athletic and took on any sport he could back home, which varied from year to year, sometimes every 6 months. He told me once it was because he wanted to stay busy, but I wonder if he just couldn't decide which one he really loved playing the most.

I signed and tapped his shoulder, waiting till he stopped the music and looked at me. "Well, we're almost there."

His look of disgust said it all, and I knew what he was

about to say. "Whatever. I wanted to stay home, but they wouldn't allow it. Sometimes it sucks being a politician's son."

"I don't think Dad's job is why they wouldn't leave us home alone for two weeks. Any parent would react the same way. Any good parent, anyway." I added, as I knew he would say, his best friend's parents wouldn't care, as they had left their son alone for three months last summer.

He just shrugged and went back to his laptop. I looked out the window again, knowing Agento was as upset as I was. I knew our parents didn't have a choice about the change in plans, as I recalled what our parents told us before they left for a business trip. Agento and I are staying with our aunt, uncle, and two cousins in Crestwood, KY, for two weeks while they dealt with an emergency call. I was so nervous about this trip because we hadn't visited our mother's brother and his family in over three years. We used to visit them every year growing up, but something had changed, and neither of us knew why or what had happened. All of the adults stayed closed-minded for years, saying it wasn't our business as children to get involved.

After we landed, we hurried through the airport traffic, meeting Uncle Basil in the baggage claim, who was waiting for us with a smile and open arms. I almost didn't recognize him after all this time. He has the same green eyes as mom and thick, dark brown hair. After a few awkward hugs and greetings, we got our luggage and headed out to the same rustic black Chevrolet pickup that he had had for the last six years. After helping us load our suitcases and backpacks, we all got settled inside the truck and Uncle Basil gently pulled away from the airport.

Sitting in the backseat, I watched as the Louisville airport faded and we shortly entered Crestwood, a small, quiet, greenery town. It was a quiet twenty-five-minute drive as nobody knew what to say or how to say it. My nerves stuck with me as I thought about how much my life could change in the next two weeks. As Uncle Basil started down their long graveled driveway, I watched the passing trees and perfectly cut grass while silently giving myself a pep talk about surviving these weeks.

I sat forward in my seat as the house came into view. It was a two-story, white house with blue trimmings and had a wrap-around porch. They have an old swing on the right side of the house, and I recalled how they have a huge yard behind the house; I wonder what is back there now. Aunt Aida was waiting for us on the porch with her shoulder-length black hair blowing in the slight breeze as Uncle Basil parked the truck near the porch, and we all got out.

"I'm so happy you all came. It's been so long. You grew up so much," she said as she hugged me and turned to Agento. "You've gotten so tall."

"That's what happens in three years." The anger was not hidden in his voice as he returned her hug and stepped back to get his bags from the pickup bed.

"Yes, and I wish it wasn't so long." We walked onto the porch and headed inside. The hallway was small, but each room surrounding it looked huge, and the staircase matched the outside, white stairs with blue railings. "Cinnia and Adacio were cleaning out the guest rooms for your stay. They haven't been used since your last visit."

"We are more than happy you two came," Uncle Basil said as he brought in our suitcases.

I smiled and spoke before Agento could say anything. I wanted to keep the peace. "So are we. We were wondering what happened all those years ago?" I hinted, hoping enough time had passed for someone to say something. After all, we were no longer children; we were almost eighteen.

But Uncle Basil just smiled, not taking the bait. "Yes, but that's a story for your mother to explain. It's not my place to interfere with my sister's business."

"Cinnia, Adacio," Aunt Aida called up the stairs, "Agento and Gemma are here. Come down and say hello."

We looked up as we heard footsteps running toward the stairs. They must be excited about us coming. Cinnia and I were close when we were younger, but I didn't think she would be happy about sharing her home with someone she hadn't talked to in years. We watched as Cinnia pushed Adacio aside and beat him to the stairs. Watching her come down the stairs with her wavy brown hair flying behind her brought up my nerves again, as I wasn't sure how to act around her anymore. I remember how she would always braid her hair before leaving her room each morning, just to keep it tamed. Adacio and Cinnia shared Aunt Aida's blue eyes, but only Adacio had his mother's black hair, a little wavy but kept short.

"I just finished setting up the guest room for you," Cinnia said as she made her way down.

I smiled, unsure of what to say. "Thanks."

"It's no problem, really. We can go check it out now if you want." The hesitation showed for a second in her blue eyes, making me realize how she feels the same way as I do. The only difference is that she was trying to be excited by our arrival. I noticed Agento and Adacio talking quietly among themselves; if he can do it, then I can too.

"That would be great. Then afterwards we can tour the

town. I don't remember much, and I'm sure it has changed since we've been here."

At that, Aunt Aida stepped in. "In fact, why don't you all go upstairs and get settled? Basil and I will put together a picnic. We have a great park in town where we can eat."

We all nodded and headed upstairs. Cinnia showed me my room, right next to hers on the right side of the stairs, fixed with some basic furniture set up neatly and ready to use. I could feel the rustic vibe as I remembered nothing had changed in this room since my last visit, except the purple blanket and pillows on the twin bed. As we set down my two suitcases and backpack near the bed, I thought about what to say.

"It's been a while. I hope our arrival doesn't interfere with any of your plans. It was sudden."

Cinnia smiled and shook her head as she sat down on the bed next to me, ready to help me unpack. "I'm glad you're here. We used to be close, and while I don't know what happened any more than you, I hope we can be friends again."

I smiled as I relaxed. "I would love that."

"Come on and let's unpack. We have much we can talk about and catch up on as we go." She jumped up and grabbed my nearest suitcase, and as she opened it, she continued, "Like, do you have a boyfriend?"

I laughed as I started on my backpack at the desk next to a purple-trimmed window. "No. It's difficult to try with a politician for a father. What about you?"

"No. I haven't found anyone that stands out at school this year, but I am hoping to before graduation in four months."

I caught up with Cinnia as we worked on organizing my clothing, toiletries, laptop, and art supplies, which I packed for something to do in my downtime. As we walked downstairs,

Cinnia explained the newly decorated house set up before we headed out the front door to meet the others. They have two female cats named Zingiber and Media Nox, and added an extra room just for them off the kitchen and behind the staircase.

We all loaded into the pickup soon after and headed into town for the picnic Aunt Aida had made for us. There was scenery all around us, making Crestwood a peaceful town, with a railroad track splitting down the middle of town all the way through. Maples Park was nearly empty as there was still a chill in the air from the snow just melting last month. They have an indoor pool with a playground on the side and separate from the picnic area, facing the road. We set up under the big maple tree next to the parking lot and unpacked the two baskets.

"Wow, this all looks and smells great. Thanks, Aunt Aida."

She looked up and smiled. "It was my pleasure. I love picnics, and this winter is finally over."

"Not much of a winter."

"No, but more than what you got, I'm sure."

I smiled and sat back with my plate full. I watched the cars drive by and listened to my family with their idle conversations about school, work, and activities planned for our visit while I ate next to Agento and Cinnia. Uncle Basil owned an auto shop, one we passed on the way here, and Aunt Aida is currently a stay-at-home mother. Adacio worked for his father and was looking to find an apartment this summer, while Cinnia was a senior like Agento and I, with only a few months apart in our births. We talked about the town, the history behind it, and the attractions we would visit over these next two weeks. As soon as we finished eating, I sat with Cinnia looking through the different books she planned on reading on kindle while the guys threw a football back and forth. Uncle Basil and Aunt Aida stood aside, watching the peaceful scene before them and reminiscing about the time they had missed out on.

After returning to the house, Agento and I went straight to our rooms to relax after a long day of touring the town. I sat down at my desk, opening my laptop to set up the Wi-Fi password and update my status on Facebook. Staying connected with my friends back home for the next two weeks would be complicated, as we were in different time zones, but not impossible. Before I could express my anxiety fully to my best friends about this place, I heard my name called for dinner. I signed off and closed my laptop, hopefully my friends would still be free to talk after dinner.

Given how Agento was on the plane, I was surprised to see how easy it seemed for him to adapt with Adacio like old buds. Dinner was steak, potatoes, and green beans; simple but more basic than I was used to back home. It was rare for my mother to cook a full meal by herself. She would normally say she was too busy with her life, and we would order take-out or eat at our friends' houses.

"How is your room?" I looked up from my seat and saw Aunt Aida looking at me.

I smiled, "It's great. I set up my laptop and messaged my friends back home."

"I know it's tough, being away from what you know, but we do hope you and Agento like it here."

"I'm sure we will. We always did on our yearly visits."

"South Oldham High is a great school and only ten minutes from us. Cinnia loves going there, and while we wait for her to get home, we can visit a lot of places. I can guarantee it won't be a lonely, boring visit." With a pointed look at her children, they quietly spoke in agreement and nodded as they filled their mouths with dinner.

I smiled and ate my own dinner. Dinner was quiet after that as nobody knew what to say. They knew we did not want to be here, but they were trying. "I'm sure we will have a great time here. Maybe this summer we can visit again for a longer time with our parents."

"I doubt mom and dad will agree to it." Agento murmured under his breath.

I shot him a dark look as I responded. "We can try. They let us come here now."

He was quick to return my look. "Because they didn't want to leave us home alone. Not because they had a change of heart." We looked around and noticed the tense, quiet atmosphere around us. I knew arguing was a moot point, but I wanted them to know we appreciated their efforts, even if it was in vain with our parents.

To put everyone's mind at ease, I kept quiet and stood up as I finished my dinner to take my plate to the sink. We all sat down in the living room after dinner and watched a movie, picked by Agento. I only made it halfway through the movie before I started falling asleep and stood up to go to bed, excusing myself. I slept like the dead, beyond exhausted from the time difference, environment, and all the new discoveries I was about to have.

I got up just after 8 am and headed downstairs for a quick breakfast of fruit before taking it outside to eat on the swing. The fresh air surrounded me and helped my nerves as I focused on breathing in the new day. The gravel driveway made a loop in front of the porch and connected to the two-car garage. The birds were chirping, and I watched as some birds hunted for food. Aunt Aida had one bird feeder, but it was crowded, and there was one bird bath that no bird was interested in. The grass was freshly cut, and the air smelled as fresh as spring could be. Trees were lining up down the driveway, making the house sit hidden from the road. I started wondering what we would do around town this week. Maybe Aunt Aida could get another bird feeder, and I can help her plant it.

"The sleeping beauty wakes." I heard as I sat down my empty bowl on the railing. I looked up and saw Cinnia sitting down next to me, wearing jogging pants and a long-sleeved tight-fitting shirt.

"Where did you go?"

She smiled and pointed at the back of the house. "We have an indoor gym behind the house. I got up two hours ago."

"What did you guys add on?"

She laughed and stood up to finish stretching her muscles. "Besides the gym and the room for Zingiber and Media Nox, umm," she paused as she thought about it. "We put in a fence around the backyard for a complete game setup, and we cleaned out the attic to turn it into an office space. Mom wanted to do an online job so she could stay at home, but she is still debating what she wants to work with the most. She has a few ideas and can't decide."

"Wow. What games do you have set up? Agento will love that. He's very athletic."

"We have a variety of goals, nets, balls, targets, bows and arrows, so we can play whatever we feel like. Just no guns, as Mom and Dad agreed, is too dangerous." Seeing my look of confusion and understanding why, she added, "The bows and arrows are plastic, not real metal. Dad and Mom keep adding more as new outdoor games come to their notice."

"We should go play. We can get Agento and Adacio to play something as well and beat them."

"I love that idea. Let me go change and get them."

The backyard was just over six acres with an indoor gym and all fenced in around the building, behind it, and connecting to the house itself. It was set up for every game you could possibly imagine. The day passed with Cinnia and me playing a variety of games against Adacio and Agento. There were wins and losses, and a lot of cursing and rough housing, but not one complaint as to this day being boring. We picked names from a basket every four rounds as to who would pick the next game or, if they chose, to continue the same game to beat the others in round two. Aunt Aida made us pause the games long enough to eat lunch, sandwiches and chips, before quietly sitting down and watching us play some more. She sat in the shade, knitting and keeping us honest and respectful of each other as the afternoon passed.

After Uncle Basil got home from work, he and Aunt Aida joined in, and we played well past dinner. It got dark out before anybody noticed the time or how hungry we were. We all picked up everything as Aunt Aida headed in to start dinner. Dinner was a lot better tonight as we all laughed and talked about the games we played today and how some were cheated until Aunt Aida caught them. I even watched the whole movie that Cinnia had picked. It was when I headed for bed that I realized I forgot to message my friends all day. I sent a reminder on my phone for the morning, to apologize for missing them, and to catch up with them before doing anything else tomorrow.

CHAPTER II

My first week in Crestwood passed with Aunt Aida and me walking around town, visiting the market, stores, and other attractions. The town's main attractions were all within walking distance, so every day Aunt Aida would drive us into town and we would walk until our feet started hurting. I helped Aunt Aida pick out a bird feeder and planted it, much to the birds' delight. I would watch them every morning as I sat on the swing, drank my tea, and ate a quick breakfast: my new morning routine.

My friends were excited about the new pictures I sent them and returned with their own pictures of things I missed back home. The people around town were nice and respectful, unlike Avalon. Keeping in touch with my friends was best done around dinner time every night. Saving the photos they sent me, I reminisced on the things I missed and felt more left out than ever before. I knew I would experience it when I returned home, but not seeing it the first time with your best friends, it loses something. The next few months were our last together before we separated for college or to travel the world. I didn't like missing out on anything, knowing how little time we had left before we went our own ways.

Agento was more than happy to help Uncle Basil in the shop rather than to go shopping with us. He stayed to himself most of the time, outside of the auto shop and family time. I missed just having alone time with him. Our parents were so busy that Agento and I were all we had for each other. There was no sibling rivalry as we knew it was pointless to try to get attention from either parent, let alone both.

I felt closer to Cinnia, much like when we were kids. As the week passed, we talked about our day every day before bed and after movie time with everyone. Adacio and I had yet to form a bond, but it's not easy, as we have nothing in common with each other. I knew he would be there if I ever needed him, but I don't see us hanging out in the same crowd in our near future as cousins. Maybe down the road, far down the road.

Our first day to hang out as a family, no school keeping Cinnia or work keeping Uncle Basil and Adacio, we all headed out right after breakfast to the LaGrange Railroad Museum. The museum was crowded on Saturday morning, but that didn't stop me from enjoying every minute of it. The three exhibits were amazing, and they had a lot of history. We stayed together as a family and got matching outfits to wear from the gift shop at the beginning of our tour. Agento and Adacio agreed only to wear the shirts for the morning, and we boarded two out of three of the trains by lunchtime. We sat down, ate a picnic lunch, and changed back into our mismatching outfits before continuing on our tour. There was so much history and videos we watched; I was exhausted by the last stop we made as a group.

The railroad splitting the town was impressive, and we all went our separate ways midafternoon. I was just turning away from the 1908 train log when I felt a chill run down my back. I turned to see someone in the shadows, apart from everyone, hidden and going unnoticed by all, just watching people go by. My breath slowed as I took in his short curly brown hair. I wanted to touch his hair, just to see if it felt as smooth as it looked. He was tall, muscular, and wore the most expensive designer outfit I have ever seen anyone here ever wear. In a white collared button-up, black jacket, and black trousers, you figured everyone would notice him, but he seemed to melt into the shadows as people walked by. That is, except me. I can't recall ever feeling this connection with anyone. I was hoping he wasn't a worker. I recalled feeling something similar in my first week here, but I dismissed it. Whenever I walked around town, I would feel like someone was there, but I never noticed anyone, that is, until now. I glanced slightly up and saw him looking right at me. I was instantly lost in his hazel eyes as I tried to remember how to breathe. Did someone turn on the heat? Why was he looking at me so intensely? Who was he?

"Gemma, oh, Gemma." I broke eye contact when Cinnia finally shook me, realizing I wasn't answering her. "Hey, are you okay?"

I looked down at my arm as she held onto me, like she was afraid I would fall if she didn't. I smiled, "I'm okay. What is it you asked?"

She shook her head as she released my arm. "Just trying to get your attention. We are getting ready to leave. I was sent to find you. Who are you looking at?"

"That guy over there…" but as I turned and pointed, I saw he was gone. "Umm, he was there, hiding in the corner."

Cinnia looked to where I pointed, but saw nobody. Was he my imagination? Surely, not. "I don't see anybody."

"Nobody seemed to. I guess that's what held my attention."

"Was he hot?"

I recalled the intensity of his stare, the posture in which he stood, and his curly brown hair, which I still hoped to touch sometime. I signed and finally answered yes to her.

"Maybe you will see him again. Let's go find my parents." As we headed out of the room, I glanced back again, hoping to see him somewhere in the room. Nothing, it was as if he didn't exist. Why was he hiding in the shadows? Has it been him around town that I felt and never noticed before now? I silently promised to pay more attention from now on. There was something about him, I don't know what, but I want to find out.

Cinnia and I hurried through the crowd, searching for any or all of our family members. We soon found everyone standing by the exit, waiting for us, and we hurried over. We headed out and stopped at the market for dinner. Uncle Basil and Aunt Aida went in alone and got pizza and fries, as it was quick and Aunt Aida was too tired to cook. As we sat in the car, I noticed just how tired everyone was. Nobody talked, even Cinnia, as we all relaxed and played on our phones.

Once we got home, I hit my friends up, waiting for dinner to cook. They loved the train pictures and the knowledge I could recall from today. I didn't tell them about the strange guy or the weird feeling I got just thinking about him. What could they do? In a week, I would be returning home, and this guy would disappear from my mind forever.

As dinner finished, we spent a quiet night watching whatever show was already on. Nobody was in the mood to fight and choose whose pick it was, so soon into the show, we slowly parted and went to bed.

Sunday and Monday were more laid back as we were all still exhausted from Saturday. Aunt Aida cleaned the house while Uncle Basil and Adacio went to work, bringing Agento with him for extra help. Cinnia and I exercised, played games, and hung out in her room until dinner on Sunday and Monday afternoon.

On Tuesday morning, I got up early to watch TV before everyone else woke up. I wasn't sure what made me wake up early, but I knew the best way to fall back asleep was to channel surf. The boredom worked every time with me. I never would have done this if I had known just how my life was about to change. Sitting down in the armchair with my feet up, I decided to watch the news as it seemed like a good way to fall back asleep. I found all the news channels were centered on the same story: a politician and his wife's death in a car accident. I sat forward, my feet hitting the floor, when I saw the pictures, knowing my parents were gone forever.

I ran to the stairs and yelled as loud as I could, not caring who I woke up, "Agento. Come quickly. Agento. Hurry." My yelling woke the whole house up as they all came running down. Concerned about my panicking yelling. I ran right into my brother's arms, sobbing as I explained, "Car accident… our parents are gone, Agento."

He gasped as he pushed through everyone with me in tow, clinging to him, to see as the news channels continued. We all watched in stunned silence until the story ended and Uncle Basil shut off the TV, unsure of what to do next. I don't know who moved first or what was happening until Agento led me to the couch. Cinnia sat with me to comfort as Agento paced the room, hiding his deeper feelings, knowing that life would forever be different, and he couldn't stop it.

Aunt Aida made the arrangements, and we left Kentucky the next day. We had people to call, a funeral to plan, and we had the media hounding us when we got back home in Avalon, California. Aunt Aida got Cinnia out of school for the week, and Uncle Basil got his manager to cover for him and Adacio at the shop.

The funeral was grand and everybody was there; in fact, it lasted all day because some people could only come to it at specific times. The reception was held the next day to ensure people got to express their grief, support, and love with the children and their family. I never knew what was happening around me; I just went with it.

My own memories flooded me, and I knew they would continue to haunt me as I wondered about having a better relationship with my father, as he was always there but always busy with the government, leaving no more time for family nights. He has grown a distance between us and himself in the last four years. My mother was there, but she never focused on us. Her life was more important to her than her children were as we got older. My parents were great, and we did have our moments, but in the last few years, I've wondered if we could turn back time. Especially now, as I wish they hadn't left our home to go on that business trip in San Francisco. Now we had to deal with our parents' death, moving in with Uncle Basil and Aunt Aida for good, and finishing school in Crestwood, KY. Life would never be the same again.

Aunt Aida and Uncle Basil were there for us all week, helping and supporting us in any way they could. The funeral ended up being the relief we needed before leaving Avalon for good. The media was a nightmare, and one that Agento and I were glad to leave behind. All of the food people left behind was packed up and given to food donation charities. Packing everything in the house was daunting and took most of the week. I barely got to grief in Avalon as I stayed busy helping Aunt Aida pack and store everything for future donations and auctions to come. Agento and I had decided to leave everything behind to give away, sell at auction, or trash as we couldn't deal with the pain that came with our parents' stuff, or our own. Material things meant nothing to us without our parents there. We wanted to start over with our lives, so we left it all behind and went back to Crestwood with our family that weekend.

Agento and I now had a new life to adjust to with our family in Crestwood. We took that week off school as we arranged our transcripts, schedules, and grieved in silence. We just didn't, and couldn't, talk to anyone other than each other. Agento and I talked about what to do, how to live here, and what happens with school, but never about the death of our parents. I do not think we'll ever be ready to talk about them.

Within the following two weeks, Agento found a part-time job working at the only phone store in town, Verizon. Agento had fewer classes than I did as he had fewer electives, which opened more time for the job after classes and still kept his weekends free to help Uncle Basil whenever he was needed. It helped that in these two weeks, we spent as much time together as possible, helping each other through this difficult change.

School had been a struggle for me, as everyone knew why I was suddenly there, with three months left until graduation. I was still struggling in these two weeks to adjust to my new classes and making new friends. I spent my first week learning the school system and my classes. I had two classes with

Cinnia, but that still left me with four without her. I was happy to follow her to our first class each day. I did manage to find someone in my other classes to help me, and everyone seemed nice here, so my nerves passed after that first nerve-racking day. I did my best to understand the town, community, and school system, but I missed home so much; Kentucky was so different from California, and my friends back home had started to ignore my attempts to stay in touch. By the end of the second week of school, I cut them out of my life completely, as they had ignored all attempts from me. That part of my life seemed to be completely over.

"Gemma, Agento, could you come down here, please?" Aunt Aida called us one night as we were getting ready for bed.

"Be right there." I called as I headed out of the room and found Agento there already, sitting with Aunt Aida and Uncle Basil in the living room.

As I sat down next to Agento, Aunt Aida continued, "We understand how difficult this has been for you right now, and we are here for you for whatever you need. We feel like it is past time to tell you this, even though we promised your mother not to. What happened three years ago was a grim time for everyone. We cannot keep this secret from you anymore."

"I want you both to promise to let me finish before you start asking questions." At our nod, Uncle Basil continued, "My sister, your mother, had a miscarriage three years ago." We gasped but stayed silent in order for our uncle to continue. "Your grandparents fought with her nonstop, and she left. Feeling I was in support of them, she would not talk to me either. She did not wait to hear from me, even though I wasn't home at the time. They made her believe I agreed with them, which was enough for her. When she had miscarried, I tried to reach out to her about my non-involvement, but she would not hear me out. I did not even find out about it until months later, when I returned home from completing my business degree for the auto shop." They sat in silence for a few minutes, letting us digest the news.

"Why didn't she say anything?" Agento asked.

"She was hurting. She felt abandoned, and I could not get through to her. I figured once we two were old enough, then she would tell you. I had hoped she would talk to me when she was ready, so I didn't push, and I let the years go by. I should have pushed her to talk to me."

"Why did our grandparents fight with her?" I asked.

He shrugged as he looked at me, "I have no idea. I was so busy starting my own business that I did not ask much at the time. I was too mad at them to talk to them myself. They had used me to push her away. Our parents were set in their own ways, so it could have been any number of reasons. We all just let our anger get the better of us."

After sitting and giving us a few minutes in silence, Aunt Aida spoke up, "The reason I asked Basil to tell you two is because of what we got today. We wanted the air cleared between us and to start fresh with you two going forward." She stood up and grabbed a large shoebox and a smaller jewelry box from the opposite side of her chair. Handing them to us, she continued, "Agento and Gemma, the large box is for everyone, but something we hope will help you the most."

I let Agento open it and saw it was the two small cremation boxes we thought we left behind in our heist to leave. Aunt Aida must have brought them without us knowing. "Thank you. We thought we forgot them. Where should we put them?"

"Wherever you two would like."

Agento looked at me, and I nodded my agreement. "We think in here would be great."

"That would be wonderful. We will find a space by the television on the wall for all to see your parents."

Next, I opened the small box, surprised by the sterling silver heart-shaped locket inside. "I found these two great pictures of your parents and had them put in it before we left Avalon." Aunt Aida explained as I opened it and looked at how happy my parents were. "The one on the left side was taken when your parents found out about being pregnant with Agento, while the one on the right was the discovery of you, Gemma." Aunt Aida sat next to me as she explained. The tears fall before I can stop them.

"This is wonderful. Thank you."

Uncle Basil pulled out our father's favorite Cartier Ballon Bleu wrist watch, black strap with diamonds circling the Roman numeral dial, and turned to Agento before holding it out. "I know your father would have wanted you to have this. As their will had said, you two decide what to do with everything, and this is the only item you two decided not to sell to charities or auction."

Agento had reached for it, and Uncle Basil handed it over without hesitation. "I actually forgot about this watch. Thank you, Uncle. It means a lot to me."

"We love the gifts. Thank you both." After hugs and kisses, we left them and headed upstairs to our rooms. Feeling some weight had lifted, I slept easier than I have in a long time that night.

CHAPTER III

I never took the locket off as I felt closer to my parents than when they were alive and with us.

As Cinnia and I walked around town that weekend, I became more aware of my surroundings. A few times, whenever we stopped somewhere, I felt eyes on the back of my neck and a chill running down my spine. After about the third time it happened, I started feeling paranoid. Nobody was there whenever I would look around, but it certainly felt like there was someone watching us. Was it that guy from the train messing with me? Was he following me around town, and why? Or was I going crazy thinking about him so much?

"The Botanical Gardens are beautiful. We should go sometime." Cinnia said, pulling me from my search.

"That sounds great. Maybe your mother will want to go as well. When do they open?"

"Mom loves going, but only once through the different seasons. They are always open, unless the weather is really bad, which is rare. Their hours are 8-4 every day."

I smiled at Cinnia. "That's even better. When did you want to go?"

She shook her head as we continued walking past the entrance. "We have another month. Mom goes a month into the season so she can see the perfect blooms of the specific flowers that grow for the season."

"That sounds good. We will go with your mom next month. Most likely after we graduate." I hinted and stopped when I thought I saw something from the corner of my eye, and felt someone staring again. We had just turned around to head back to the house, and I glanced behind me, just a quick glance, just to make sure, but saw only a shadow, then nothing. It had looked like a shadow, but where was it now? Shadows don't disappear that quickly. This feeling made me think about that guy at the museum again. Maybe I was seeing things. Maybe I just wanted a little mystery to happen in this quiet town. I shrugged it off and walked home with Cinnia before she noticed my hesitation. I started thinking about school tomorrow to distract me, and how I plan on making the most of it.

I invited my new friends to join me as I sat with my brother and cousin to eat lunch at school. As I tried to figure out what today's lunch was, I compared schedules with Medea and Christabel. Medea shared the second and sixth periods with me and became friends when we shared the history book during the second period this morning, as she forgot hers. Christabel shared the third period, and we started talking when Mr. Tacio paired us for a computer project.

South Oldham High School, home of the dragons, was one of three schools built as a big community within Crestwood. I finally adjusted to this school and started getting comfortable. The elementary and middle school share the space with the high school, but with separate buildings. It was crowded as the schools, middle and high, got out at the same time, but there was a roundabout at the entrance, and we moved along pretty quickly.

At the entrance of the high school sits the Veterans Memorial Park. This holds monuments that represent all the different wars in which people in this community have fought and died. As Uncle Basil drove past it each morning, the monuments, benches, statues, and gazebo, as well as the beautiful walk path of regular and red-tinted cement with the years of U.S. military personnel embedded in the cement blocks, always drew my attention.

Oldham County has a lot of history in this small town and much to appreciate. People here are like a big family. Not at all like Avalon. This week passed with my newfound appreciation of history in this town and through the schools.

I spent time with my friends learning and exploring all it offers as we all walked around town that weekend to the market, the park, and other attractions. Medea has six siblings, so she loved getting out of her house. Christabel normally only leaves home for church, so she loved the change and escape from her parents' watchful eye.

This Saturday was full of fun for everyone as we got to know each other outside of school. I still miss my parents and home at times, but my new friends have already been there for me more than my old ones, making this move all the more bearable.

We all joined Christabel at her church on Sunday. St. James Episcopal Church was history itself, built in 1869 with its stone walls, red doors, preschool on the right side, and the eerie feeling of old: a historical church. Church wasn't normally my thing, but I loved art, and this building was architecture in the making.

I was excited to go to school on Monday. It was a rainy day, and one I enjoyed spending indoors at school. I sat down next to Cinnia, waiting for Mr. Peck to start class. American History passed with Medea and me passing notes behind Mr. Woodward's back. Christabel and I finished our project and turned it in with Mr. Tacio while some other students begged for an extension. And I actually got to English class early. I soon realized my nerves were suddenly on fire as I took in the only other person to arrive early. I gasped and lowered my head.

It was him, the guy I saw in the shadows at the train station, the shadow nobody seemed to notice, and quite possibly the same shadow I thought I saw that day in town. On occasion, my nerves would tense up throughout town, but I pushed it off and soon ignored it. I never actually saw him, so I thought I was going crazy, but I felt the same intensity now that I felt since that first time. He must be new, as I have never seen him before in school. He did not seem to notice me in the slightest as I sat down in my normal seat and looked away, watching as other students and Miss Thurlow finally arrived. I tried my best to ignore him as he ignored me.

He became an obsession for me by the end of English. English was my only class with him, as I looked in my other classes but never saw him again. He would sit with others at lunch, distanced from most students. They quickly became school gossip as they stayed to themselves, dressed in high-end clothing, and only sat there, talking among themselves, and not actually eating lunch. There were five in total, all with this intense aura around them, no student approached them, and the teachers respected their boundaries.

In the next few days, I learned he and his family were new to the town. They were rich, stood out, kept to themselves, and the intensity I felt that first day seemed to stay. I could always feel his eyes on me when he looked my way, and without consciously understanding it, I watched him as well. Everyone talked about the Leigh family, but nobody could get inside their circle to learn more about them. A classmate found out that our favorite secretary in the office was actually this family's aunt.

On Friday, Miss Thurlow went on and on about this weekend's assignment, an essay I needed to do great on in order to get my grade back up. I soon realized how little I heard. I took my compact mirror out of my backpack to stare at Errol Leigh, three rows behind me and to my left. I first focused on my own reflection before moving the mirror to see him. I was so transfixed with watching him as he wrote down the assignment that I did not even hear the bell ring or that the class was leaving until he stood up himself.

"Gemma, I would like a word with you," Miss Thurlow called to me as students rushed past. When a sign, I waited until most of the students were out of the way before making my way to her desk. I stood at her desk as the last of the students left.

Miss Thurlow set her reading glasses on top of her pixie brown hairstyle and stared at me with her brown eyes. "I'm wondering if the work is becoming too hard for you or if you just don't care to pay attention…"

I cut in, "It is not either of those things. I love English as well as my other classes. I know I need to pay more attention."

"So, do you think you can blow off your classes? I know

you are going through a tough time right now, but this material is essential in passing my class and graduating in a month. There is no makeup work this late in the year, and you need to get your grades up and fast in order to pass."

I knew that unless I wanted to confess to the truth, that's how Miss Thurlow would see my lack of attention. "I promise to try harder."

She stood up, "That is all I can ask for. Just try harder. And I am sorry for your loss."

I nodded and left the classroom only to rush to lunch to meet my family and friends. After dropping off my books at my locker, I took a corner too fast and ran into someone near the cafeteria. When I looked up to apologize, I saw it was Errol. He simply stared and seemed undisturbed as I regained my balance and stepped back.

"I'm s-sorry," I stammered before taking a breath and trying again. "I was walking too fast. Are you okay?"

He just nodded, "I understand. Lunch is an important part of school."

I hesitated; did he make a joke? Unsure, I agreed, "Yes, well. See you around sometime." I hesitated as I walked around him, unsure if it was a question or a statement. He seemed to acknowledge he heard me, but did not reply as he walked around me.

One last glance behind me, I realized he was walking in the opposite direction from the cafeteria. I thought that was weird, shouldn't he want to eat? Remembering how late I was, I hurried and got in the short line for food. The food here paled in comparison to Avalon, where everything was cooked fresh. Back in Avalon, I would get lasagna most days; here I ate mashed potatoes, meatloaf, and green beans. With my food paid for, I found Agento sitting with Cinnia and some of our friends at our usual green with gray-trimmed table and matching chairs. I could not concentrate on the conversation at hand as I ate my lunch. Errol has always been on my mind lately, and talking to him didn't change that one bit; it only made it worse. What was it about his family? Where were they if not here, eating lunch?

I got the English assignment from Cinnia over the weekend and finished my essay on Sunday afternoon; I know, last minute, but I needed the time to recharge and focus on my paper so I could write my best one yet. I was determined not to have a repeat with Miss Thurlow or any other teachers. By the time I went to bed, I was feeling great about myself and my classes, and I was ready to achieve anything thrown my way by Monday morning.

This week I paid more attention in classes, enough that no teacher said anything. I normally do great in school, but the Leigh family was never far from my mind, especially Errol in English. Some days, the family sat in the cafeteria, but most of this week they did not enter at all. I wondered where they went during lunch and why, when they were here, they just sat there watching everyone from a distance. Unlike last week, I even noticed Errol watching me more, which made it difficult for me to ignore him completely. It is like my body was on high alert every time he looked my way, but I kept my grades going up and felt more settled in than ever before. I became the best of friends with Medea and Christabel. We had a sleepover planned on Friday night.

Cinnia and I went to the mall on Saturday afternoon after Medea and Christabel left. I was dying for new clothes, for a fresh look in this town. Aunt Aida agreed to drive us and pick us up in three hours, after she finished all her errands. Cinnia and I's idle talk came to a stop when I realized I had said too much about the Leigh family, particularly Errol. Cinnia would not stop grilling me until she was satisfied with all the information about my secret crush as we walked the mall and shopped. We spent over an hour talking about Errol while we ate Chick-fil-A for an early dinner; we split our deluxe chicken sandwich and grilled nuggets with waffle fries and two medium sweet teas.

We were in our last store, H&M, when I noticed Clarebelle and Garcia strolling toward us, Errol's sisters. I have noticed a lot about this family in the last two weeks from a distance, like how they never eat at school, they don't talk to anyone, they are obviously rich, and they have great manners towards adults, but distance themselves from everyone. The weirdest thing I noticed was how they watched everyone as if they suspected that person might be dangerous. All five of them, not just Errol.

Cinnia leaned toward me and whispered, "They are coming over." I just nodded and looked through a rack of shirts, hoping for one more new outfit before we left, making a full week's worth of clothes. I watched out of the corner of my eye as they stopped in front of us, instead of walking by like I thought they would.

"Gemma, right?" I looked over to see that it was Clarebelle who spoke.

"Yes." I was just as stunned as Cinnia. I knew Clarebelle and Garcia only from the gossip at school, but nobody, no students that is, talked to them or expected a response back.

Clarebelle had pulled her long, wavy, brown hair back into a ponytail, while Garcia left her black hair down, which just passed her shoulders by a few inches. They are both stunning young ladies that anybody would envy. Up close, I could see the highlights in Clarebelle's hair, there but barely noticeable. I could not think of any reason for this sudden change in behavior, in which they stopped talking to us, of all people.

Garcia stepped closer and moved a strand of hair back from her face. "Hi, I'm Garcia, and this is Clarebelle." After we nodded in greeting, she continued, "We are having a dinner party, just a small one, and thought you would like to come. So, would you? It is at our place tomorrow night."

Wait, what? I was too stunned to answer, so Cinnia responded, "Would she ever? Could I come too?"

"I'm sure that would be fine."

I pulled Cinnia back and finally spoke up, wondering about this sudden change in attitude. Was it safe? We did not know them, and why now? "Why are you inviting us over? You have never talked to us before."

Clarebelle stepped forward, making me uneasy with her blank expression. "Well, we have seen how you and Errol have been watching each other these last two weeks," she whispered, "a lot," and spoke louder as if we did not hear her. My face started getting hot. "We are inviting you because we want our brother to be happy. We think you two would be great together."

I stared at them in silence, and I hoped they didn't notice how red my face was. This didn't stop Cinnia from accepting on my behalf, however. Just how much did they notice? I did not have any classes with them and only one with Errol. They must be paying more attention than I thought. Cinnia got directions to their place, and we waved goodbye as they walked away.

"I cannot wait. Tomorrow night will be memorable if not fun."

"Cinnia, only you could think that. There is something weird about that family. I'm not sure we should go."

She shrugged. "Weird is hot. It is mysterious and sexy. Our popularity will be skyrocketing after tomorrow night once this gets out. And you know you want to go."

CHAPTER IV

Cinnia could not stop talking about how lucky we were, the only people known to talk to the Leigh family, let alone get invited into their home for dinner. I was trying not to feel embarrassed as I recalled the attention I had, apparently, caused by looking at Errol so much.

On the whole way home, she quieted down, only because she didn't want her mom to hear us. We talked as we went through our new outfits, folding and hanging. We started in my room, then I helped her with her bags. She seemed unaware of how little I responded to her. I was lost in my own mind, wondering if I should have said no or if this was the start of something great, like Cinnia thinks it is.

Sunday morning, Agento and Adacio helped Uncle Basil at the shop, and Cinnia and I helped Aunt Aida clean the house. My mind wandered, and I tried to quiet it but couldn't. Once cleaning was done, we left Aunt Aida to play with Zingiber and Media Nox under the stairs. They were hyper cats, only two years old. Zingiber was a ginger color, after her name, while

Media Nox was pure black, except for a white spot circling her right eye.

When the guys got home, Agento and Adacio took showers and went out with friends. Uncle Basil and Aunt Aida hung outside while I hid in my room, uncertain what was to come.

The afternoon soon came, and Cinnia and I took turns showering and getting ready for our dinner with the Leigh family. As we applied our makeup, I recalled how much we have bonded as sisters over the past month, and I know I can count on her for anything, even against Leigh's family if there's a problem tonight. I don't know why I thought having someone with me should be comfortable when I didn't believe I had anything to fear, but caution was good to have when dealing with anybody nobody in town knew about. I will say I was curious to see how Errol and I would hit it off tonight. I now knew from his sisters' that he was paying as much attention to me as I was to him.

"They sure do like their privacy," Uncle Basil commented after we had a 10-minute drive through the forest outside of town before reaching the mansion-sized, black house with an eight-car garage on the right side.

I admired the house as I compared it to my childhood home back in California. It was the same Victorian style with modern-day windows installed, but while our own place was in the open and white, the loneliness felt the same. My parents were great, and I knew I could count on them, but, to be honest, they were self-centered and only bothered us when it helped them in some way. Aunt Aida and Uncle Basil have already proved to be better than my parents at parenting, but I would always miss my parents, no matter how they were. I knew they were trying to be there, and that's what counted.

Uncle Basil promised to pick us up in two hours, reminding us of school tomorrow, before pulling away after we reached the porch and knocked.

We were greeted by Mrs. Palma Lacey, their aunt, and our school secretary. Her green eyes still hold the sparkle we all know at school, and her short, light brown hair frames her face without a strand out of place. She had a magazine in her hand, which she had folded when she answered the door. She smiled and invited us in. "Dinner is almost done. You girls are right on time. Welcome."

"Mrs. Lacey, I didn't realize you would be here as well," I said as I took off my jacket and hung it on the black jacket rack inside the door.

Cinnia copied me and turned to take in everything. "Wow. It looks great. It looks like a museum in here with the paintings and velvet gray walls."

"Thank you. My nieces and nephews will love to hear it," Mrs. Lacey turned to me. "I am here as the only adult supervisor for the evening. Just to make sure everything goes smoothly. Oh, and you girls can call me Palma as we are not in school." Her smile faded as she turned to walk away, stopping first to make sure we followed.

The Leigh family was together in the living room, I assumed, as every room was just as big and open. I remembered a few of them from school, but there were apparently more to this family than we thought. Clarebelle and Garcia were sitting on a couch with two guys, one of whom I knew as Paio from school. He has blue eyes and wavy, thick, honey blond hair, and his arm was around Garcia. Weird, right? They seemed to be in deep conversation when we walked in. The guy sitting by Clarebelle sat with his arms folded while Clarebelle played with his short spiky brown hair with one hand and the other resting on his chest, smoothing him for some reason. His brown eyes showed anger as he watched us enter. I wonder why he would be upset about it; maybe he didn't want us here. There was another lady here, one I did not know either. She shared the same blue eyes as Paio, but her wavy blonde hair was to her shoulders, and she had platinum highlights in her hair, barely noticeable in this lighting. She sat in the chair, facing everyone. Errol was the last one, standing by the stairs, as if he had just come down them.

"I am sure you girls remember Clarebelle, Garcia, Paio, and Errol from school," Palma went on, "the man sitting by Clarebelle is Citino, her boyfriend, and Pagan is the oldest sibling." She said, pointing out the only two people we did not know.

Cinnia smiled and nodded, "Hi, everyone. I am Cinnia, and she's Gemma. I am curious. Where are your parents? Why is Mrs. Lacey the adult here tonight? I thought they would be here as well."

Clarebelle spoke before anyone else could. "They died," she paused and continued, "shortly after we moved here four weeks ago."

"Oh, I am so sorry. I had no idea." Everyone noticed her anxiety spike as she became uncertain as to what to do.

"It is okay, really. Only a few people know."

"What happened to them?"

Palma stepped forward, ready to change the subject, "We appreciate your concerns, but let us eat. Dinner is now ready."

Dinner was nice and lovely. We started with a salad, and I only ate half-heartedly. I could relate to the loss of a parent, especially both. I kept touching my locket as I ate. I had to remind myself to remember the good times I had with my parents, in order to not cry in front of everyone. We had mac n cheese and riblets for dinner. No dessert. I noticed the family barely ate anything at all and wondered if their lack of appetite was not something strange after all. Maybe they were just grieving.

After dinner, we moved into the living room, just to talk and get to know each other. Cinnia was natural at this, while I stayed unsure and unable to blend in with this family. Some of their conversations gave me a weird vibe, like they were unsure themselves of what to say. Errol had tried to stay away from me most of the evening, watching from afar, except when Garcia made him sit next to me by taking the only other spot before he could. With a pointed look aimed at his sister, he sat next to me awkwardly, making me more nervous than I thought possible.

He kept quiet, and the atmosphere only made me want to leave even more. Maybe Clarebelle and Garcia were wrong in trying to get us together. The hesitation, exchange of looks, and some wording, there but forced, were off as I listened to the conversation around me. Sometimes I get the feeling they haven't socialized with others in years. A little of their conversation seemed old-fashioned, but they remained polite and nearly emotionless. After twenty minutes of silence and barely any eye contact from Errol, I had had enough and got up to use the restroom, which Clarebelle was nice enough to direct me to its location. In the hallway on my way back, I heard voices coming from the kitchen, quiet but stern. I did not want to eavesdrop, but it's difficult not to when you hear your own name.

"...should not be here. What if something happens?" I recognized Mrs. Lacey's voice right away.

"You should not worry so much. We all know what to do and what not to. You told us everything we needed to know. All that could happen is Errol finally finds someone after so many years of being alone." I could not be sure which lady spoke, so I leaned closer to the door to hear better. I wondered what was going on and what was so important to keep quiet about.

"You all are in danger, and keeping quiet about who and what you are is essential to keeping you safe. You have never been in this situation before. You have more pressing problems to deal with than your brother's loneliness."

"That is where you're wrong, Aunt Palma. We love you, but my family's happiness will always be at the top of my priority list. My family is everything to me, and I will not let Errol torture himself when the one person who can change that is right there in the parlor right now." Her voice got louder, but not enough. I listened and knew it had to be Clarebelle or Garcia as the voice was a little familiar to me, but I was not sure which one.

"Your family's and your own safety are more important. You could very well be bringing even more danger to their lives as well as your own. Least of all to Gemma and her family. How will your brother feel if something happens to her?"

She signed and lowered her voice again, so much that I could not hear what was said. I had to wonder what was going on, but the voices soon stopped, so I left before I got caught eavesdropping. As I slowly made my way back to the parlor, I noticed Clarebelle and Palma coming from the kitchen at the same time from the opposite door that I was at. So that is who was talking. About what I had no idea, or what their big important secret was.

After my return, I noticed how Errol was slowly starting to speak with his family, and occasionally with me. His hesitations and forced words were better than his ignoring me. I answered his questions and asked for a reply in return. Most of which were basic 'getting to know you' questions any friend would ask, like my favorite color, places I wanted to visit most, and favorite hobbies. I listened to the smoothness of his tones more than the words themselves. Could he be happy with me? I am not someone special, but Clarebelle seems to think I am. The night left me with more questions by the time we left.

That night, I laid awake, my mind completely distracted as I knew they had a secret, one that made them different and dangerous to be around. I recalled the problems and dangers mentioned surrounding the family. What was the Leigh family and Mrs. Lacey hiding? How did their parents die? What situation have they never been in before that Mrs. Lacey had to teach them how to behave? Why would I possibly be in danger just from talking with Errol? Talking to him tonight, even the little bit that we did, has relieved some of my butterflies while being around him. The tension was still there, but manageable. Errol and I have turned a corner, even if it is a small one.

My wandering mind eventually quieted down, and I fell asleep that night knowing I would do what it takes to find out what the family is hiding and why I cannot keep Errol off my mind. Am I in love? How could that be so fast? Last week, I started making a list of questions, trying to piece together the answers surrounding the family, but I am lost. Now I had more questions, and very few answers.

After school the next day, I pulled Cinnia into the home

gym when she had returned from her jog. I knew nobody would hear us, and I wanted her opinion. I could not concentrate on my homework since we got home. "What did you think about last night? We did not get a chance to talk afterwards or this morning."

She started stretching as she replied. "I had a fun time. I wonder if they will talk to us more in school."

"You think they will?"

"Definitely. I mean, they did not today, but I still have hope for the week. At least Errol will. He slowly opened up to you last night." Cinnia's grin said it all. She was on his sister's side, and now I was not escaping their notice.

"I doubt they will talk to me, especially at school. Last night was awkward, and I eavesdropped on a conversation that hinted they have this huge secret to hide."

She shrugged as she finished stretching her muscles. "We all have secrets. You should not eavesdrop on someone."

Ignoring that last comment, I continued, "This was different…" I hesitated, unsure how much to tell her. "I mean, it just sounded weird with everything I heard."

"What did you hear?"

Replaying every word I could recall, I told her who I eavesdropped on, what was said, and how it sounded. I also told her how awkward it felt being invited to their place when we knew next to nothing about the family. All the weird aspects I noticed about the family, including the way they sometimes talked and while I knew she was listening, she could not provide any comfort as she had no explanation as to this family's behavior.

Cinnia signed and, watching me carefully, she answered. "If all that stuff bothers you, you should ask them about it. Not eavesdrop on them. I can tell you have feelings for Errol, as I have heard his name multiple times in your explanation just now and saw you two last night. I bet you have not stopped thinking about him either since then."

At her pointed look, I looked away. Maybe I do have feelings, but I am not sure how to act on them. Right now, a boyfriend is not at the top of my to-do list or shouldn't have been with all I'm dealing with, but something's going on and I'm not sure what it was.

I was still mulling it over as I got ready for school the next day. My latest look was a hit, lining it up with the school colors. I wore my new black heeled ankle boots, navy blue jeans, belt, and plaid long-sleeve forest green and gray button-up shirt complete with my heart-shaped locket. Cinnia waved my hair with her curling iron before school. My classes were going great, now that I am keeping up with them. English went by slowly as I tried not to open my mirror to look behind me, and when the bell rang, I jumped. Everyone rushed out to lunch, and again I was left last to leave, or so I thought.

"Would you mind eating lunch with me today?"

I looked up and gasped when I saw who was speaking to me. Errol was standing beside my desk, waiting for an answer. I slowly nodded, unsure if I could speak with how shocked I was. I stood up with my things in my backpack. He waited for me to walk out first and walked slightly behind me. Between his polite tone and gentlemanly ways, I knew I liked him and was glad he was speaking to me. He did not seem to mind as I stopped at my locker on the way, as he waited patiently like a statue nearby. I was not sure if he knew what to say or if he was waiting for me to say something first. We walked silently to the cafeteria, and I wondered where he wanted to eat, with my family or with his. As I picked out my food and paid for it,

I kept wondering why he did not say anything or buy any food for himself. We did spare glances at each other, making me believe he was waiting for me to start the conversation, but I did not know where to begin.

Errol finally spoke as we turned from the line. "Let's go eat at that table." He said as he pointed out the only table that was empty and far from both my family and his family.

"Sure." I said as I followed him to the table. What made him talk to me today, let alone have lunch with me? I also noticed the silent look between him and his family as we walked by. I seem to pay more attention to his family than ever before. I am surprised I was even able to focus in school at all. I do not know why, but something about them just drew me to them. I wonder if I can get some answers out of Errol today. I have been debating about him for a few weeks now.

As soon as I sat down, I started on the easier questions, hoping for at least one to be answered today. "So, what made you talk to me today of all days? After your normal quiet behavior and again at your place, I did not expect any further communication from you."

"I know what my sisters have said to you." He paused before continuing, "I also knew how you have watched me these last few weeks. I figured it was time to talk."

"I'm sorry." I mumbled, embarrassed and looked down at my tray of food to hide it from him.

He spoke softly, making me look back up. "Do not be. I have been watching you as well. I was hoping we could try to be friends and see where it goes. I do not want to push you in one direction or another."

I ate my mac n cheese and what should have been a hamburger, but lacked the flavor of beef as I considered this. "I have noticed you, all of you in fact. I mainly notice how you all never eat at school." I hinted as I pointed out the lack of food in front of him.

"We eat a heavy breakfast. We do not eat in public." His statement sounded rehearsed, but I did not push. At least he's talking, and his answers kind of make sense.

"I know your parents passed. I am sorry for your loss. I lost my parents just over a month ago in a car accident."

"It's been hard." He did not seem to know what else to say or not to say; this just drove my curiosity more.

"If you do not mind my asking. What happened?"

"They were murdered, just shortly after we arrived here in town. We do not know who did it or why."

"That is horrible. Is that why you all stay to yourselves?"

"It is a part of it, but mostly we just like our privacy." Before I could continue questioning him, the bell rang. Never before have I wanted to break that bell. I was just getting him to talk.

"So, friends for now," Errol continued as he stood up from the chair, "I would like to spend time with you outside of school as well. How about tomorrow night after school, we meet up at the Jefferson Mall in Louisville? If you want to, or you can pick the place."

"No, that sounds great. I love shopping, and we can walk the whole mall to get to know each other. I will see you tomorrow."

He nodded and walked away, back to his family, I am sure. I am afraid I only got answers and ended up with more questions to think about. I rushed to class before I was late. Nobody has ever gotten close to this family, and now, I am friends with the guy I have a crush on.

CHAPTER V

I was still shocked by this development as I made it to gym class. Cinnia and Medea knew something had happened, but I would not tell them, so I waited impatiently for Mrs. Finley to start gym. Mr. Damico had started the minute he could in our last class, forcing Cinnia to hold off on her questions until later. Cinnia managed to drag me aside as we waited in the parking lot after school let out. Uncle Basil was late getting here today, so I finally told her everything.

"O-M-G. This is great. You are friends with the strange but hot guy at school. Everyone is going to be talking about it." She exclaimed after impatiently listening to everything said today at lunch.

I shrugged it off as I watched for the pickup. "Don't get too excited, we are only friends."

She pointed at me, "Friends, for now. You just wait. I bet before the end of school, that will change."

I shook my head as I knew telling her how wrong she was would bring an endless argument, and I was tired. School was out within the month, and I doubt I would see Errol after that. "Your dad's here. Let's go."

As we headed for the truck, in which Agento beat us to, Cinnia continued, "Tomorrow you get to hang out with him, outside of school, and at the mall, no less." As we climbed inside, I could tell her excitement was not going anywhere anytime soon. "I am so doing your hair. It's beautiful and the perfect length for a Dutch braid."

Talking about hair was all Agento knew we were discussing as we stopped talking on the way home. I did not want to go into it with Agento just now. I only hope to pick out my own outfit tomorrow. During the quiet time before bed, I silently thought of the great couple we would make if that ever happened. I wouldn't get my hopes up, though, not like Cinnia, although I have to admit it's never far from my mind. In my head, I started changing some of the questions I had written down since I did get answers to some and added much-needed others. I knew I needed all the answers before any relationship could really start.

I woke up anxious for school the next day. I wondered what was in store for me as I got my boots on, wearing denim jeans with a belt, and a red T-shirt with my heart-shaped locket. Cinnia argued, but I would not budge on my own outfit today. I laughed at her expression of disappointment, which changed to ecstasy when she started in on my hair before school. Cinnia braided my hair, and as she was finishing, I touched my locket and remembered all the picnics, family outings, and good times we had with my parents, back before my father became a politician, which forever stopped all the family fun.

I thought about how most of my family's favorite memories were from before my father's political days. I knew my parents would forever be in my memories, but even after all this time, I still feel lonelier than ever before. Thinking about the secret my mother took to her grave, I could not help but be angry as well. How could my mother keep such a secret from her own children? Why? What would have happened if she had our younger sibling? Why couldn't she bring herself to talk to her brother? Why did our grandparents fight with her? I realized that by keeping the good memories I've gotten through rough times, but this secret is starting to destroy them. Did I really know my mother at all?

Somehow, I focused on all my classes and even managed to avoid looking at Errol before heading to lunch with him. My teachers are happy with my progress and how it shows in my assignments.

Errol and I sat down at our table, and I ate in silence as I watched him look around for something. It seemed he was looking for someone. "Who are you looking for?"

"What?" He stopped looking and saw I had finished eating. "Nobody. Just looking."

I decided to let it go, for now. "So tonight."

"Yes. We could meet at the main entrance at 6 pm."

I nodded. "That is great. I will have my aunt drop me off." He nodded and looked away again. My curiosity got the better of me, and I had to say something after all. "We don't have to stay here if you don't want to."

"No, I like it here. We have our own space."

"Okay." I hesitated, unsure which questions to ask, if any. He obviously was looking for someone, but he refused to answer. Before I could decide which way to go about it, the bell rang, and we headed out of the cafeteria.

Before we parted ways, he finally spoke, "I like your hair pulled back."

I smiled, happy that I finally got a reaction. "Thanks. With my long, thick hair, it is hard to keep tamed."

"It is an innovative idea to pull it back then. Well, I do not want you to be late for class. See you tonight."

As I watched him walk away, I wondered what he was hiding. Was he embarrassed to be seen with me? I doubt it, but I am not ruling it out. Tonight was a night for answers. Hopefully, I will get many answers tonight. I do want to see more of him, but I need to know he does too and what he was hiding.

Cinnia and I sat together to do homework at the dining table and discussed what had happened today. Even she was suspicious about today at lunch. She noticed him staring as she was watching us. She was full of cheer when I told her about Errol's comment and how he noticed the fantastic job she did with my hair. She promised to try out assorted styles each week to see which he prefers and/or notices.

Aunt Aida was more than happy to drive me to Louisville, where she had plans to shop as well. As Aunt Aida found a parking spot, I looked at and admired the mall. It was done with beige cement and deep brown bricks in some areas. The main entrance was surrounded by beige cement and orange designs on each side of the glass doors. The sign, Jefferson Mall, was in blue with silver line designs, similar to the orange ones, above the glass windows and door. Aunt Aida and I parted ways shortly after entering the huge mall. This mall was one floor but huge, and the ceiling inside was beautifully decorated with diverse levels, bringing a peaceful, beautiful atmosphere to the mall. The multi-colored tiles of brown, gray, and white gave off a classic feel to the mall.

I sat on a comfortable chair just inside the entrance, next to the colorful mobile car-shaped carts for kids, waiting for Errol and hoping not to get stood up. The problem is we never exchanged numbers, so I hoped he knew where I would be and would show up soon. I wasn't sure if I should have waited inside or outside the doors.

"There you are."

I looked up and saw him walking towards me. I smiled as I saw he was wearing jeans and a black T-shirt. The normality of his clothes made him look even hotter somehow than at school, and his expensive designer outfits made him and his family stand apart.

"Hi, I was hoping you would find me." I said as I stood up, ready to get going.

"Yes, I should have thought about that before." As we started walking together, he continued. "Before we leave here tonight, we will have to remember to exchange numbers."

"That would be great." I realized I was not paying attention to where we were going when we walked into the first store. Not one of my favorites, but I am not going to be meticulous tonight, not with the company I had with me.

I got to know him a little more personally as we walked, but he did not seem to answer any of my more pressing questions as we went from store to store; he kept dodging them. Most of the time, his tone was smooth, but here and there, I detected hesitation in his speech, one that I was unsure as to what caused it. The longer we walked, the quieter he seemed to get. When we got to one of my favorites, Bath & Body Works, I had this strange feeling again and looked at him, only to notice how attentive he was to everyone else. "Who are you looking for?"

He jumped and looked at me in shock, "What do you mean?"

Weird. "You seem to be watching everyone else so intensely, so I just figured you were looking for someone in particular."

He shrugged. "No. I guess I'm just more careful now…" he hesitated as he was debating what to say, "We don't know who killed our parents, so we don't know if we are targets as well."

That made sense. So, not a possible girlfriend. I finally relaxed. "Did the police tell you guys to be careful?"

"Not particularly, but they don't know everything, like they seem to think." His matter-of-fact tone stopped me in my tracks.

Looking at him, I questioned him. "Wait. You mean, you did not tell them everything?"

"We told them what we could. It is not like we saw it happen. Sometimes, it still feels like it happened yesterday. Aunt Palma has been here greatly to help us through."

Maybe I was too harsh. I understood grief as much as the next person, and I was acting like he was holding out on the police. "You all must still be grieving greatly. I know if my parents were murdered, I would not be able to function normally for months to follow."

"We are managing."

"My parents died in a car accident, and I understand the struggle to function normally sometimes. I still keep them close with my locket." I said as I instantly reached up to touch it. We had stopped walking and were standing outside the store when he reached over as well to touch my locket. He opened it, and I could hardly breathe with him standing so close to me and touching me without actually touching me. He seemed so sincere that I could not move away. I tried everything to focus on breathing normally as he looked at the pictures of my parents. Why was I reacting this way? The tension was so thick, and I wondered if he felt it as well. His fingers brush against my skin, but he was only looking at my locket and the two pictures inside. It did not seem to mean anything to him, so why did it mean something to me?

"I wish I had a picture like this to keep them close." His voice was quiet, and I leaned closer to hear it.

Realizing what he said, I asked. "You mean, you don't have a picture of your parents?"

He just shook his head and moved away, gently setting the locket down against my chest. "We do not have any pictures. We only have strong memories. Our family is not big on photos."

It must be a religious thing, so I didn't ask. "I still have moments where I hide in the bathroom when I feel a break-down coming. I understand how hard it is, but then I remember how heartbroken they would be if I did not continue with my life, and it helps."

"That is helpful. Thank you. Hopefully, we can continue on without them as well."

I nodded as I recalled the conversation, the one I overheard Clarebelle and Mrs. Lacey have last week. She was a great, friendly secretary; we all loved seeing her in the office, more so than the other school secretaries. She must have been a great aunt as well to get them through this tragic time.

As we continued shopping, I stayed careful and cautious about what I asked. I did not want to bring up any more bad memories for him. We kept the conversation light as we got to know each other. I learned his likes and dislikes while telling him mine. Halfway through the mall, I realized I already had a few bags and did not make too much in allowance, so I had to plan better on my continued spending. Once the bags became heavy, Errol offered to help carry them. He shopped, but my shopping still put his to shame.

When we finished the walkway of the mall and got back to the entrance, I ended up with three more bags, which he carried along with his two. I saw Aunt Aida sitting on a chair by the entrance, waiting for me. I turned to Errol for his number and my other bags. He set my bags down at my feet and got his phone out before I could say anything.

"I had a wonderful time, and I cannot wait until we see each other again. Next time, we will find something to do in Crestwood." I gave him my number and waited for the call to go through on my phone. He said goodbye shortly after and walked away as I saved his number, grabbed my bags, and finished walking over to Aunt Aida. Hauling our bags out to the car, I noticed I couldn't stop smiling. Aunt Aida never once questioned me, maybe she knew more than she let on.

The half-hour drive home went by fast with my head spinning with Errol. When will we spend time together next? Will it count as a date or just as friends? Was the family in as much danger as they believed? Walking up the three steps to the front porch with my bags, I called out to Uncle Basil to help Aunt Aida with her bags. I walked through the front door, almost running into Agento and Uncle Basil as he went outside to help. Agento waited until our uncle was outside the door before stopping me from going upstairs.

"Whoa there," Agento said. "I take it your date went great."

"It was not a date." I huffed as I took off my boots and pushed them aside, out of the walkway. "We are just friends." I bent over and grabbed my bags before I started around him to walk upstairs.

"Sure. That is the term we all use." He chuckled as he went outside to help. I pretended not to hear him as I continued into my room, my nerves were all over the place. Cinnia knew the second I walked by her room to get to mine, and I knew my night was not over yet.

"You're back!" She ran from her room in her pajamas and pulled me into my room. We barely sat down with my bags spread on the bed and floor before she started again. "Did you kiss?"

I shook my head as I started undoing my braid. "No, of course not. You do not kiss your friend."

"You both know that's going to change."

"Nobody knows if we will date. His sisters and you included."

"What did he wear?"

"What's that got to do with anything?"

"Everybody knows a man dresses his best while he's courting."

"While then, that proves he is not. He was wearing a T-shirt and jeans. And courting, really?"

"He seems old-fashioned. So yes, courting." She shrugged and frowned, deep in thought. I used this to get up and put my bags away. I got my pajamas out, ready now more than before for bed, before she continued. "Wait. Maybe that is his way. You know how his family dresses in those designer outfits every day at school. Maybe his T-shirt and jeans are the same as our expensive, dressy clothes to us."

"You can think whatever you like. It was not a date, and the next time we spend time together, it won't be a date." Maybe, but I secretly hope that it is a date next time. I had such a wonderful time, but I was not ready to let anybody know it yet, especially Cinnia.

"You can deny all you want." She shrugged as I got dressed for bed. She decided to change the topic, knowing her cousin would not say anything else. "What did you find out about him and his mysterious family?"

"Not much, but they are grieving and a little paranoid over their parents' death."

"Wait…why would they be paranoid?"

I sat down next to her on my bed. "They watch everyone like they are suspects. He would not relax much tonight as he kept looking around at everybody who walked by. They think they are next to die. Who else would think like that? And I think they did not tell the police everything. They are hiding a lot."

"Wow, your boyfriend has baggage."

"He's not my boyfriend!"

"We will see. Good night. Sweet dreams about your future, guy." She ran out the door laughing before the pillow could hit her. I shook my head, as more thoughts spun as I tried to sleep.

What was the Leigh family hiding? Was Mrs. Lacey behind it as well? I can talk to her, although I doubt she will say anything. There is just something about him that keeps me interested, to the point of doubting any kind of good relationship with him would come.

CHAPTER VI

Being at South Oldham High for almost three months now has gone so fast that I was surprised when I realized graduation was right around the corner.

Today, Errol managed to switch seats with the person next to me in English. Now I can forget about paying attention in class; he looks better next to me than three seats behind me.

I smiled as I sat down, and he just smiled back. "I hope you don't mind me sitting here from now on."

"Not at all. It is distracting, though." I hinted. Maybe one day we will be more than friends. Not much has changed from our evening at the mall.

"Understandable. If it becomes too much of a problem, I will move back to my old seat."

That, surprisingly, made me pay attention to Miss Thurlow as she started the class. No way would I be the reason he moves back behind me. If he could deal with sitting next to me, then I could too. English went by quickly today, and I actually remembered what we had learned. I was more than ready for the homework tonight.

When we walked to the cafeteria together a few days later, I got lunch for myself, but instead of going to our table, we sat down with his family. This whole time, not once had he hinted at sitting with his family at lunch. We would always sit at our table, and today made me wonder, why now, why today? All week, we kept to our table. I was so nervous sitting down that I almost fell into my seat instead of sitting.

I was sitting between Errol and Clarebelle. It was so awkward as I knew everyone was watching us, me in particular, and I did not know we would be sitting together with his family today. Errol sat down with Paio next to him, and Garcia was across from me. Sitting with them was awkward, mainly because I felt undressed and unsure as to why today had changed.

Garcia spoke first. "We have been wondering when we would get to hang out with you."

"Yes, it has been debated for some time now." Paio said dryly.

"Now, do not be rude, Paio. She could very well become a part of this family." That definitely made lunch more awkward. We had burgers and fries for lunch, and I always brought my own drink, water in my tumbler, as I do not trust cafeteria milk. Only Clarebelle and Garcia had a plate in front of them, but nothing on it, so I was not sure if it was for show or if they were already finished before we arrived.

Errol changed that subject quickly. "Any news from the police yet?"

Paio shrugged. "They know something, but they won't tell us. I can go over there and ask them, again, this weekend." The look they exchanged caught my attention, that is, until Clarebelle leaned toward me.

She drew my attention away from Paio and Errol's conversation and whispered, "I do hope sitting with us is not too much for you. I know our family can be intimidating to most." Garcia was paying attention to both our conversation and Paio and Errol, making me wonder if they were purposely drawing my attention away.

I took a deep breath and whispered back, "No, I am glad to sit with you all. Errol and I are just friends, though." As I spoke, I never thought I would mean it as much as I did. This family felt like a second family, but I did not know why.

"I know, and I also know how quickly those things can change. I started as friends with Citino."

"How long have you guys been together?"

"It has been a couple of years now, maybe a little less. Time sure goes by fast."

I sat back, only realizing then that the others were watching and listening to our conversation, even though we were whispering, they all seemed to know what we were saying. I was quiet after that, focusing on eating and barely listening to the conversation. My questions never seemed to be answered, and if they were, they only raised more questions.

I only turned back into the conversation when Errol touched my shoulder and leaned into me. "So, I was wondering if you would be okay going with me to the Yew Dell Botanical Gardens. There is a lot there that we can do, like walk the gardens, shop at the gift shop, and even better, we can eat lunch at their Cafe."

I nodded. "Yeah, I heard about the Gardens. That sounds like fun."

"So maybe Saturday, or is Sunday better for you?"

"Either day works for me."

He seemed to think it over, but I wondered if his decision came from their exchange of looks. "I believe we would benefit more from going on Sunday morning. There will be less traffic, given the church."

I smiled and agreed to Sunday. We all stood up as the bell rang, ready to go our separate ways. I started to walk away to dump my trash, promising to see him tomorrow, when I heard something behind me. "So that's him."

I jumped. I turned from the trash and saw Agento behind me. "Don't scare me like that."

He just shrugged as we walked from the cafeteria together. "You only did not notice me as you were so focused on them. I was behind you since before you left his table."

"What's it to you?"

"You're my sister, so I have the birthright to judge any guy that looks at you twice." He finished as we reached my locker.

I pulled it open and started grabbing my books as I replied. "We are just friends."

"That is why you are going on a date with him on Sunday. You do not know anything about that family."

"I know more than you."

"Right, because a few conversations make you an expert."

I signed as we turned from my locker. "Shouldn't you get to class?"

"Yeah, right after you do. Where are you going?"

I barely looked at him, knowing where he was going with this. "The Gardens in town."

"Really?" His arched eyebrow said so much as he contin-ued, "And you don't think that's a date?"

"Think what you want and go to class." I replied, walking away from him. I knew I would hear more on the way home, but I needed some space right now. Siblings are a pain sometimes.

I barely paid any attention to my classes after that. I already had a lot on my mind with the Leigh family, and adding in my conversation with Agento was more than enough to keep me focused. I did not need Agento reminding me how little I knew about the Leigh family. I wonder how much I will get out of Errol on our day out this Sunday. I hope to finally put an end to all my confusion and learn everything, or at least get a good explanation for what I have seen with them. I was still debating how to ask some of my questions and which ones to focus on when the final bell rang for the day.

Everyone had something to say on the ride home about the Leigh family and my 'date' with Errol. Agento had beaten us to the truck, in which Adacio and Uncle Basil were together, finishing work in time to get us. Agento had already told Adacio about today, in which they both started in on me the second we all got in the pickup, and Uncle Basil pulled out of the parking lot.

I refused to back down. "I am eighteen. I'm not a little girl who needs an adult supervisor. It is my decision who I spend time with and where, and with or without supervisors."

"Not with that family. They are outsiders. Nobody knows anything about them except that their aunt is our school secretary," Agento argued with me, facing forward. I knew he believed he had won the argument, but I was not finished, and he would not have the last say.

"That's why I'm going in three days, and you can't stop me."

Uncle Basil interrupted before Adacio could jump in to define Agento and his decision, "Now, while I am on Agento's side about not wanting you alone with someone nobody knows, this argument is over. Agento, you have to work with me and Adacio on Sunday at the shop. Gemma, I know I can trust you will be careful and smart about this guy. You two have been through more than most have, and this small argument is pointless."

"Dad, you could easily tell her not to go," Adacio tried.

He shook his head, "I will not use my role as uncle against Gemma any more than her own father would have."

I nodded, "That is true. While I know my parents would not have liked the idea, they would not have stopped me. They have made that clear every time we did anything reckless back home."

"Both of you are being silly anyway," Cinnia interrupted in my defense, "She is going because she likes him, and he obviously likes her. He would not have invited her to the Gardens otherwise. Gemma is not a little girl in need of her big brother to defend her. Errol is strange but respected by all of the teachers, so that is something. I am sure nothing bad will happen. Agento, you will just have to get used to it."

"I will not." He stubbornly stayed facing forward, but I knew he was trying to control himself. Just the talk about our parents still had me clenching my locket in my hand. Our grief is forever a part of us. When could anybody truly get over the loss of a parent, especially both, and so suddenly?

I flashed back to the one time when Agento came home late, so late that our parents almost called the police. He had started dating a girl that our parents disliked and said she was born from the 'poor, dirty folk' and she didn't deserve his attention. Our parents argued away from us the next morning about it, and I overheard it. Agento never knew how badly they did not want him to date her, but I did. I knew he had to know something just because they did not openly argue around him, and he knew what they thought about her and her family. I remember telling him how much they do care about him, and their reason for not yelling at him was because they did not want to control him, not because they did not care about him. They were afraid of how he would rebel, so they kept all of their arguments away from their children. Agento had dated her for a month after that incident before she finally left him, telling him it was 'to find someone who didn't have a politician for a father.' I stayed with him through his heartbreak and kept him going after that. Coming back to reality, I knew he would do the same for me, if and/or when Errol turns out to be like her.

Friday passed slowly, making everyone fidgety for the great weekend plans to begin. Medea and Christabel, in our shared classes, kept asking me about Errol and how close they noticed we had gotten recently. Between them and Cinnia, I was more than ready to leave for the day, and then the weirdest thing happened. I got called into the office over the intercom fifteen minutes before the final bell rang.

I am so nervous when I enter as a call to the principal's office, as it is never fun, especially on a Friday and during the last period. Some of my nerves lessened, though, when I saw Mrs. Lacey sitting behind the only occupied desk. She was on the phone when I entered, so I sat down, wondering when she would tell the principal I was here.

"I'll be right with you shortly." Mrs. Lacey spoke to me before quickly returning to the call.

My eyes wandered the room, looking for something to focus on instead of wondering why I was called into the office. There were degrees in picture frames behind every desk, except the one desk that had three, with Mrs. Lacey's. That did not help my nerves, so I looked elsewhere. The forest green walls with navy blue desks and gray trims everywhere were decorated with our variety of winning teams covering them. The long mahogany wall separating me from the four secretary desks.

"Alright, I'm done." I did not even notice her leaving her desk and standing next to me. I jumped and tried to focus on the matter at hand. "Are you okay?"

I nodded. "Yes. I am. The principal wants to see me?" I asked when I stood to follow her to the principal's office, but she did not move.

She waved me back down. "No, I called you for me. I wanted to talk to you about something," she hesitated before saying, "before you and Errol go out on Sunday."

"Oh, umm," this was awkward. She called me because she was their aunt and not my school secretary. Was I about to get a third degree again? I was not looking forward to this. It is making this weekend difficult to deal with, and I am wondering why everybody is interfering with a possible date when it shouldn't be important between two friends.

She hesitated as she read my questionable expression. "If you do not mind, that is. I figured you might also want to ask me a few things. We have only about ten minutes."

I sat back down and realized how I could ask her some of my own questions. I started relaxing as I spoke in a quiet tone, "I don't mind, and I do have some questions."

She sat next to me and crossed her ankles. "Well, ask me anything. Then I will give you advice, if you want."

I wondered where to begin, "I have noticed Garcia and Paio-"

She cut me off, "Yes, I am sure a lot of the students have. I told them to cut it out around others. Garcia should know better." She added under her breath. She took a deep breath and continued, "Garcia and Paio are not siblings like everyone believes."

I was taken aback. "I thought Garcia, Paio, Clarebelle, and Pagan were all Errol's siblings."

"Garcia is by marriage. They are older than people think."

"How much older?"

She signed as she thought of the best way to answer. "They have been together for a few years now, but they never went to a normal school, so they are pretending to be younger for the experience. I do not want to say more as too much could get out."

"I will not tell anyone. I promise."

She smiled. "I knew I could count on you, which is why I am glad to talk to you now. I do not want to keep you for long. The bell will ring in less than five minutes. You can ask me one more thing, and I will answer as best as I can. Then, I wish to ask you something."

I hesitated; there were so many questions. I decided to confess to my eavesdropping. "I overheard you and Clarebelle when I was at their place. I did not mean to. I have been wondering what you meant about the bigger risk. Are they in danger like their parents?"

"I am not surprised that you overheard. I suspected it was due to how you reacted afterwards." She looks away, hesitating and thinking about how to answer. "Yes, they are in danger. They saw more than they should have. They know more as well. That is all I can say." Her answer was not comforting at all. I thought they did not see or know anything. What were they hiding? She took a deep breath and continued, "Now I understand right now you don't know how you feel, but I believe we both know you feel something for Errol." I looked away, unsure where she was going with this. "I do not want to see anything happen to you, so I must ask. Will you keep your distance from Errol for the time being? I ask for yours and his safety as well as others."

I hesitated and debated whether I could keep lying to myself or not. Should I lie or go with the truth? I decided to let the truth be told, I was tired of lying and keeping my feelings to myself. Mrs. Lacey seems to understand and will keep my secret. "I know I feel something. I must see this through. I cannot stay away from him."

She nodded. "I see. I figured you would not leave if asked. I had to make sure I was right about you. I want what is best for my nephew. Thank you for being honest. I hope everything works out for you two, but I know there is a lot you will have to deal with before long."

Right then, the final bell rang, and I was forced to leave the office with conflicting emotions. I want to go out with Errol, but his aunt has just told me how dangerous it is, how much danger he could be in, and how I still have a lot to learn about him. What did they know, and why were they lying to the police? Would I be able to oversee their big secret if it means I get to stay with Errol? Is this what I want? I now know I will get answers one way or another. By it from Errol or from his aunt.

CHAPTER VII

Cinnia and I locked ourselves in my room the moment we walked inside. Cinnia spent the two hours with me before dinner, trying out different hairstyles for Sunday. She took the clothes choice after I said I was planning to wear jeans and an old, but clean, long-sleeved blue shirt. She had gasped in horror, and I laughed, knowing that it worked faster than if I had put in an effort. It was a garden, so I knew I was not going to wear anything too classy, and she had the perfect outfit in mind, just like I knew she would. I got her to hurry up by mentioning the food I could smell from downstairs. It was bacon cheeseburgers and homemade fries night. She finally settled on pulling out my nice dark wash straight-legged jeans with three buttons and no zipper and a nice navy-blue three-quarter sleeve shirt, classy but not too dressy and perfect for a garden date with an off-white vest if it gets windy. I hung the outfit on my door with my white ankle boots.

Agento and Adacio were quiet during dinner, but that was fine with me. I knew that Uncle Basil had told Aunt Aida about the date and the argument that followed because she had steered all conversation far away from it. As I made my way back to my room for the night, forgoing family movie night by pleading exhaustion, Agento followed me.

"Hey, I am sorry about arguing with you. You know I just care, right?"

"Yes, you always have, as I do." We turned into my room.

"I know things have been crazy around here. I want to spend more time with you, but work is getting busier and between school and work and helping Uncle Basil with the shop…"

I stopped him there, "Do not. You do not need to feel guilty about not spending time with your sister. I know how busy and hectic it has been. Between our parents' passing, the move here, school, your work at Verizon and with our uncle, I do not expect you to find time to spend with me. I know you're pushing your schoolwork to finish early, and I will not be the reason you do not finish and graduate. You are working hard now so you can provide for your family. You never need to apologize for that."

"I am off next Saturday. We could do something then. That is, if you do not have a date."

"That would be great, but how did you get the first Saturday of the month off?"

He grinned as he walked backwards out of my room. "I asked, in hopes of spending time with my sister."

I am glad that the move has not affected our relationship; we have always been close and more like friends than rival siblings. After I got ready for bed, exhausted from my wandering mind and crazy day of school, I fell asleep quickly.

The next morning passed with some of our friends coming

over to hang out, giving us more people to play games against each other until they all left in the late afternoon. I was cleaning the living room for the night when I realized how Mrs. Lacey had managed to avoid a question: 'How old are they?' It made me wonder just how old they all were; were they all pretending to be younger, and if Clarebelle and Citino were really dating or married, like Garcia and Paio were married? I was getting tired of adding more questions to my boundless list to ask them. When would the mystery end? The night passed the same as always, family movie night. Although my mind was elsewhere.

Cinnia braided my hair back on Sunday morning and helped me with light makeup to match my outfit. I decided to walk to the Botanical Gardens as it was only a 20-minute walk, and I did not want another lecture.

The streets were quiet with Sunday churchgoing. The sun was shining, making it perfect for a picnic and walking in the gardens. The walk was brisk, and I got to the Gardens before I knew it. When I stood by the entrance, I started texting Errol.

> I am here at the entrance. How far away are you?

Less than a minute later, my phone chimed with…

> Turn around.

I turned and found him walking toward me. My heart started racing, and I took a few slow, deep breaths. I knew from day one that I was attracted to him; why else would I constantly think about him? Right now, wearing just a black tee and plain blue jeans with black boots, he was hotter than the sun. It always made him look better than in his designer outfits, and it made me wonder if he knew it.

"Are you ready?"

I smiled and nodded. We walked into the barn entrance of the Botanical Gardens, and he paid the entrance fee for both of us. Looking around me, as the person explained the map to Errol and what was open and closed, I noticed the cute little gift shop on the left and wondered when we would get to shop, hopefully on the way out, not on their way in, as other people were. I did not want to carry what I bought with me inside the Gardens.

"Thanks." I heard him tell the nice lady as we walked through the barn into the Gardens.

"Wow, it is beautiful here. I did not think a garden would thrive in this small town."

He nodded. "I know. The flowers that grow here are different for each season. The castle and fairy houses are the main attractions. We can see the castle from a distance, but we cannot enter as it is being repaired. The cafe is after the castle unless you want to go there first."

I shook my head. "I want to walk the whole place in order. Cafe after the castle."

As we walked the path, taking in the beautiful flowers, statues, and sculptures, he reached out and grabbed my hand. I was not complaining. The castle was first and huge. Made of stone, it looked straight out of medieval times. I took lots of pictures as we walked together, enjoying each other's company. I waited to start the conversation until after we saw the old castle and were walking toward the cafe. "I hope you don't mind, but I do have a lot of questions to ask about you and your family."

He walked in silence for a minute before answering, "I

know you do. This date was a way to get you alone so you can ask me anything you want. I will try to answer the best I can, but some things cannot be answered now."

I hesitated at the mention of the word 'date' but let it go as I took pictures of the cafe as we came upon it. "Well, I have noticed a lot from the beginning. Like how you and your family stay with yourselves, which I now know from your aunt today, that it is because you are in danger. Do you know who killed your parents?"

"We should grab something to eat." He stalled.

"Okay." I waited in line as I looked around me, taking in the beautiful, quiet cafe. It was black with the kitchen on the left in a square-sized building and the bathrooms on the right. The walkway separated the kitchen and bathrooms, with a balcony overlooking the gardens, which had chairs, tables, benches, and umbrellas to block the wind. We ordered and sat down, waiting for our food, and looked out at the great scenery around us.

"We do not know who killed our parents," he said as he finally looked at me from across the table. "We saw our parents at the scene where they were killed afterwards. We were there before the police and would like this to stay quiet."

"But shouldn't you tell the police?"

He shook his head. "They cannot know. They will ask too many questions, ones that we cannot answer."

"Because you don't know who it is." I asked in confusion.

"That's part of the reason."

"What else is the reason?"

He signed as he looked away, debating what to say. We were called to get our food, and he jumped up before I could blink. I watched him and saw the sun's glow reflected on his face as he walked back to me with our food and drinks. As we settled into our seats with our food and jackets hanging behind us over our chairs, he continued. "We know the police cannot stop the killer."

"How?"

He started eating his rare burger before he swallowed and spoke. "We know enough to know the killer is beyond the police. That is all I can say about it at the time."

"Okay, but you will explain soon, right?"

"Yes, I will. To answer another part of your question, we stay away from others because we are new to this situation. Our community is completely different from yours, and we like sticking close until the danger passes, and we feel more a part of this community and understand it better. It allows us to feel safe."

That piqued my interest, and I stopped eating my gourmet sandwich. "Where are you from?"

"Lake Las Vegas. It is a small town outside of Las Vegas, Nevada."

"What's it like there?" I asked, returning to my sandwich.

"Our community is different from all others, so different that some people would say we are an unusual species. We do not have a mayor, politicians or a government. Our town is run by one person, whom I will not name, and his own beliefs are to be followed. We all grew up there, and there were a lot of new laws passing that my family could not deal with anymore, so we left."

"I can imagine that it is horrible to live by one person's means." I plan to go home tonight to research more about Lake Las Vegas. It was difficult to believe a town, even a small town, could and would live like that in the States. We finish off our sandwiches. "Where to next?"

He looked out over the gardens as I cleared the table. "We follow the path. We still have plenty to see."

I have never known a guy to eat so little, which reminded me as we got on and walked out. "How come you all eat so little? I know you said before you eat a big breakfast, which is why you do not eat lunch at school, but a big breakfast would not last you all day."

"We survive on extraordinarily little food. We are used to it."

"But why? You cannot tell me you cannot afford it. I know by now you all are rich."

"We just don't have the need." His vague answers always frustrate me as they only leave more questions than answers. I stayed quiet as I hoped that he would continue, but after waiting a few minutes, I figured not. I walked to the fairy house, across the path from the cafe. I thought about my next question, wondering if he would answer it.

"How old are you?"

"I'm eighteen, almost nineteen." His answer was without hesitation, still making me wonder, but not enough to push.

"And Garcia and Paio? How old are they? Your aunt told me today they were pretending to be younger so they could have a normal high school experience."

"Garcia is twenty and Paio is twenty-two."

My mind went blank. How? "I thought they were married. When did they meet?"

"They met a few years ago. I know you think it is strange, but you need to remember we come from a completely different society than you."

"They are still too young to want to be married."

"Not from our home. Some people there are married before their twenties," he hesitated before he continued, as he was not sure he should. "Clarebelle and Citino are married as well. They actually just got married before we left home. Clarebelle and Citino are both twenty-four."

I was so shocked, I stopped taking pictures of the stone fairy house and looked at him, watching me. "What? Why?"

"Our community is small. We were all expected to marry young so we would have more years together, although I do not see why that should matter."

"What do you mean?"

"Our society lives longer than the average … person." His hesitation gave me the impression that 'person' was not what he was going to say. Before I could question it more, he changed the subject, "We have not talked about your family, which I do have questions about as well. Starting with this locket you wear every day." He reached out and gently handled the chain in order to look at the silver heart and open it to see the two pictures I had memorized. "When were these two pictures taken? They seem so happy."

He was so distracting, even though he did not seem to know it. It took me a few moments to remember what he asked. I forced myself to try to breathe evenly as I told him the story of my parents' love. "The one on the right is when my parents found out about Agento, and the other is from my mother's pregnancy announcement of me. My aunt and uncle explained how our parents said those were the best pictures they had ever taken, as they were so happy about the pregnancies." I hesitated, waiting as he let go of the locket, because continuing, "My father was a politician, and they were away on urgent business when the car accident happened. Agento and I were only supposed to stay with our uncle, aunt, and two cousins until they could get back home. Now we live here permanently. My aunt and uncle gave me this so I would always have them close."

The tension in the air lessened as he dropped his gaze. "That was really nice of them. You must miss your parents a lot. Where did you live before coming here?"

"Avalon, California. It is beautiful and sincere. We actually had a house much like yours here, except while yours is dark and in the forest, ours was white and in the open for anyone to just stop by anytime they wanted."

His soft, full-hearted chuckle was breathtaking, and I had to look away to remind myself to breathe. "We do like our privacy. I do not think we have time to continue further, it is already the afternoon, and I am sure you want to check out the gift shop. We should head back. I have something to do by four with my family."

I agreed and we walked back quietly, holding hands and each in our own thoughts. When we made it back to the barn, Errol stopped and turned to me. "I know you still have questions, as do I. Hopefully, everything will be cleared up soon. My family and I have a lot to do, but hopefully it gets resolved and we can talk more about us."

I hesitated, wanting to ask him what they were doing, but knowing I would not get any more answers today. I smiled, "Sounds great."

We shopped together in the gift shop, looking for unique gifts for people. I secretly found something I hoped he would love, but I do not know when I will give it to him yet. Hopefully, I will not be returning it or giving it to someone else in the future. We paid separately and headed outside to say our goodbyes, unsure when the next time we would see each other, at least outside of school.

I watched him walk away as I turned to walk back to my place. My heart was still racing by the time I got home from what I learned. I still do not know where we stand, what his secrets are, or if he wants to see me in more serious settings. Where do I go from here? If I did not have problems sleeping before, I definitely would tonight. I knew Errol and his family were different; how different, though, I do not know. I sneaked into the house to get ready for the night and school tomorrow.

The next week passed without any new knowledge gained by Errol and his family. Errol and his family, including Mrs. Lacey, were out all week for unknown reasons. Aunt Aida and Uncle Basil brought us all out that weekend for a family night and to celebrate the near end of school. We were all doing so great that there was no doubt about us graduating. Agento would even be finishing school early, giving us more to celebrate. I do not know what I will do without him after the next two weeks; school will be vastly different.

I was very conflicted over the weekend. I heard nothing from Errol. I wanted to text him, but did not want to come out as needy. I tried to distract myself with chores and exercise. I spent time together with my family and talked to Medea and Christabel over the phone. Before I knew it, Sunday night came, and I started passing out during the movie time.

CHAPTER VIII

Disaster struck at Uncle Basil's shop, and Aunt Aida had a doctor's appointment, so we got to school early. We all spent time together, waiting for the teachers to start arriving. We estimated we had twenty more minutes to go before they started showing up. The first car to arrive was in fact not a teacher but the Leigh family in their dark blue Rolls-Royce Phantom with tinted windows. After Paio, Garcia, Clarebelle, and Errol started walking toward us, the driver, Citino or Pagan, drove away. This must be why nobody saw what they had for vehicles.

They stood on the opposite side of the main entrance from us, but were still within talking distance. I guess I will be an icebreaker today. "Nice car."

Paio nodded. "Thanks. It was a celebration gift."

"For what?"

He smiled and looked away, but not before I saw the gleam in his eye. He really did not want us to know. What was there to hide?

Clarebelle jumped in and changed the subject, which did not stop the awkward pause with us or the confused looks between Cinnia and Agento, I noticed. "So, I was wondering," she hesitated, looking back at her family before looking back at me, "we were wondering if you would like to visit our place again. We had a wonderful time last time."

"Oh, well, that depends on when." I did have plans, a few, but Agento is not the only busy one. Aunt Aida, Cinnia, and I were planning our own trip to the Gardens, and Agento had another Saturday off, so we planned to drive out of town for more fun opportunities than Crestwood could give. Not that I did not like Crestwood.

"Whenever you are free is good for us. We do not have many visitors. We would like to get to know you more. You all can come if you want." She shifted her gaze among my family, who all stood in silence.

"I would like to see your place," Agento said after a moment's pause as he stepped forward. "There is a lot we don't know about you all, either. I, for one, would love to know who my sister is spending time with."

She smiled and held out her hand. "Great, so Errol and Gemma can figure it out when while they go on their next date and let us know. I am Clarebelle, by the way."

"Agento," he said as he shook her hand. Thankfully, the parking lot started filling with teachers and early students and the doors were soon opened. The tense atmosphere lessened as we all parted ways and headed to first period.

All morning, it bugged me how Clarebelle mentioned a date, and nobody interpreted it as anything else. Since when did we date? We had much to discuss. Why were they all out last week? I thought by now I would run out of questions, but they just kept piling up as days passed. Going from class to class, I wondered if any of my questions would ever get answered. Did Errol even want to date me, knowing there are secrets between us?

As Miss Thurlow started English, Errol pasted me a note and waited as I read it.

> *Sorry about this morning. I know that must have been awkward. Clarebelle has been on me for weeks to ask you out, and I have pushed it off. That is a lot to discuss, but I was hoping to see you this weekend. How about a night out on the town? We can go anywhere you want.*

I wrote back at the bottom of the small sheet.

> *Sounds great, and there are no worries about Clarebelle. I know you were not behind it. I have plans with my brother on Saturday. Does Sunday work for you?*

Passing the note back as Miss Thurlow looked down at the book, he read it and nodded to me. I smiled and paid attention to Miss Thurlow as she went over the homework from last night. Surprisingly, I never had a problem paying attention with Errol sitting next to me, as we were just comfortable in each other's presence.

Errol and I ate lunch today with my family and friends. Between Agento and Cinnia, I barely got to say a word. I mostly daydreamed about certain places in town we could walk to while listening to my family and friends question Errol. Agento and Adacio saw it as a way of getting to know Errol, and he did not seem to mind. Cinnia and my friends were naturally curious about any subject they asked. I did notice how Errol was hesitant and vague in his answers, at least the ones he would answer. I look forward to our next outing, hoping he will not be vague with me.

More than once this week, others and I have asked why they were out last week, but he just said they were busy or would change the subject completely. I guess they just did not want to go to school, or maybe they were grieving suddenly over their parents and didn't want people in their business. I hope they had a good reason, but his answer just made me wonder more. I know I have had moments where I could not stand being around people, but I didn't get to skip school. The family did not get in trouble for skipping, so I'm sure Mrs. Lacey had their excuse solid with the principal.

All week, Errol and I talked more, never answering or asking any of the more pressing questions. We spent lunch with his family for a few days, and the others with mine. On Friday, though, we ate alone, at our table away from others.

"What time did you want me to come get you?"

I hesitated as I thought it over. "Seven works for me if we are still planning on a night in town. We normally eat at six, so unless you want to eat out?" I questioned him as I was unsure what he wanted.

He nodded. "Seven works for me. It will give us more time to explore the town if we eat before we go out."

I smiled. "Great." As I ate, I tried to think about something to ask, but I was sure all the 'getting to know you' questions were answered through this week. I could not think of anything to say. I felt like I'd known him for years, even though at times the truth came rushing back, shattering my illusion. There was much to discover.

"I can't wait for this weekend." He said after a few moments of quiet. I finished my lunch, and he reached for my hand. "I know we said we had to discuss a lot before we started to date, but..." he hesitated, as if he was unsure how to say it. "I hope this weekend we can change that." He watched me, uncertain of how I would react.

I smiled to ease his uncertainty and covered his hand with my other one. "I agree that while I have more pressing questions, we can see where this weekend leads us."

"And I promise to answer any questions you have once you come to my place. There is a lot I can't say in public. I appreciate your patience."

"Your place is out there."

"Yes, and for many reasons. I hope it goes well. Do you have an idea when you would like to visit?"

"I honestly do not right now. I have thought about it, but I need to compare schedules with my family to see who is going with me and when we are all free to go."

"I understand. When you know, just let me know. We have a lot going on right now as well, but I think the sooner it happens, the better it will be. For everyone."

I agreed, and we sat comfortably, staring into each other's eyes, wondering what the other was thinking. The bell soon rang and we stood to go our separate ways, promising to talk again before Sunday night. The rest of the school day went by with friends and Cinnia asking for a play-by-play of today's lunch. After caving, I got an earful of what to do, how to, and what to say for the date. How to act is where I finally tuned everyone out. I planned my own way to do things, and nobody knows me better than myself.

Saturday morning, Agento and I left the house to walk into town to his favorite take-out place, and we waited quietly for our food before continuing on our day. We continued walking to The Maples Park to sit and hang out. I could not remember the last time we just sat down, ate, and enjoyed the serenity around us back home. Avalon was insignificant compared to San Francisco, but it was so crowded that there was no peaceful scenery around to enjoy. In times like these, Crestwood was better than Avalon. We listened to the kids in the distance playing while the cars drove by. We breathed in the grass around as we finished eating.

"So now, how do you feel about Errol?" I asked hesitantly, wondering if this week made him more comfortable or not.

He took a deep breath before turning to me. "I am never going to be comfortable with you dating. That is something you will always deal with. I am never changing that."

"But?"

"He is not the worst, I am sure you could find. He is secretive, so I'm still unsure, but I've seen you two together."

"Are you going with me to his place?"

"Of course. I need more information."

I laughed, picturing him quizzing his family at their own place. "You are so like dad, you don't know it."

He shrugged as he took in the trees and grass surrounding them. "Some days are better than others."

I agreed as we sat quietly for a few moments. "All I want is to turn back time to stop them from going, but then I think about Errol and how we never would have met."

"You really like him that much?"

"Yes, I do. I know it has only been a few months, but it just feels right. I do not know how to explain it."

He nodded as he pulled me to him. I leaned my head on his shoulder. "I get it. I promise not to be too hard on him then. But then again, if he lets me run interference, he is not worthy of you."

I tasked him and pushed him away. "Not funny."

He just laughed. We planned to hang out all day, but as we walked around, after leaving the park, we debated our next move when Uncle Basil called Agento.

"Come on. There is something Uncle Basil has for us back home." He said after hanging up. We hurried home after that, a little paranoid that something was wrong. Twenty minutes later, we reached the driveway and ran the rest of the way to the house. When we entered the house, we saw everyone standing in front of the living room in the hallway, blocking the room from entrance.

"What's going on?" Agento asked everyone, just as confused as I was.

Aunt Aida spoke up, silencing her daughter with a sharp look and a hand on her shoulder. "We are sorry to pull you two away from your time together, but we did something we could not wait to show you. It is a way to express our appreciation and remember the good times over the years. Please close your eyes and let us show you."

We looked at each other and shrugged. "Okay." I said as we closed our eyes. Someone pulled me forward, anxious to show us whatever it is. Once we stood where they wanted, they moved to the far side of the room and told us to open our eyes.

Tears came to my eyes instantly as I took everything in.

Pictures made from when we were born to recent ones of us in our new home filled the right corner of the living room. The far wall was filled in the shape of a tree for each of us; our parents' lives, Agento's, and mine. At the center of the trees sat our parents' ashes on a brown, rustic shelf built into the wall. Turning, we saw they even had a wall for their own family trees, opposite ours.

"This is great. I love it. How did you do this so fast?"

Uncle Basil smiled as he stepped forward. "I got up at five, and I am sure you remember Aida wouldn't let you two in here this morning. She did an amazing job finding all the pictures and frames while Cinnia and Adacio made the trees from wood they found in the forest around the house. We finished quicker than we thought, so we added our own family trees."

I did remember Aunt Aida saying something about the living room being off limits, but I did not pay attention as Agento and I were leaving this morning anyway. "Thank you."

"I just wish we had not let three years go by without reaching out again to your mother. My sister and I were close growing up, and I am sorry I didn't try harder to reconnect."

Agento shook his head before stopping our uncle from beating himself up. "Stop. It is not your fault. I think she did not blame you either. At least not in the end since she did send us here."

He smiled. "You are right. We cannot change the past, but we can keep it with us now." We all looked to the two walls and stood there for a while reminiscing about our past and great, sometimes embarrassing, memories before we slowly went our separate ways for the day.

My mind was racing the next day as I got ready for my date with Errol. Walking around town at night was strange but unique for a first date, especially with someone like Errol. I was not going to question it if it meant I got to spend time with him. Eating breakfast, getting showered, and hanging out in my room with Cinnia for date outfit ideas was my morning, and one I would never regret. I was too nervous to think about a proper outfit for tonight and appreciated Cinnia's help. The silver blue long-sleeved shirt with a fold-over look on the front paired perfectly with my form-fitting light wash blue jeans, a light white jacket to fight the cold breeze at night and white cowgirl boots, comfortable with sole inserts.

"You should go into fashion," I told her as we studied the perfect outfit lying out on my bed, standing in my robe.

"Maybe I will. Next is your hair."

Lunch passed, and we ate in the room, going through hundreds of unique styles in all of our magazines to best match my outfit. We settled on the fish-tale braid to crown the top of my head and turned to my jewelry next as the afternoon slowly passed. Cinnia hurried through my hair as I put on my diamond stud earrings and fastened my locket around my neck before we rushed downstairs to eat dinner.

I ran upstairs to change quickly after I finished eating. I stood in front of the mirror and admired the look. Cinnia did light makeup to finish the look as I turned from the mirror and headed downstairs to wait for Errol to text me that he was here. Everyone was waiting at the bottom of the stairs, not shy with their pictures.

CHAPTER IX

The comments continued nonstop as I tried to push past them to answer the door as the doorbell sounded. Errol stood with his hands in his pockets, looking uncertain. His outfit matched but through darker shades of color with his navy-blue shirt, black leather jacket, and black jeans. The contrast of black with the night made him look even more pale in the moonlight; eerie even.

"Are you ready to go?"

I nodded as I turned from him to my family behind me, waiting for introductions. "Everyone, this is Errol Leigh." Before I could continue with the introductions, each member of my family surrounded us and introduced themselves, shaking hands, even Agento. We left soon after with promises to return by ten to reassure everyone it would not be too late, at least in my uncle and aunt's eyes.

He drove the Phantom tonight, and we parked at the edge of town in the first parking lot, closest to my place, so we could get out and walk. At this late at night, in this small town, there was next to nothing open, or at least all were close to closing.

"It's different at night."

"Yes, and a lot quieter." He answered as we walked down the road. We walked hand in hand as I debated which questions he would feel comfortable answering tonight.

"Do I finally get an answer for the week you all were out of school?"

He signed and looked down at me, being a foot taller, "I guess now is a good time." We settled on a bench before he continued. "You know how we know more than the police about our parents' murder," I nodded so he knew to continue. "We were following a lead. We got an anonymous letter that led us to multiple places that we could not solve. It is a game to him and one we don't understand yet."

"Wait. Now you all are looking for the guy."

"Yes."

"Why not just go to the police?"

"They cannot know. It is not safe to explain the full explanation here. We are always on alert."

"Okay, but you will explain soon, right?"

He smiled and stood up to continue our walk. I thought for a minute I would not get an answer. Holding his hand out for me to take, he finally continued. "Yes. A lot more will make sense then. Which reminds me, when did you and your family want to come over?"

"I know Agento wants to go with me, but I do not think a crowd is a good thing. Especially if your family is in danger," I hinted. I debated my and Agento's schedule before continuing, "Saturday afternoon? I know Agento works in the morning, so we can come over after he comes home."

"What time?"

"He should be home by 4 pm, so we should be there by 5."

"How long do you think you will be able to stay? There is a lot I have to explain."

"I know my aunt and uncle aren't happy with us being out too late, but five, maybe six, hours should be good, pushing it, but good."

"That is perfect. Saturday it is. I will let my family know. Oh, and I promise, no danger will come to you or anyone associated with you."

I nodded and smiled thanks as I turned up to see the beautiful, clear night sky. The scenery was different at night and more peaceful, with the crickets, the stars shining, and the slight breeze; no danger or uncertainty in the air as we walked to the only store, a fast-food restaurant, still open. McDonald's was closing up soon, but we got ice cream cones to enjoy the spring night with. We sat down outside at their seating to eat them as they slowly closed up.

Halfway through the cones, we startled as someone came up behind us. "What are you two doing out here?"

I jumped as Errol stiffened, but smiled as he looked up at his sister, Pagan, and a guy slightly behind her. "Pagan, you know I had a date tonight. What are you two doing here?"

She smiled as she sat down next to him. "Okay, you got me. I just had to see you, and Gemma," she nodded to me as she continued, "everyone has had their opinions about you two, and I just wanted to see it for myself. I do not like pretending to be younger for school, so I don't see you two as much as the others get to."

I tried to ignore the guy standing behind Pagan as Pagan and Errol continued their sister/brother banner, but he was impossible to ignore. He was tall, possibly taller than Errol, but it is hard to tell with us sitting and him standing. His biceps barely fit in his black T-shirt as he folded his arms across his chest. He wore worn-out blue jeans with holes in them, but what held my attention was his dark eyes, black and reflecting nothing, much like a black hole in space. His face was expressionless except for the dark gleam in his eyes as he stared back at me.

"Gemma," I pulled my glance from the man when I heard Errol speaking to me, gently shaking my shoulder, and looking between me and him. "Are you okay? I called to you twice."

I nodded. "Yes. I am sorry. I blanked out for a minute." Looking back at the man standing, watching me with a smirk, I gave my own smile. "Hello, we have not met yet. My name is Gemma Sheard."

He looked on without responding. This only brought on an uneasy feeling in my gut as I waited. Pagan stood up, wrapping one arm around his back and reached for his thick black hair to push back a strand that covered his ear, before turning to me. "This is Daimon Cree. My new boyfriend. He is new in town, so I'm sure that's why you haven't met before."

"I am new as well. I moved here with my brother to live with our aunt, uncle, and cousins after I lost my parents in a car crash."

"I am sorry. I understand what the loss of a parent is like." Her sympathetic look was sincere, and I fought back tears.

"It has its good and bad moments."

"That's true."

"Pagan, as much as I love seeing my siblings, I am on a date and would appreciate some space."

She smiled and moved back as she waved off Errol.

"Brothers!" She exclaimed, with a look at me, one I understood greatly and smiled back. "We will leave you now. We have our own night planned."

"Sorry about that." Errol said, drawing my attention from their retreating forms.

I shook my head as I turned back to Errol. "No, it is fine. I do not know Pagan and like seeing her. How long has she been dating Daimon? He is something else."

"A few weeks now. He is anti-social, but we are happy if she is."

I smiled as I recalled the conversation between their aunt and Clarebelle; this family really does only want the best for each other. Over the next two hours, we found a few places to hang out at, goofing around, looking for attractions for future dates, and just enjoying the night.

We found a clearing and were lying down in the freshly cut grass on the opposite side of town from the vehicle, when I remembered a couple more questions I wanted answered tonight. "I know your family's reason for moving here, but what is yours? Did you just move here to stay with them, or was it some other reason?"

Rolling onto his side, he looked down at me. "It was a little of both, actually. I have never been apart from my family, but I love exploring. This move has given me this opportunity."

"Even though it's a small town."

"Yes, small towns are wonderful as they are more like a family than a big city is. Seeing the difference in the environment and society here and in Lake Las Vegas has taught me a lot. It makes me want to see more of the world, though. Everywhere you go, there is a uniqueness about it."

"I never thought of that. I just believed that all small towns were too small for any enjoyment in life, but I did learn a lot by being here. They have such a history, and it is a great community here."

"You know, there is a history museum here. We could go to it."

"I would like that. History tells us a lot about ourselves and helps us find a connection to others from before us."

He nodded as he leaned down, closer to me than ever before. "I know this is fast, but I feel more connected to you than anybody else."

"Me too."

He was too much of a gentleman for me to think he would try to take advantage of me, so I smiled and sat up ever so slightly, enjoying the tension in the air and the uncertainty in his eyes. As I used one elbow to hold myself up, I reached into his short, wavy hair. I was finally ecstatic, and I finally got to feel its smooth locks. He signed as I combed my fingers through his hair and waited until I looked back into his eyes and laid my hand back between us before he spoke again, his voice low and husky.

"We should stop. Now really is not the time for us to." He hinted but could not seem to say it. I knew I would love to kiss him, but he did have a lot of secrets, so I guess, for now, I will take his advice.

"You are right. We have some stuff to talk about first."

"I don't mean to hide it from you, but it's life-changing, and I want you to know, but here is not a great place for it."

"I get it. In time and at the right place." I smiled to show I understood, but deep down, I really did not.

What did the place matter? What is his secret, which is so huge that it is life-changing? Could I handle it? He leaned down and pulled me close as I laid back, unsure what to say or do after that. I felt the grass tickle my arm as the breeze blew, and I moved my hand to rest on his chest. He kept his arm around me, moving ever so often up and down my back. I listened to his heartbeat, never changing, and watched the stars. We laid there for a few minutes in silence, enjoying the birds chirping and the slight breeze in the air. My next question came out before I stopped myself.

"Have you had a girlfriend before?"

"Yes, and no, it was never serious."

I looked up at him, embarrassed that he read me so well. My heart skipped as his finger trailed down the side of my face, then down to my neck before stopping there to rest. The tension was still there, lingering like a shadow and one that did not want to be ignored. I turned away and broke the tension as I grew uncertain of what to do.

"We still have an hour. Did you want to head back through town?" He said as he sat up as well.

"Yes. I do not think it's smart to stay here much longer."

He helped me up, and together we slowly headed back through town, holding hands and enjoying the quiet night as we went. I debated what to ask him and decided to stop wasting time and just ask.

We made it halfway through town, and I asked the first question that came to mind. "What do you like the most about Crestwood?"

"The trust in the people. This town really is a suitable place to be, and not much happens here. The serenity of this place and its history." He smiled as he continued. "It almost makes me regret coming here. I always wanted to explore the world, as you know, but I do not feel like leaving anytime soon."

"That's good." I said, secretly hoping his need to explore does not take him away, at least not without me. That very thought made me anxious as I did not know why I felt so close to him or where my desire came from. I also regret not having the courage to kiss him when I had the chance. I have never kissed anyone before, and while he does have sound reason to wait, I do not want to.

He pulled me from my thoughts as we walked in front of the museum in town. The huge historical building was history itself, with its bricks and stones making up the foundation. "We should go when it is open. I would love to see inside."

I nodded as I took in the museum. "I agree. I would love to see it. When do you think we can go?" I was so glad to spend time with him, no matter where it was and maybe on our next date, I can work up the courage to kiss him. I hope his secret does not end up being our end; that would really suck if it were.

He smiled and turned toward me. "We already have a date planned, so I think it is best to wait and see what happens next. I hope within the next two weeks we can go, but I do not know how well you will take my secret." My hesitation was all he needed to push me forward. "Come on. We should continue our current date."

We walked and talked, getting to know our less important secrets, ones I did not mind sharing and ones he only told his family. Why should any secret stop us from being together? I still have secrets I will not tell him, and I understand their importance, but I knew, no matter what they were, I would respond with an open mind.

We ended the date by going back to the car, and he stopped me from getting in. "I hope you don't mind waiting."

The tension never did fully leave us, and I looked into his stunning hazel eyes as I responded. "No. It's for the best to wait."

His eyes seemed to glow, but it must have been my imagination. "Great. Maybe next time." I nodded and looked down, unsure of what to expect.

"Let us go then. We do not want to be late. I am sure your family is waiting up for you."

"Probably. Given that they all were as excited as I was about tonight." I blushed as I turned away and got in. I cannot believe I just admitted that. What was I thinking?

I sat in the seat, lost in my thoughts as I kept pondering what his secret was. Could everything I questioned be connected somehow? All of the weird aspects I have noticed. If I thought I was nervous before about going over with Agento, now I was more anxious, but at the same time, I could not wait. Finally, I knew I would find out the truth, the whole truth.

He held my hand as he drove me home and walked me to the door. "See you in school." He said as he walked back to his truck, waiting there for me to enter the house before driving away.

The house was dark and quiet, given the hour, I had hoped nobody would stay up. I welcomed the silent house, that is, until I saw Aunt Aida was waiting up for me. She was just making her way downstairs as I shut the door behind me. She stopped in her tracks, probably going into the kitchen for a late snack, when she saw me.

"So how did it go?" She asked as she hugged me and led me, arm in arm, to the kitchen.

I smiled as I sat down at the table, and she sat next to me.

"It was great. He was a complete gentleman, and I cannot wait to go over to his place next weekend."

"I am glad. I think you two look great together."

"Agento and I are going on Saturday night after he gets home from work. We promise we are not going to be out too late." I hesitated and added, "If you are okay with it."

"Honey, of course it is okay with me, and your uncle. We are glad you found someone who makes you happy. I know this move has been difficult, and you are still struggling some days to keep going, but seeing the happy moments and seizing them are key in getting through life."

"I know you are here for me, and Agento, when needed. I will not take advantage of your help. If you need anything, just ask. I know we changed your life as well."

"I am fine, really. I love having you two in our lives, and I would not change it for anything in the world." She patted my hand and stood up. "Now, go to bed. You have a long week ahead of you."

I walked upstairs as Aunt Aida stayed behind to get her snack before heading up herself. Stunned by how easy tonight was, I got ready for bed and climbed in as I shut off my thoughts. Tomorrow will come soon enough, and I will have plenty of people asking me questions then, but tonight, all I wanted was a peaceful, quiet sleep.

CHAPTER X

The next morning, before we left the house for school, Adacio stopped by my room as I was going through my backpack, ready to leave. "Do you really like him?"

I looked up toward him as I answered, "That was unexpected from you." I signed as I smiled and sat down. "Yes, I really do like him. I cannot explain it. I know it is fast, but it's like I've known him much longer."

"Your face tells me more than I asked for. I know we have not talked much, but I am here for you. I just want to make sure my little cousin is doing what she wants and not what someone else wants."

"I'm not that little anymore."

"You will always be little to me." I pushed him away from me when he stepped closer and messed with my ponytail. "I am not your brother, so I do not need to warn you away from dating anyone. That's Agento's job."

"It is nobody's job. I have liked Errol since the beginning. I am just lucky someone could like me back. I do not exactly fit in here."

"You have adapted pretty quickly to this little town."

"Yes, but it doesn't mean I will change my personality."

"Good, because I like your personality. Do not change for anyone."

"I do not plan to. Adacio, nobody has ever made me do what I do not want to, and I won't let anybody change that now."

"Good," he smiled as he walked away, "little cousin." He left me frustrated as I laughed off his comment and continued to the door to leave for school. He knew I would get him back for that comment when he least expected it.

Medea and I got caught passing notes in class, but only got a warning from Mr. Woodward. She wanted to throw a party while her parents were away this weekend. I declined as I had plans with my brother and Errol. I have been fitting in nicely since coming to live here, and I could not believe school was out in four weeks. As the day progressed, English was the only class I looked forward to, but when I entered, Errol was absent again. I tried to hide my disappointment behind my book as class started. He was never sick, so it must be something new that was uncovered with his parents' murder. I pondered this development as I listened to Miss Thurlow and even answered a few questions when called upon.

I held out hope as I walked to lunch, maybe they were just late today. I looked for him and his family, but they were all absent from their table. I tried casually asking everyone at my table who would talk to me about the family, but nobody knew anything, much like before. Gossip started about the Leigh family and favoritism in the school office. They were all that everyone wondered about as they were so secretive and absent more now than ever before. Maybe Mrs. Lacey was in today, and she could shed some light on this for me.

My afternoon flew by as I debated when to ask Mrs. Lacey. I found the excuse to leave when Ms. Clara started us with homework today. It was an easy day, she said. I finished my artwork and left my last class five minutes early, pleading for the bathroom. My breath left me in relief as I saw Mrs. Lacey was quietly reading at her desk when I showed up.

"Why is none of the Leigh family in today?" I asked as soon as I entered, not caring about hiding any emotion from my face. She had to know, being their aunt and all.

She looked up from her book and motioned for me to sit, waiting until I did. "They had an emergency. Very last minute."

"What kind?" I was not falling for it. "Wouldn't you be with them if they did?"

"Not this time. I am not a part of this. They found something and are investigating it."

"Wait…you mean, their parents' killer?"

"I do not know what you know, but given the look on Errol's face this morning, I am going to say soon you will know everything. I cannot tell you right now. Hopefully, you will understand it all this weekend when you visit their place." She went back to reading as if dismissing me, which only frustrated me more.

I was tired of all the secrets. "Are they going to the police with this new knowledge?"

"No."

"Why not?" I heaved a sigh.

"You will know soon enough. You should leave. I am sure

your family's waiting for you, as the bell had rung a couple of minutes ago."

I hesitated, wanting answers, but knew she would not give any, and I knew my uncle didn't like being kept waiting. Later that night, I tried texting Errol, but he never replied. I ignored my family that night at dinner, lost in my own thoughts. I stayed in my room, knowing my family was concerned, as I ignored them and my turn for movie night, but I could not give them an answer until I knew what to say. I was so conflicted, wondering what was going on and afraid of what could be happening. Why would they investigate their parents' murder? Why hide it? What would I someday understand? Errol texted me extremely late, so I didn't see it until morning, explaining we would talk soon.

Errol was back in school today, but his family was not. He did not even look at me in English class, but at lunch, his focus was completely on me as we sat down at our table. I was so frustrated that I just wanted to know what was going on. Why did Errol come to school without his family? What secret was I supposed to understand? Why are they hiding it from every-one? I wish he would just tell me.

"What happened yesterday? Your aunt said you all had a lead in your parents' murder and were hiding it from the police. Why are you investigating your parents' murder?"

He traced the lines on the table before he spoke, without looking back up at me. "We were contacted, and we investi-gated it. I told you before that the police cannot help us. They would not understand what they are facing, and we cannot explain it to them."

"You were contacted? What happened? Why wouldn't the police know?"

"Because the killer is from our community back home."

I touched his arm and waited until he looked back up at me. "You know who it is."

"No, we only know where it all started. I understand if you want to cancel dinner this weekend. It is not safe right now to be around me. Maybe we can reschedule it for two weeks out, just to be safe."

"What?" I pushed my half-eaten food aside as I leaned closer to him. "If you expect to have a relationship with me, how could you think I would leave you alone to face whatever this is?"

"I do not know that we should continue dating. I do know I want you to know more about us, but what is going on right now is extremely dangerous. There is a lot to cover with us, and we could always wait till it's safer before we continue this relationship."

"No. We are not cancelling. Agento will be suspicious, and I want to know everything about you. This threat will not stop me." I smiled as I sat back into my seat and continued, "Besides, if it's from your town, I doubt I will be a target."

Errol's look of astonishment as he quietly tried explaining, unsure how to without saying too much, which just made the threat lack the danger vibe that I felt. "Anybody...everyone in contact with us is a target...I can't explain it...there's a lot we know and a lot we don't."

I ate my lunch silently as I pondered what to say. Errol was warning me, but at the same time, I wanted to prove I could be a great girlfriend. What girlfriend would leave at the first sign of danger? My strong attraction has kept me awake most nights, wondering what it would be like to be a couple. He is strange and has great secrets, but his kind, quiet nature makes me want to know more.

"I want to be with you. Honesty is the best policy for any great relationship." I hesitated as I recalled how he dodged a question earlier, and before I could ask it again, the bell rang.

"Well then, we will have plenty of time to talk when you and Agento come over at 5 pm."

"I look forward to it."

The day progressed quickly, leaving me with my friends and Cinnia in the parking lot, waiting for our families to come. Christabel had just invited us to her church again this weekend, saying she could use the help with her parents.

"They must really not want you to leave town for college." Medea commented upon hearing Christabel's parents' argument.

Christabel signed as she adjusted her backpack straps. "They want me to attend a college nearby. That way, I will not be far from them. It is just not what I want."

"Why would the church be a place for this argument?" I asked, concerned for Christabel.

"They think they can ask Reverend Adamus for his advice, hoping he sides with them since he's all about family values."

"So, if we went, you would have us on your side. The plan has terrific value to it as we would outnumber them, but would they even care to listen to us?"

She smiled and nodded. "The benefits expressed from each of us would make them hear our side more than just my own."

"We are here for you, then."

"Count me in." Cinnia added.

Medea agreed as well, as we all started walking away and toward our families waiting. As Uncle Basil drove us home for the afternoon, I pondered my weekend plans and how much busier I was here than back in Avalon. The rest of the night passed as usual, with homework and a fun family night.

The Leigh family returned to school for the rest of the week but seemed more distanced than ever before; concerned even. Errol and I ate alone at our table for the rest of the week, making me wonder why he was just as distanced as his family. He kept glancing at his family, watching them as they whispered about something I had no idea of. I barely got any information from him, so I stuck to the basic questions any girlfriend would want to know about her boyfriend, only to get vague answers in return.

By Friday, I could not take it anymore and asked Errol to eat with my family and friends; that way, I had someone to talk to when he went silent. Everyone noticed this sudden change with Errol and his family, which brought more gossip spreading like a forest fire. I was exhausted by the time I entered gym class. Mrs. Finley made us play baseball today. I was told to walk on the track, doing one mile before I could return to the game, after accidentally running into a classmate and causing him to sit out, nursing his hand from the fall we took.

I did my best to focus in my last class, but I am not sure how successful I was when the next thing I knew, school finished for the day. I made my way to the parking lot. I followed the crowd of eager students leaving school for the fun weekends they had planned when I heard someone calling my name.

"Gemma."

I turned to see Errol pushing through the crowd to me, and stood aside to let other students pass to wait for him. "Hey."

"I am sorry for this week. I did not mean to ignore you." He explained as he stood next to me.

"That's okay."

"No, it is not. I just cannot tell you what's happened, at least not yet. It has been frustrating hiding this from you."

That grabbed my attention, making me miss Cinnia's wave. "So, what happened?"

He composed himself before saying, "Hopefully tomorrow everything goes well because I do want you to know. There is just a lot happening, and my family and I are distracted right now. I hope you can understand I…"

He was cut off as someone stepped close to us, asking, "Are we going to wait on you all day?"

I turned to Agento with an ignored look, hoping to silence him, but he ignored it as Errol spoke up first, "It was my fault entirely. I had to apologize for my behavior this week."

He nodded as he weighed Errol's words. "Good. We all were wondering about that."

Changing the subject, smoothly and without much suspicion, Errol continued, "I cannot wait for you two to come to my place. We can get to know each other better. It is great that you want to know who your sister is dating. It shows you care."

Agento shrugged as he pulled me to him. "Yes, well, she is all I have left. We do have to leave now. I finished school today, and I cannot wait to never set foot here again."

"I understand."

"See you tomorrow…" I called out as Agento pulled me to the vehicle, where everyone else was waiting impatiently. Uncle Basil stayed late today at the shop, so Adacio came to get us.

"That was rude." I told him before we got into the truck.

"I'm not happy with you dating, and you know it."

"Errol is a great guy. Once you agreed to visit his place, if you have forgotten."

"Does not mean I have to be nice. You are not married to the guy."

Before I could respond, Cinnia and Adacio started laughing. Cinnia tried to stop but could not, that is, until I pushed her. "I am sorry. I cannot help it. You two remind me of Adacio and me last year."

"That guy was a loser." Adacio gave a pointed look to Cinnia.

She rolled her eyes as she turned back to me. "My point being. It is great having you two here and knowing I'm not alone with an annoying brother."

"I know." I said as I turned to Agento. "And some days it's unfair having an overbearing, know-it-all brother."

"That is true, but at least you have someone to look after you. There are a lot of single children who hope for a sibling."

"You are forgiven, like always. Just do not be mean to them tomorrow. We are guests at their house."

"We will have to wait and see what happens. If he really is a great guy, I will know. If he is not, you dump him and move on."

I ignored his last comment, hoping he would behave himself. The last thing I want is not to get any answers I was promised because Agento started a fight with Errol or one of his siblings.

As we walked into the house, Cinnia and Adacio were walking purposely behind us, and we were stunned into silence. The hallway was decorated with graduation streamers and balloons. Aunt Aida and Uncle Basil jumped out from the living room to yell in surprise and hugged Agento. I guess Uncle Basil did not have to work late.

"We know you haven't had a graduation ceremony since you finished early, so we decided to throw you one." Uncle Basil said as Aunt Aida pulled us into the kitchen. "We even got you something special to complete the day."

Lying on the table beside a huge, two-layer cake with black frosting and yellow stars decorating the sides was a flat rectangle gift wrapped in matching paper to the cake. Agento opened the gift first, revealing his graduation diploma. "They told me I had to wait for all the diplomas to go out. How did you get it?" Agento said, astounded.

"I have my ways." Aunt Aida said mysteriously.

"She persuaded the principal with her baking goods." Uncle Basil revealed and earned a push from his wife. We all stood laughing and enjoying the admiration on Agento's face as Aunt Aida started cutting the cake to serve. Removing the topper that said 'Congrats Agento' and grabbing the cake knife, she started serving the cake, evenly among us, leaving Agento the top layer for later.

I stepped away for a bit when my phone chimed, and I saw it was Errol.

> Hey, I know you are most likely busy, but I wanted to make sure everything was good between us. This week has been difficult, I know.

I took a deep breath, debating how honest I wanted to be.

Everything is great. I just have a lot of questions and concerns by not knowing the answers.

His response came quickly.

> I have the answers. Hopefully, you will understand and have an open mind tomorrow.

You could always tell me now.

> I cannot. It is best in person and definitely in private.

There will not be much privacy with my brother coming with me and your family there. Right now, it is just the two of us.

> My family will not be a problem. Hopefully, Agento will be fine with us stepping away for a bit without him. My family will keep him company.

Can he know?

> Right now, no. Maybe in the future we can. Right now, I'm only concerned with you knowing.

How bad can it be?

> See you tomorrow. I have to go out for a bit with Paio.

Okay. See you tomorrow.

I did not hear anyone coming into the hallway, and I jumped as a hand landed on my shoulder. "Are you okay? Sorry, I did not mean to scare you," Adacio reasoned as I started breathing regularly again. I sat down on the stairs, leaving space for him to join me.

"No, I am fine. I was distracted." I said as I held up my phone. "I was texting Errol."

"Is everything okay?"

"Yes. Why wouldn't it be?"

"I do not know. I just wanted to see how you were doing. It does not seem like you to disappear on your brother."

"I am great. Nervous about tomorrow with Agento going, but it's like Cinnia said. It is what annoying brothers do." I hinted. "I had to see what he wanted. It is not every day I get a text from Errol."

He signed as he considered what to say. "Cinnia and I have a great relationship, but so do you and Agento. He will not make a scene tomorrow unless he needs to. You should see it from his side. He is just worried for you, your safety, and possibly losing you."

"That is crazy. He will never lose me."

"That is what you think, but coming from his side, he's not going to be the only guy in your life now on. He likes taking care of you and knows someday someone else will be there for you. He will be yesterday's news. You cannot promise him by constantly arguing with him that it won't happen."

I signed as I realized just how much we used to hang out and how little we do here. Maybe Adacio was on to something.

"I will reassure him. Nobody will stop me from going to Agento if I need to."

"That's all he wants from you."

We hug and sit for a minute, debating what happens next. Adacio and I were not as close as we could be, but we weren't enemies in the least. We were cousins who had nothing in common; I liked shopping, hanging out with my friends, caring for people and animals, and dance, while Adacio loved sports, much of all like Agento, running, doing God knows what with his friends, and driving out of town to see more places nearby. He would be gone for hours over the weekend, and nobody questioned him; he was a free spirit. I love this small town, and I have not had as much spirit in traveling as he does. I do wonder what it would be like to travel one day, but right now, I am happy staying in one place.

"We should go congratulate your brother."

"Yes, let's go."

CHAPTER XI

The next morning, I started my morning routine, only for Cinnia to interrupt with a dance video in the gym for our morning exercise. Soon, we spent the rest of the morning with everyone, except Agento, as he left for work, playing board games in the living room. I was anxious, waiting for five o'clock to come around. The games were exciting, and we had an enjoyable day, but my anxiety persisted in the back of my mind. I have been wanting answers for a while now, and now that it is here, or about to be, I was nervous, wondering if I could handle it.

Late afternoon, I started getting ready, knowing Agento would be home soon, and I did not want to wait longer than I needed to. I went through everything in my closet, unsure what to wear as I did not know what would happen. Would we become official today? Would I be able to see past whatever this great secret was? Should I dress as a girlfriend or a friend? My thoughts wandered for a while as I searched through my outfits. Seeing my frustration as Agento came home and started getting ready himself, Cinnia stopped by and helped. Casual, friend, but possible girlfriend, I found the outfit. Cinnia was a lifesaver. I do not know how she does it, but she should never stop.

Agento and I were finally heading to Errol's place. I was so nervous as Agento drove. He, like everyone, commented on the forest surrounding the place and why they would live in the middle of nowhere, on the outskirts of town. Secrets will be revealed today, and I ignored Agento, focusing on my own thoughts.

My only previous relationship had lasted two months, which ended because I found him cheating with a rival of mine. My lifetime school enemy revealed she only made out with him because she blamed me for telling her secrets in elementary school, which I later found out she was not my friend after all. Which never got fixed before I left Avalon. I had a tough time trusting any of my friends after everything that had happened with her, and now I wondered if I was even wrong to begin with. None of my friends from back home had tried to stay in contact with me since I moved here.

I knocked once we reached the door and waited for someone to open it as Agento took in the house and the surrounding scenery. The grass was luscious as ever, with a variety of trees surrounding the beautiful home of the Leigh family. I never looked around the house, but imagined it to be just as green and luscious as the front was. Palma Lacey soon opened the door, stopping Agento's observation of the garage.

"Mrs. Lacey?" Agento asked, surprised to see the school secretary here.

"Hello, Agento. It is nice to see you outside of the school.

We are not at school, so call me Palma. And congratulations on an early graduation. You deserved it. Please, do come in."

"Thank you. Why are you here?" He added as we walked in.

We walked down the grey hallway with its paintings on the walls to the open room; now known as a parlor, not a living room like I thought last time. "I am here as the adult. I know you know I am Errol's aunt. I do not know how much you know about their parents, but they are no longer with us."

"I am sorry. I did not know." He looked at me with a pointed look, one I ignored as Palma called out to everyone and we sat down, respectfully waiting for them to come.

"Yes. It was a tragedy, but one we are coping with. My sister and I were remarkably close. Now I help out when needed."

"I understand. We lost our parents in a car accident just over two months ago, if you do not mind me asking. What happened? How long ago did they pass?"

"It's been just over three months now, and they were murdered, not far from here, actually."

"That is terrible. Do you know what happened?"

"No. Nobody does. It is an open case." Changing the subject, she announced, "Here they come."

I stood aside, next to Errol, as Palma made introductions for Agento, and he shook everyone's hands. We apparently had arrived at an inconvenient time, as Pagan and Clarebelle were in the middle of an argument. It seemed to be about us and, as I remembered, Daimon.

"This is a really bad time."

"No, it's a great time as we already have guests."

"But these guests are not-"

"Clarebelle, Pagan, please. You are being rude to our guests. What is going on?" Palma said as she interrupted their argument, standing between the ladies.

"Pagan invited Daimon over tonight. He will be here shortly."

"What?"

"He has been here before. I do not see the problem."

Palma glanced at us before turning back to Pagan. "Too many guests are the problem. Not everybody knows about certain aspects of you or this place."

I felt awkward as it was obvious she was talking about Agento and me, but I had met Daimon before and felt they were overreacting. Wanting to keep the peace, I said, "I do not mind. I met Daimon, and I am okay with Pagan wanting to have someone else over. This house can fit everyone." Everyone looked at me in shock, except Agento, who agreed with me.

Pagan broke the awkward silence and smiled at me. "Thank you. See? She is fine with another guest coming tonight."

"This is not just another guest. He is completely different from Agento and Gemma. Putting everyone together is not a clever idea. We will discuss this later." With that pointed look, Palma walked into the kitchen, most likely to see to dinner.

After everyone slowly recovered and hid their expressions, Garcia got everyone sitting in the parlor, with Agento at the center of the conversation as he started asking questions, much like how my relationship with Errol started. As long as he stayed basic, I was fine with that. He did not need to know more than I knew about this family. Clarebelle and Mrs. Lacey were the main responders, but Garcia jumped in when the conversation turned to her and Paio. I noticed

Citino was quiet but responded when needed, and Pagan ignored everyone as she texted Daimon, most likely, on her phone.

Errol invited me outside to see their garden, which was behind the house in a large greenhouse. After telling Agento and making sure that Agento was okay with it, Errol and I walked outside, through the back door. We waved to Palma as we walked through the kitchen door. Errol explained, as we walked, how everyone built the garden shortly after our date at the Botanical Gardens.

"It gave me inspiration," he explained as we started looking around. "I bought a lot of flowers and herb seeds while we were there. I even got you a gift. It is at the center of the garden, where we can talk without the others hearing our conversation."

"It is lovely here. You did a great job of planting and getting them started. It will take time before it fully grows, but it still looks wonderful."

"Some have already grown while others are slower, but it is enjoyable to watch. It definitely has my wandering mind entertained."

"Where do you want to travel to the most?"

"I am not sure yet. I have been preoccupied with a lot lately, and I have not thought it through."

"I understand."

As we reached the center of the garden, I saw the lifelike white oak log-shaped planter from the Botanical Gardens and wandered over to it. It had such a lovely flower, fully bloomed. "You got some rose glow lantana for me. They are lovely."

"I was not sure how you were with plants, so I got the one that only needs water once a week. I also was not sure which one you would like best, as you took pictures of all of them, but this one is one of my favorites."

The dark green foliage and rounded bicolor rose pink and creamy yellow flowers sat beautifully in this white oak planter. "They are beautiful. I love these flowers and the planter you chose. And I never owned a plant before, so I am grateful you thought of taking care of the flower. I would have most likely killed it quickly if you chose a more demanding flower."

He clears his throat while I gently touch the flower buds, wondering what the meaning behind them is or if I should read into it more or not. Our relationship was rocky at best, and I was unsure where this was going. I stepped back and looked at him, watching me with wonder in his eyes. The air intensified as we stared at each other, unsure who would break the quiet first.

Errol soon broke eye contact, looking to the flower before gesturing to the bench. "We should talk now while your brother is with my family. They can only do so much, and they know this may take a while for you to understand." I sat nervously on the bench, waiting anxiously for him to continue. I knew I wanted answers, but this was basically a confession, one I knew I would not have to jump through hoops to get him to tell me anything right now. "I know this will be hard to believe, and there are many ways to tell you this. I find it is best just to come out and say it. Then I can explain in depth afterwards. If you do not run screaming." Errol, still holding my hand, turned to me and looked deeply into my eyes.

"Whatever it is, I am here. Tell me. I will not run."

"Before this goes any further, you need to know," Errol hesitated as he debated whether she could handle his deep, dark secret. With a deep breath, he continued, "I am a vampire."

I sat stunned in silence, unsure where he was going with this unrealistic secret of his. Was he insane? "I am sorry. You are what?" I asked in disbelief. This had to be a joke, right?

"A vampire. My whole family is, including everyone back home, except Aunt Palma and a few others. I know this is difficult for you to believe; my people make that happen in order to keep the secret."

"I don't understand." Why was he insistent with this crazy notion? Did I fall in love with a crazy person?

Seeing my disbelief, he signed as he let go of my hand and stood up. He took a few steps before turning back to me. "I had hoped it would not come to this, but it does seem to work best from what I heard. This is what I mean."

My disbelief soon turned into horror as his face stayed the same, but his canine teeth grew into two pointed, sharp fangs, right in front of me, and his eyes took on a shimmering glow, as if the light reflected against them, even though the light did not change. "Do not be afraid. I will not hurt you." He said as he knelt in front of me. I did not realize I had retreated until he kneeled in front of me, pleading. I was stunned, staring at the fangs and did not notice the concerned look on his face, only his lack of expression in those reflecting eyes. His fangs soon retracted, and his eyes lost the shimmer in them as I watched. I tried not to pull away from him anymore, but what just happened? I couldn't believe it, yet I knew I wasn't crazy. I saw what I saw.

"How is this possible? Why?"

"It is a lot to explain, but I was born like this. My kind is different from most. My family and a few others were cursed over a millennium ago. I will tell you the story later when we have more time, if you want, but we are born vampires. Pagan,

Clarebelle, Paio, and I are the children of our parents, Antico and Maya. Citino and Garcia were turned into vampires shortly after meeting Clarebelle and Paio."

"They turned them?"

"No. Our parents did. Once they discovered the connection they had. They are soulmates. This is difficult for our kind to find, but they are out there, one for each of us if we are lucky enough to find them."

The pieces started to fit as my mind processed this discovery. They barely ate at school, they distanced themselves from everyone, they were loners, but model students in the teachers' eyes. The danger, the differences in who they were, and the way they sometimes spoke. They had a hint of an accent and hesitation in their speech that made them seem like they were unsure what to say, how to say it, or if they said too much. I now understand it all. I was still unsure about this secret and did not know what to make of it, but I was also curious to know more. After all, how else could I possibly explain his fangs and eyes? And all the aspects that made them stand out, and how it drove me crazy, not understanding why.

"Wait…that is what celebration Paio meant when asked at the school about the Rolls-Royce Phantom. It was his marriage to Garcia."

"Yes. But it is more than his marriage; it's about finding his soulmate. Our parents' main concern was our happiness." The sadness in his eyes was apparent as he mentioned his parents.

"Have you found yours?" I asked, and without knowing it, I had leaned forward, unable to stop myself.

"I have."

The meaningful look in his eyes brought hope to my heart, but I did not want to assume, so I backed off and leaned away.

He sat down next to me again as he realized I was not running away from him.

"I won't stay in your way then." I said, heartbroken but sincere.

But as I got up to walk away from him, Errol grabbed me, and I ended up in his lap. I gasped and placed my hands on his shoulders as he leaned in. "You are my soulmate."

The tension thickened in the air, making it difficult to breathe as I looked into his eyes. Being this close to him, I wondered if I was ready for this to happen. He slowly leaned forward, waiting for my response. Could I really believe him? Could I trust him not to bite me? I moved without thought as my hand moved into his wavy hair, and I leaned into him. He quickly closed the distance, and our lips touched. The air thickened as the kiss deepened, and his arms wrapped around me. Feelings elevated, and I leaned in for more, lost in the kiss, and my fingers tangled in his hair.

The excitement of being with him, understanding his secrets, and still wanting him became so intense, but still terrifying as I realized how quickly this could end. With my heart racing, I soon realized that I was making out with a vampire. How weird my life could get. After what felt like hours but was only minutes, I tried to move away, a little too quickly, but got stuck as his hands were still on my bare back and my shirt pulled tight, keeping his hands in place.

"I'm sorry." He said as he realized I wanted space.

CHAPTER XII

Untangling ourselves from each other, I stood back and concentrated on getting my breathing under control. "I am sorry. I do not know what came over me." I had to take a deep breath to try to get my racing heart under control before continuing. "I just do not want to get hurt. I have been through a lot. There is still a lot I'm not sure of."

"I understand. I got carried away. I know it is fast to you, and you just found out about a whole species you didn't know existed."

"I do want to know everything. I have so many questions."

"You can ask me anything."

"How do you survive? What are your abilities? What really happened to your parents? Is the killer like you?" The questions kept pouring out of me when I finally managed to stop and wait for his answers.

"We do feed on people, but we do not kill. We have superior hearing, strength, eyesight, speed, and hypnosis, which we only use when feeding or in dire situations. We are still trying to find the whole story behind our parents' deaths, but we know it was a vampire who followed us from Lake Las Vegas. We do not know why, but this person is rivaling something our parents knew and didn't tell us about. When we were contacted, it was a scavenger hunt the killer sent us on. We still do not know why or what he or she wanted. It is a puzzle we are still working on."

"How were, are, you guys killed?"

His hesitation was almost enough to make me regret asking. Before I could change my question, he answered. "There are a few ways to kill us. Given we are born, we can die through a stake, silver if used correctly, if you cut off our head, or if our heart is ripped out. Those turned into vampires are more vicious and have an immunity to silver, but a stake, cutting off their head, or ripping out their heart works for them as well."

"Are they stronger than born vampires?"

"No. It is more like they have less control when put in the wrong situation. We were cursed as a means to an end, but turning a person into a vampire changes that curse," he hesitated as he tried to find the right words, "It changes some aspects, like the control we have in an intense situation. It is also why they are not killed by silver if ingested by it like we are."

"So silver kills by you eating it?"

"Not so much, it can damage us permanently. It needs to be ingested into our blood and kept there for days as it slowly kills us."

That is terrible. It is definitely time for a change in subject. The first thing that jumps to my mind is Palma. "Is Palma really your mother's sister?"

"Yes, my mother was human, and yes, my father was a cursed vampire like us. After he changed her, he wanted her to cut all ties to her family, but Aunt Palma insisted she stay connected. My father did not like it in the beginning, but soon became close to Aunt Palma as a sister-in-law, and if an easy escape should be needed. She has really helped us with everything. We do not know how to fit in with humans or what is coming for us, but she's here for us because she kept in touch with our mother."

"So is Daimon…"

"Yes Daimon Cree is a vampire. I am not sure which category he is in. We have not met much, but my sister really likes him, so I'm giving him the benefit. For now, that is."

I laughed as I recalled my feelings about Agento. "You sound like Agento. I hated him interfering with my personal life, but I learned it comes with having a brother."

"That it does." We sat for a few minutes as I tried to gather my thoughts. I could not believe it. I was sitting with a vampire, discussing their vampirism, and hopelessly in love with him. "I have a question for you. I know I need to give you time, but I just got to know."

"What is it?"

"Could you possibly be okay with dating me? I need to know if my secret is something you cannot handle or don't want to. We do not have to rush things like my siblings did. I can be patient."

I thought it over, wondering how much I should confess and remembered honesty is key. He told me everything I asked; it is only fair that I be honest as well. "When I first saw you, it was around town and even then, I felt something. I could never understand what it was or why. How could someone fall so quickly for someone else? I liked you from day one, and I do know I need time to come to terms with this world of vampires, but I am not going to do it alone." Looking at him, leaning my head against his shoulder, breathing into his neck, I continued, "Yes, we can totally keep seeing each other."

He wrapped his arm around me and sighed in relaxation. "I felt the connection as well. I was so stunned by it and hid from you after first laying eyes on you because I had to be sure."

"Wait," I said after a few quiet moments, leaning back and looking at him. I continued, "What do you mean, you hid from me? I saw you on your first day of school and at the train station."

"I have been in town for weeks before going to school. The train was not the only day I saw you walking around town."

I gasped as I recalled the times I felt something, someone. "That shadow I saw once was you?"

"Yes, but I was there every day, so I saw you more than just once."

I thought for a moment, wondering if I should have been creeped out or not. "Why? Were you stalking me?"

"Not at all. My family and I were constantly looking around town for the killer. I was not sure if you were for real or luring me to my death, so I stayed hidden. I was not expecting to find my soulmate so quickly."

It seemed I was not creeped out after all. I would have done the same thing if our roles were reversed. I let it go as I relaxed back into his arms. I do not know how long we stayed there before Errol drew my attention and sat up. "My family and Agento are looking for us."

"I don't hear…" and I stopped as I remembered. "You do."

He smiled as he moved me aside and stood up. He held out a hand to me. "Yes, and you caught on quickly."

Using his help to stand up, we continued back to the house, with my planter in hand. I took in everything I learned and pondered ways to live my life with Errol, and not letting this secret interfere.

Agento was waiting for us inside the door as we reentered the house. "Where were you?"

"In the garden they had built, like I said. And he gave me a gift from our time at the Gardens." I said, showing him the planter and handing it over to him before going over to the couch to sit next to Errol.

"How did it go?" Clarebelle asked Errol and me after making room on the couch for us by sitting in Citino's lap herself.

The pointed look shared between everyone gave them away. They were happy and could not wait to include me in their lives, but the secret still needed to stay a secret. Agento did not know, and they weren't ready to share this with him.

"Great." Errol responded just as Agento entered and sat across from us.

"What was great?"

I rolled my eyes. "Stop being a guy. I just walked with him and we talked. Which was great."

"I am not being a guy. I am being your brother, and if more happened, I have the right to know and handle it however I see fit."

"No…"

Errol interrupted, "Nothing happened. I would not take advantage of Gemma like that. I care about her, and I understand why you are protective of her. Maybe one day we can all sit down and talk about what Gemma and I talked about."

"One day soon."

Errol nodded, hoping the conversation would steer away from us. All conversations died when Pagan brought in Daimon, and everybody stared. Citino whispered something in Clarebelle's ear, much to her delight as she laughed under her breath. Errol smirked but did not join her, making me give him a confused look, one he whispered that he would explain later, nodding toward Daimon.

Palma announced dinner was ready, and we walked into the dining room to sit down and enjoy dinner. Dinner looked like a feast; a bit small, but huge given how little everyone ate. I wondered about that, but was not sure if Agento would leave my side again since we left him hanging and out of the loop for over an hour, so I couldn't ask. Dinner was quiet, a little tense, but mostly comfortable, as conversation was kind of steady.

But when Agento tried asking Daimon a few questions and only got vague, uninterested answers from him, the tension grew tenfold. I wondered if Daimon was Pagan's soulmate. They seemed to have eyes only for each other, but Daimon's personality is not an easy one to overlook. Maybe that is what soulmates do: overlook all the flaws everyone sees in order to stay together and be happy. I hope I do not have that many flaws to hide from Errol; I would never make him overlook something that bugged him. It would only make me nervous; what if someone had another soulmate, or would they prefer to date random people the rest of their lives, should their soulmate suffocate them? What did this even mean for us?

There was so much left unsaid that I knew I would not let it go until I got the answers. I pulled Errol aside as soon as dinner finished so I could ask him when I would see him next.

"Whenever you would like."

"I still have a lot to ask you, but I doubt we have time tonight. Agento most likely will stay close to me."

"I agree. We have a lot of time to figure this all out, but I will always be available for you."

I hesitated, unsure if I should ask or not. I chickened out. "Can you come to my place next weekend?"

"I would love to."

"Great. Saturday or Sunday?"

"I will work around your schedule as much as I can. Just let me know which day is better for you. Your brother is staring." He added, looking over my shoulder.

Looking behind me, I saw how right he was. Agento was leaning against the wall by the dining room door, watching with a stony look. I signed and decided to ignore him. "That will be an obstacle."

"He will never fully trust me until he knows all about me."

"How long do we wait?"

"I do not want to tell everybody else until we stop the killer at hand. I did not want you to know either, as you will now be a target."

"But only if the vampire finds out." I whispered as I sensed an audience approaching.

He smiled and turned toward everyone. "How about we all spend time together in the parlor? We can play some games as a family with our guests."

"I would love that. Come on," Garcia said as she pulled Paio behind her. Paio sent Errol a dark look, which Errol returned with a grin.

"What was that about?" I whispered to Errol as others slowly made their way to the parlor.

"Paio dislikes family games. He believes them to be 'too human.' He knows Garcia does loves them and he will not turn her down."

"So, you took advantage of that to distract them."

"Yes, I did. I will pay for it later, but it will be worth it. I told you, our hearing is superior. Whispering does nothing, and I do not like an audience."

"Right." I looked down at my phone and texted him.

Text works great. They cannot read our minds, right?

He smirked as he texted back.

No, we cannot. Very private.

So, we text to talk in private so that I can get questions answered without others' knowledge.

All the questions you want.

I smiled and put my phone back in my pocket as I grabbed his hand and pulled him to sit on the love couch, the only place left; on purpose, I bet. Soon into the games, everyone felt like family. Something about games brings people together; even Daimon seemed to have a fun time. We played again, fought, and laughed like we had known each other our whole lives.

Before we knew it, Agento and I had to leave. Errol and I stole another quick but passionate kiss as he walked me to the hallway and reminded me to grab my plant before heading out with Agento shortly following behind.

In the car, my phone chimed.

I miss you already.

I do too. Everybody had a wonderful time.

Yes. You were just as distracted; I got no private texts from you.

What can I say? I love games.

They are the universal way to pass time.

We could meet up tomorrow if you are free.

I look forward to it. I will text you in the morning.

Looking out the window, I notice Daimon watching with dark eyes reflecting. I shivered as a chill ran down my spine, and I looked away. Hoping that he is going hunting soon, which explains the reflection. Somehow, the reflection is scarier than the fangs. It looked like a window with no soul staring back at you.

Ready to relax, I turned to Agento and asked. "So, did the family pass your brother's test?"

Agento signed as he drove through the forest and into town. "I have no brother test. I just love you enough to watch out for you."

"If you weren't driving, I would slap you."

He laughed, as I knew he would. "The family is great, and I have no complaints. Right now, that is."

I relaxed and settled back in my seat to watch the scenery go by.

After a few minutes of silence, Agento continued, "Why didn't you tell me about their parents?"

I looked at him, stunned. "It never came up. Also, I felt…" I paused as I debated what to say and how much to tell him.

"What did you feel?" He prompted when I remained quiet.

"Trapped, I guess. I did not want to think about it; I still had unanswered questions. I did not want you to feel worse about our parents when someone else is going through something worse, because our parents' death was an accident, theirs is murder. We were still grieving ourselves, and we needed to, but this situation is complicated."

"You should have told me. I am not close to them. I would have been here for you."

I said nothing as I pondered what to tell him. The situation was more complex than I originally thought. I still needed to keep some things a secret, but surely, he should know more. I do not want him to question everything like I did. I cleared my throat and started with, "What if I told you they are in danger as well?"

"What?" His exclamation made him swirl into the opposite lane before regaining control of the vehicle. Luckily for us, it is late and not busy with traffic. He soon pulled into a nearby parking lot and stopped the truck before looking at me. "Come again."

I hesitated, maybe I should not have started with that question. "They found out they are being targeted like their parents when the killer sent them on a wild scavenger hunt, leading them to no answers as to why."

His disbelief was evident. "And you think you should date him."

Firing back as my own anger surged up, I folded my arms and glared at him. "I know I am dating him. You cannot stop me. I am not a target, and I know nothing can happen to me when we are together. I cannot explain it, but one day soon you will understand."

"Screw that. You are not seeing him again. I'm not letting some guy put you in danger by being associated with him."

"Agento, you do not get it. Not being around him right now will only put me in more danger. He will not let anything happen to me. You are being unreasonable."

"No, you are. Some person is out there killing people, and he is a potential target. What does the police have to say about this?"

"He will protect me. And as far as I know, the police are clueless as to the killer's whereabouts."

He shook his head and turned away from me. Taking a few deep breaths before continuing, he looked back at me. "Protecting you is my job right now, and staying away from that family is necessary. If, and that is a big if, the killer is found and the police arrest him, you can start seeing Errol again."

"You're not keeping us apart."

"I will if it's the only way to keep you safe." After a few moments of silence, as I looked out my window, he continued softly, "I know you are mad at me. I cannot lose you, too. We have lost too much already."

I signed as I looked at him. "You will not lose me. I am not going anywhere. But this does not change my relationship with Errol. We are being careful, and I promise, I am safer with him than anybody else in town."

"How do you figure?"

"I cannot tell you that now. It is not my secret to tell."

He debated whether arguing would help his case, but slowly came to the realization that he could not control his sister, and he didn't want to. She was raised by his side, and he had to remember how strong, stubborn, and persistent she was. She refuses to let anyone control her, even our own parents.

He pulled me into a hug and soon pulled back onto the road. "I guess that is all I need for now. I trust your judgment, right now, but if anything happens-"

"It will not. I promise. One day soon, you will understand."

"You sound like a monk." He scoffed. I laughed and turned up the radio as background noise while Agento drove the rest of the way home.

Later that night, at an old warehouse, danger struck while everybody slept soundless and was left unaware of what was coming.

"That family will pay for what they did. We shall get what we came for. Stealing from us, how dare they?"

"Yes, sweet revenge. They will not know what hit them before it's too late to stop us. With your help, we will return to glory."

They laughed and enjoyed the slaughter they brought to the warehouse. The screams were heard as people were killed. The Leighs were too late to save them.

CHAPTER XIII

The next morning, I slept in, only waking up to Cinnia jumping on me, huffing in disbelief when she saw my eyes open. "Sleepyhead, what are you doing lying in bed still? We have church today for Christabel."

"Shoot, I am up. I forgot, and my alarm did not go off."

"No, because you forgot to change the alarm to the correct time." She said as she showed me the alarm. I quickly pulled myself together and grabbed my church dress to run to the bathroom to quickly shower, and hurried through my morning routine. Because of me, we had to run to the church; everybody was already gone for the day.

"You slept for over ten hours last night. Dreaming about someone specific?"

I scoffed as I paid attention to where we were going. "No. Just couldn't sleep."

She became concerned as I didn't banter with her about her teasing of Errol and me. "Are you okay?"

"I do not know. I just feel like I tossed and turned all night. One time, I thought I heard something."

"What did you hear?"

"It sounded like screaming. Weird, right?" I looked at her questioningly, hoping she heard it as well.

She shrugged as we slowed down, out of breath. We started walking as we were almost there. "I didn't hear anything. If there was a coyote nearby, it could have been that. They can sound like a person."

"Maybe. I just have a really bad feeling. I do not know, but something happened last night."

My phone chimed with a text from Errol.

> Sorry, but something came up. I cannot hang out today.

I frowned as I texted him back.

> That is okay. Is something wrong?

> Yes. Something happened last night. I will tell you about it tomorrow.

> Be safe.

> You as well.

I looked up from my phone to see Cinnia smirking at me. "What?"

"Nothing. It is just that I see that look on your face and I am reminded of my parents."

"Stop it. It is not that serious."

"Oh, please." She scoffed and fanned herself, acting faint. "You keep telling yourself that. But I know better."

We soon got to the church after a few more teasing words exchanged, and immediately looked around for Christabel and Medea. We found Medea doing the same near the door, and we sat down together, curious as to why we could not find Christabel. She is usually one of the first people sitting.

"Where is she?" Medea asked as the church started, as Reverend Adamus entered.

"I hope we did not miss the fireworks. We were supposed to be there for her." Cinnia complained after the singing started, and soon after, the reverend started the sermon.

I shook my head. "I do not think we did. Wasn't Reverend Adamus supposed to talk with them?"

"Yes, but they could have finished before he entered the room."

"I hope not."

We all shared a look of concern. "Maybe we should excuse ourselves and try to find her," Medea started, but before she finished, Christabel entered the room, upset but contained as she stood in the back with her parents. "She is upset. Hopefully, we can fix that." Cinnia and I nodded in agreement, but we all sat still as we listened to the reverend and his sermon.

We rushed to Christabel as soon as Reverend Adamus and everyone stood to gather their things and leave. We ignored the impatient, rude looks that were sent our way as we pushed through to Christabel and pulled her aside so others could still leave, talking to the reverend on their way out.

"What happened? Don't tell me we missed it."

"Only my parents' insistence." Christabel said. "They are here to wait on Rev. Adamus to talk sense into me."

"We are here for you."

She smiled and we group hugged. "Thanks. I know you all are not into church."

"It's not that," I commented. "It's the early hour that we don't like."

"Yes, I don't believe a lot of people do."

"My parents are talking to him right now. Maybe we should head over before they get his full attention."

We made our way over as the last of the people left the church, and her parents stood aside with him. We listened to the conversation and jumped in to explain the benefits of Christabel choosing her our college choice as she is the one benefiting from going, not her parents. This made an argument happen as her parents argued their side, leaving Reverend Adamus an outsider to this conversation and not so much the advisor.

"Please, everyone, give me a moment," Rev. Adamus interrupted as her parents were about to interject yet again. "You are here to hear my side, not to argue yours."

Everyone stopped, feeling ashamed for their behavior, and listened to the reverend as he explained. "While I am all for parent ties, Christabel clearly doesn't want you two to choose a college for her. Independence is an important thing to have, and Christabel has shown she does have it. Everybody learns from their mistakes, and yes, Christabel will too." Turning to her parents as Christabel held her breath, he continued, "Controlling someone's wants will only result in pushing them away. I love my family and wouldn't want to cause such a rift between us. This is why I'm against you two. I don't see how family ties will strengthen if you push your daughter to do something she doesn't want."

Leaving the church in a daze, we let out our breaths as we took in the fact that Christabel's future is up to her and not her parents.

"I can't believe that happened. I was sure he would side with them. I'm glad you girls came. For support and for talking on my behalf."

"Adamus had no choice but to listen." I concluded.

"You're right. Thank you all. I don't know what would have happened, as I knew I couldn't defend myself like that. It really did take all sides for Reverend Adamus to see the truth."

"That's what friends are for."

We spent the day in town, shopping and talking about school and boys. In fact, I found out Cinnia has a new crush, one she doesn't plan on acting on. We bugged her about it as she had acted ready for a boyfriend in the last few months, and yet, when she found someone, she wouldn't act on it. Something was up with her.

"You should say something to him. Summer is right around the corner. You said you hoped to have a boyfriend before summer came. You don't want to wait long before asking him out."

"I've actually been thinking that waiting is better. If I see him this summer and things happen, then I will feel better about it."

"What do you mean?" Medea asked, as confused as I was.

"If I ask him out before summer and then break up because we don't see each other, what happens then. But if the summer proves to be on our side, we stand a better chance."

I shook my head as we continued walking around town.

Sometimes I'm lost in her logic. "You pushed Errol and me to start dating now."

"That's different. You two have stared at each other for over a week straight without acting on it. This guy and I barely see each other as it is, and we haven't stared at each other every chance we got. We only barely pass each other in the hallway, no classes together, and I doubt he knows I even exist. I don't want to be the one to make a move."

I looked away, wondering if we were really that bad. Surely Cinnia was exaggerating for her benefit. Maybe not, remember, soulmates. My thoughts were a jumble, and one I didn't appreciate. I almost missed something, no, someone. Someone caught my eye across the street. It was Daimon, and he was waiting for something, or maybe someone else, standing outside the market. He didn't notice me, and while I thought I was rude if I didn't go over there, I also didn't know him well enough to want to start a conversation with him. I forgot the conversation I was having while I watched, and a few minutes later, Pagan walked outside. He hurried to her side as they started walking away, engrossed with each other.

Errol had said they were busy investigating, so why was Pagan here with Daimon and not helping her family? Or maybe Errol lied. I felt like texting him, but I hesitated as I don't want him to think I was suffocating him. I'll wait till tomorrow and ask him in English.

"Earth to Gemma, what's up with you?" I was pulled back into my conversation as Cinnia waved a hand in front of my eyes.

"I'm sorry." I noticed Christabel and Medea were gone. "Where did Christabel and Medea go?"

She scoffed. "They left like over a minute ago. They tried

to say goodbye, but we couldn't seem to get your attention. What's got you so distracted?"

"I saw someone I knew."

"And?"

"It was Pagan and her boyfriend. Errol told me they were busy today, like the whole family."

"Ohhh, so you think he lied to you."

"I don't know. Maybe they finished what they had to do early."

"But you're not sure."

"Right."

"Call him and find out."

"No, I don't want to smother him."

"It's not smothering if you call and see if he changed his mind about hanging out with you. You don't have to tell him why you're really calling unless it comes up."

"I will wait and just ask him tomorrow. Back to your problem," I added, changing the subject. "You should at least let the guy know you're interested. Fear holds you back. Besides, who is he?"

"No way am I making the first move, and I'm not telling you who he is. I doubt anything will happen with him, and I don't want your interference."

"I care about you. You knew about Errol from day one, before we were even a thing."

"Like I said. This is different. Why tell when I doubt anything will happen between us?"

"You know, I will find out who he is, so just tell me." I pleaded as we left town, heading home.

She shrugged and smirked, unwilling to give in. "Worry about your own guy. He's the one who has the secrets."

"Believe me, I am." I whispered.

The next day before school, I wrote a letter for Errol that I plan on passing on to him before English class begins. I tried to keep it school-safe and had to rewrite it a few times as I wrote too personally and in-depth about their secret. I reminded myself not to reveal too much in the letter, just in case it fell into the wrong hands.

All throughout the morning, Christabel, Medea, and Cinnia tried to get my attention, but I was still in a daze. What was going on? Should I have believed Errol so easily about his secrets? I know what I saw but were we really soulmates or was I a sucker pining for love? Luckily for me, classes began quickly as the morning went by, and I didn't have too much time with my cousin and friends grilling me about my thoughts.

I ended up not giving the letter to Errol at the beginning of English, as he was late to class and gave Miss Thurlow a tardy slip from the office, most likely from Mrs. Lacey. He sat down as Miss Thurlow continued the class. *What happened?* I whispered, catching his eye. He wrote out family drama in his book in pencil, erasing it after I saw it.

I passed him the note discreetly as Miss Thurlow wrote the homework assignment on the board before going over it with the class. I waited for him to read it, but he had to stop reading every time Miss Thurlow turned to face us, which made him take what felt like forever to read it.

I saw Pagan and Daimon in town yesterday.
What happened the night before? You said you all
were searching for, you know, as a family, because of

the night before that. I heard something I'm not sure was real or my imagination that night as well. Did you find what you were looking for?

Instead of replying to my note, he put it in his book and closed it. Bell, he mouthed to me, seeing my confusion. Just then, the bell rang, and he stood up, waiting for me with his hand out. We walked, hand in hand, toward my locker and waited as people passed before I asked, "Well?" and opened my locker.

"We will talk in the cafeteria. Away from prying ears."

"Right." I said as we made our way there. "Where anyone could hear." I added in a whisper.

"Only my family will hear us, and they will already know what I'm about to tell you."

"That's true." I answered, recalling the safe distance of our table. After grabbing a plate of food, we headed toward our table to sit down and talk as I ate.

"Okay, so you're wondering if I lied to you yesterday. I didn't. Pagan just got tired of our search and was called by Daimon. She chose to hang out with him and not help us. We were still dealing with her drama this morning, which made us all late."

"But you didn't show up until last period. You fought with her for hours this morning?"

"Yes, she was relentless."

"Okay. What happened that night?"

He signed and hesitated, unsure how much to say. "A lot of weird occurrences. What did you hear?"

I shrugged. "I'm unclear if I really heard anything. That's

why I wanted to ask you since you confirmed something happened. I thought it could have been a coyote. I woke up thinking I heard someone screaming."

He looked surprised. "Wait, you heard that?"

"You mean, I wasn't dreaming and that it wasn't a coyote that night that I heard."

"No, it was five people, humans were killed that night. It was a warning of some kind."

"What do you mean?" I lost my appetite and pushed my tray aside.

He took a deep breath, glanced at his family, and backed up to me before he answered. "We heard the screaming, but even with our speed, we got there too late to save them. The five people killed were dressed expensively, with wigs, matching them to each of us. The killer wanted us there for some reason, but was gone before we got there. How you heard them and nobody else did is confusing even to us." He nodded to his family.

Glancing at them, I could tell they were listening and agreed with his statement. Looking back at Errol, I answered, "I don't get it either. Where were they found?"

"At an old warehouse. We discovered it was bought by an illegitimate name and can't find the sale report. The warehouse was on the same side of town as your place."

I gasped as I recalled the close proximity it had to be to me. "That warehouse could only be five miles from me, my place is in the center of that side of town." I tried to stay quiet and not bring attention to us, but how can one not react to such a discovery? A few people had glanced my way before returning to their conversation. Maybe the killer used the warehouse because he knows about me, or maybe it was a coincidence.

"It's actually only three miles from you. I double-checked yesterday. I am surprised your family didn't hear them, and why you did."

"Maybe because I couldn't sleep. I must have been awake, or somewhat awake, to hear it. Why would the vampire kill those humans? And why dress them like you all?"

"We don't know why he or she would dress them up, but…" he hesitated until I nudged him on, "the five humans killed were the same ones we all fed on that morning. It's not a coincidence. They were targeted to draw our attention." I felt sick. He continued, pretending to ignore my expression, even though he was sickened by the whole situation as well. "We had a lead as the vampire left behind a note, signed with an O. Pagan didn't want to help and left us shorthanded for hours, unaware of letting the trail run cold. She is the oldest and has the most experience in hunting our kind. This town is small but has many hiding spots. We couldn't find the person, and we didn't stop until night fell."

I looked at him, unsure how I could help. "I'm sorry. Maybe Pagan learned her lesson, and you will find the vampire soon. What did this note say? Maybe I can understand something you all overlooked."

He shook his head. "Not here. It's too crowded. We have to use caution from here on out. The note was detailed without revealing secrets of our parents or why he was after us."

"Okay. Well, you know that person is trying to rattle you. Maybe you could get with the police. Do the police know anything?"

"No, we burned the place down, with the bodies inside."

"Why?"

"Because there would have been no explanation for how

and why they were killed. The police would have been on us twenty-four/seven because of the look of the bodies. We can't find this killer with a police escort following every one of us around town. We had to cover it up and stop him from using that warehouse. We don't like that he used it in the first place, considering it's so close to you, but maybe it was a coincidence of location."

"Let's hope. Agento will never forget this if he finds out. He already wants us to stop dating as it is."

"I thought he liked me now."

"He does, but then he asked me about your parents. He doesn't want me involved with possible danger."

"I understand. I will keep you safe, no matter what happens to us."

"I told him that. That doesn't mean you can be reckless yourself."

He laughed, despite the intense atmosphere. "I'm always reckless. I love adventure, but I know how to be cautious when needed. It's the advantage of being born like this."

"That's good to know."

The conversation went light after that as he tried to calm the situation and get me to finish my food before the bell rang. "See you tomorrow." I called as I left before him, leaving the family surrounding him, discussing something of utmost importance.

CHAPTER XIV

The rest of the week passed with me learning more about Errol as a person. We have plenty of things we don't like, differences, and hobbies, but we like learning about each other. We haven't fought about our differences, but we appreciate the likes in between. We avoided vampire talk because of school, and I still looked forward to Sunday with him. Some of Errol's speech is well-developed now, whereas he was hesitant and slow-spoken before. Now I understood why, and it wasn't due to a speech impairment but his natural hesitation to not say something best to refrain from an outsider. He grew up in a vampire community, and while he is modern, he didn't know anything about humans before moving here. I love how calm and relaxed he was with me.

Saturday morning, my family and I left town for a change of scenery. Crestwood only had so much you could do, and I felt like I'd seen, heard, and smelled it all by now. We spent the day in Louisville at Jefferson Mall, taking our time and enjoying the relaxing day after such a long week. I limited myself to four bags, that is, to carry. Aunt Aida and Uncle Basil pushed cart after cart in each big store, only to end up walking it outside to load. We had two loads already by lunch and knew we would be crowded on the drive back home, but we had such an exciting time that none of us cared.

"Hey, come here for a second," Cinnia called as we headed to dump our trash from lunch. She pulled me slightly away from the trash bins and pointed out a guy standing in the food line for an Asian place. He had a leather jacket on even though it was hot outside and black jeans with combat boots. His sandy hair was short, cut like a marine's.

"Who is he?" I looked at him to see her blushing cheeks and gasped. "Wait. Is that him? Your crush."

She nodded, not taking her eyes off him. "What is he doing here?"

"I don't know," I smiled and nudged her. "Maybe he came to see you. What's his name? I don't remember seeing him at school."

"Marino."

"Nice. So, is this the first time you noticed him outside of school?"

"Yes."

"Which grade is he in?"

"Senior."

I was tired of the one-word answers. "We should head over there. This could be the opportunity for which you've been waiting. We can pretend to run into him, and you can have an actual conversation with him."

"No way. I wouldn't know what to say."

"Come on, girl. You are overthinking this. Just act like yourself."

"I can't. What if he pretends I don't exist?"

"I bet he won't."

"We should head back to our family. I'm sure they are waiting. This is family day after all."

I was sad and upset that she would let this opportunity pass her by, but I knew I couldn't push her. Why was she suddenly nervous? This wasn't like her at all. I let it go as I knew when she was ready, she would find her own way to him, or whoever else came her way.

As we were nearing the exit, after yet another walk to the truck, Cinnia and I stopped at the bathrooms. As we waited in the lengthy line together, it slowly moved. Uncle Basil took the last of the bags to the truck and would wait for us there, with Adacio and Agento. Aunt Aida promised to wait for us by the entrance so we didn't have to walk out alone. Once we finished using the facilities, I saw that the opportunity was about to happen. Cinnia was so focused on me that she didn't notice someone right behind her until she paused at the last second, and he accidentally ran into her. I gasped and tried to pull her aside from the crowded hallway, where he followed, to make sure she was okay.

"Yes, I'm fine," Cinnia started, but stopped as she realized it was Marino. "I'm really sorry."

"No, I ran into you. I'm sorry." I stayed silent as I let them work it out. Realization formed on his face as he recognized the girl he ran into. "You're Cinnia, right? We go to the same school."

"Yes."

He grinned as he held out his hand, but hesitated when she didn't shake it, too, in shock at what was happening in front of her. "Well, it was nice to see you. See you around."

As he walked away, Cinnia buried her eyes in her hands. "Oh My God. I told you I wouldn't know what to say."

I hugged her in comfort. "I'm sorry. I figured the opportunity presented itself, and I wanted to stay out of it. Next time, I will assist if needed."

"That was horrible. Now, how am I supposed to go to school? I've embarrassed myself in front of him. He probably thinks something is wrong with me."

"He seemed more confused than awkward. Maybe you will be fine in school. The good news is he knew your name. Maybe he has paid more attention than you realized." I added with a smile.

"Great. So, now he knows to avoid me in school." She signed as we started walking again.

"I'm sure he won't. He did say he would see you around."

She wouldn't talk to me about it again all night. She hid in her room as soon as we got home, much to her family's confusion. If she isn't better by the end of this week, I plan on assisting her. However she needs it. I don't want her to chicken out on life. When I first came here, she said she wanted a boyfriend, but now? What really changed her mind? I don't know, but it seems like a talk was in order. Marino seemed like a nice guy, and we were graduating soon. Maybe a little intervention was in order.

The next morning, I was woken up by my phone chiming.

Morning beautiful.

That's modern.

I'm not that old. I'm eighteen, like I told you.

I could hear his scoff at my comment, and I smiled as I replied.

I know. I know. I guess I'm not used to
vampire and modern in the same sentence.

I didn't believe you were used to vampires
at all.

Haha. You got me. All I knew was fiction, but
it was always so old-fashioned. Modern day
doesn't have a place where vampires are
concerned.

True. But that's the way we want it. Nobody
will think 'vampire' when they see us
walking down the street. Right after that
text, I got another. When did you want to
meet me in town? I have many answers to
give you.

That's great. Let me get up, get dressed,
and eat breakfast. Give me two hours. I
have a feeling I'm lazy today.

Two hours. See you at the town market.

I smiled all through getting ready. I was so happy; I didn't notice anybody until I was stopped by Cinnia in the kitchen while making my breakfast. "Errol?"

"Yes. We are spending time together all day. You know, the getting-to-know-you part of our relationship."

"That's wonderful. Did you find out any of his dark, mysterious secrets? By now, I figured you two would have passed the basic stage and onto more exciting aspects of the relationship."

I had forgotten I confided in her about my concerns after our dinner with them. "Yes, in fact, I did. He told me when I had dinner at his place with Agento. I can't tell you much as it's not my secret to tell. Today I will get all the answers I want, so I'm excited to see him. We have no big secrets between us now."

"Good. I do want to know what this big secret is, and I can't believe Agento gets to know first."

"Agento doesn't know. Errol and I went outside to talk while Agento grilled his family."

"Well, that makes me feel better. One day soon, hopefully, I will know too. I'm dying with curiosity now."

"I will never keep you out of my life. Someday you will know. I have to ask him."

"I'm here for you for any reason at all."

I smirked. "And so am I. I have a feeling tomorrow will be interesting for you."

"Yeah, right. Go see your man."

"I have to eat first."

"Then I'm going. I don't want my tragic life to interfere with your terrific one. I've seen enough to last me for today."

"It's not a tragedy." I called out as she ran upstairs.

After cooking sausage, egg, and cheese bagel for breakfast, I put on my shoes and walked outside. Breathing in the warm air, listening to the birds chirp, and watching the grass and trees sway with the wind, I was reminded of the peace I always found here. I saw Adacio waiting for me at the end of the driveway and headed his way. I was walking to town with Adacio as he had friends to meet up with. It was a slow, quiet walk, not awkward but interesting as we both didn't know what to say, how much to say, or to say anything at all. But we were comfortable with each other. I doubt I will ever be close to Adacio like I am with Cinnia or Agento, but I hope to keep what we do have, and maybe one day, extend upon it.

Errol was pacing back and forth in front of the watermelons when I arrived. Adacio had previously cut paths with me as his friends waited for him five minutes back. "Good morning. Where are we going first?" I asked as I stood next to him.

He smiled and leaned in for a quick but sweet kiss before saying. "The museum to start. I have an outdoor picnic ready for after since I'm sure we will be in the museum for a couple of hours, maybe more."

"Sounds great."

The Oldham County History Center was amazing and so full of history. As we walked, we would occasionally bring our phones out and text each other. It would have been easier to talk, but we didn't want to disturb the people around us. And what we talked about was not for their ears. We spent over three hours holding hands and talking about our likes and dislikes with museums when we weren't texting.

Are there other creatures of the night I should know about? Other than what we talked about.

Only witches, vampires, and a few werewolves.

Curious but aware of my surroundings. I asked.

What's your community like? Do you all live together, or are each species separated in different towns?

Lake Las Vegas is full of vampires with one ruler. I can't reveal his name. The witches live in Las Vegas. And the werewolves, I don't know.

I took a deep breath before debating what to ask next.

Where did your name come from? It is unusual.

So is Gemma. Uh, ok. It's my great-grandfather's.

Was he a wanderer like you?

Yes. He had many adventures before he passed. I will show you some pictures he took one day.

Is Palma Lacey your only family left?

No. Aunt Palma is married, but we are not close to him. We have an uncle, my father's older brother, back home. But we left without him knowing we were leaving, so I don't know where we stand with him right now. Aunt Palma is such a godsend to us. She has been helping us adjust to life among humans.

How does grieving work with you all?

The same applies to you, except we grieve more briefly and feel grief strongly in the beginning. We always get revenge or come to peace with death, if it was an accident, which is rare for us.

I still grieve more some days than others.

I know.

I hesitated, unsure if I really wanted to say anything, but I decided I really had to know.

I noticed your speech is different. Is that common for your kind?

What do you mean? I talk funny???

Lol. No. Just hesitant and unsure of what to say. And you do have an accent. Which I'm assuming is from Lake Las Vegas?

That makes me sound funny.

Sorry, but I don't know how else to explain it.

Watching me as he replied. I kept my eyes ahead, looking at a sculpture of which I was unsure.

Sign. Okay, so no and yes. Nobody talks like that in our community. When we got here, we knew our secret was and always would be a secret to keep. I just don't want to say something and have someone to take it the wrong way. I can't risk slipping up. It's not just me I will be exposing. And I am sure everyone sounds like us; we never thought of it as an accent, but it makes sense.

That makes sense, but it's not human-like to talk like that all the time.

Noted. I will try to do better.

When we left the museum, I was on air. I felt more connected to Errol already, and the day was only halfway over. We walked back to the market, where he left his car, and I noticed the sleek, smooth, deep blue of a two-door, expensive car. Seeing my look of disbelief, he chuckled as he held open the passenger door for me. The leather seats were amazing; I felt like I was at a spa getting massaged by the seat.

He spoke as he turned on the engine. "Custom-made. Flying Spur Speed hybrid Bentley. It is a gift from Paio."

"Why?"

He looked over at me and squeezed my hand before answering. "Because of you, of course. Paio wanted to keep the tradition going. It has top speed and it benefits from the automaker's most advanced chassis-"

I stopped him there. "I am not into cars. I have no idea what you are about to say. I do know it is a great car, and the seats feel amazing. I am happy with it if you are."

He smiles as he pulls out of the parking lot. "I doubted you would be interested, but I had hoped that you would like it. I do not want a car expert anyway. Now onto our next stop."

Our next stop was huge, a clearing outside of town, close to his place but far enough from anybody that could or would hear us. It had wild flowers growing under the trees, but was an empty field of grass; a perfect circle with a variety of trees around it.

"This is the perfect place to talk. I found it one day, wandering around and clearing my head." He walked to the center and spread out a blanket from the basket he carried.

The slight breeze added to the quiet, serene scene and made me breathe it in as Errol set up the picnic with the food. Once he finished, I sat down and started eating. It was a lovely picnic; one I planned on enjoying for a change with a guy I really liked.

"So, you all obviously don't eat much. Do you still need some nutrients to survive?" I asked before grabbing some fruit after finishing my chicken salad sandwich.

"No, but we can eat regular food. Blood is all we need, but food for us is like gum, I believe, for you. It helps with the hunger."

"Yes, that makes sense."

"Next question," I paused as I thought it over. "Do you have more powers than what you already told me?"

"We are immortal, but besides the superior abilities and hypnosis, we are very ordinary."

"There is nothing ordinary about you." I murmured under my breath; a lot of good that did me.

He chuckled. "Immortality is tricky with our kind. My kind

of vampires can control the aging whenever they want, but turned vampires are stuck at the age they were when turned."

"Wow. Are there a lot of turned vampires?"

"No. There is but a small town of all vampires, with a few here and there in the world. We are not a huge species, and most are born vampires."

After I got full, I sat back and asked the biggest question of all. "What's the curse surrounding the born vampires?"

He leaned back and looked into the blue sky as he explained. "Vampires were created during the Black Death in the Middle Ages. They were created out of fear of death, loss of control, and the unknown of what was coming. A witch created the curse as she wanted people to represent the desires of power, freedom, and transcendence in order to survive and stop the panic. She created the spell that brought forward the desires and fears of humanity, their eternal struggle between light and darkness. It was only four of the best warriors she chose to perform her spell on. And from then on, the truth of our strengths and weaknesses came to bear through time. All born from those warriors were born with the curse intact. They never knew the cost until it was too late. It took over a century for them to learn everything that we know today. And some secrets are still hidden."

I sat in silence, unsure of what to say. That was some dark stuff, and I couldn't see any comfort coming from saying anything. I leaned over and laid my head against his shoulder, waiting for him to speak. Having one's destiny decided for him before he's even born is difficult to defend. How could he live his life, knowing it was never his decision? We lay there peacefully for what felt like hours, but was mere minutes.

"Is there anything else you wanted to ask?"

"There's a lot I have on my mind, but I didn't want to break the quiet serenity we have here."

"You're right. It's very peaceful," he shifted and we ended up looking into each other's eyes, lying on our sides before continuing, "and romantic."

CHAPTER XV

I instantly moved closer to him, my hand slid up his chest, into his hair. He took the cue and leaned over me as our lips touched. The air heated, and we ended up flat on the blanket as he lay half on top of me. I wondered just how far I would let it go. Would I want to stop? Feeling his hand on my lower back ignited my body for more, and my mind shut off. Before I knew it, I was gasping as he moved from my lips to slowly work down to my neck. Light kisses covered me as I tried to remember where I was.

"We should stop," he whispered as he slowly worked his way back to my lips. I tightened my hands in his smooth hair, keeping him close, not wanting to stop. Why should he? I wasn't ready to stop.

"Why?" I murmured against his lips, after much more kissing. Did I miss something?

He soon pulled slightly up from me and stared into my hazy eyes, breathing heavily. "I don't want to lose control." He said, running his hand through the few strands of hair covering my face, watching as the strands fell through his fingers and lay on the blanket.

"We've kissed before."

"Yes, and I have loved every moment of this. But-" he moved completely off me but kept his arm securely around me, back, moving me with him before continuing, "I never kissed your neck before. I almost lost it for a minute."

I shrugged and tried to move closer with no success as his hands kept me in place. "So don't kiss my neck."

"Making out with you is difficult enough. Add in our teenage hormones, and kissing you, wherever, is nearly impossible to control. Including your lips. I also don't just feel my hormones, I feel yours as well."

I leaned slightly back, surprised and confused by this knowledge. "Wait, you are saying you can feel my…" I stopped, uncomfortable with saying arousal to him.

He smiled. "Yes, I can. Very much so."

"How? You said you only have superior senses."

"I do. It's a part of the five senses as it combines them all together. Making us aware of a lot of things around us."

"That's…" I hesitated, unsure what it was.

"Strange. Confusing. Embarrassing. Unreal." He suggested as he touched my cheek and held my eyes to his. "You need to understand more about us before we don't seem strange to you. I have no secrets, so whatever you want to ask, please do. And, lastly, I don't ever want you to be embarrassed by me. This situation is difficult, and while we are teenagers, I won't push anything on you. I know we have a long way to go in learning each other's ways. We have all the time in the world that you want."

"Have you ever?" I asked hesitantly. "With anyone."

"No. I didn't want to be with anyone other than my soul-mate. But I'm not as sheltered as you are."

"If you lost control of me, would I die?"

"No. I could never hurt you. I don't kill to feed. I have always been careful with the people I feed from."

"Would it have been so bad if we didn't stop then?"

He sat up and frowned at me. "Yes, it would have. I would still have fed on you. Or worse, you would have regretted the whole ordeal had we not stopped."

"Why would I regret it? I've heard it brings pleasure."

"Only when it's the right time. You are not ready for that. I'm not either."

"Didn't your sister and brother enjoy it when finding their soulmates?"

"Clarebelle and Paio are older than we are. They have had time to figure out what they want in life. And our community is a lot more demanding than yours is."

"So, we are not to want to be together for the next five years?" I asked, confused. "What does age have to do with it?"

"It's maturity, not just age." He sat us up, barely touching each other, before he continued, "There is nothing I want more than to be with you, in every way possible, but we are not there yet. We need time first to get to know each other. I want to travel the world. I don't know what the future holds for us, and neither do you. We don't even know what will happen within the next month because of this vampire out there."

"But, Errol, I would love to travel with you. I know I would prefer to stay here for the time being, but that doesn't stop me from wanting to be with you. How long are you going to make me wait?"

"As long as it takes for you to be completely sure this is

what you want. Don't be controlled by your hormones but led by your heart and mind."

The birds were chirping around us, and I listened, lost in thought as to what happened, or in fact, didn't. I don't know how long we sat there, but my toes started to fall asleep, and I was so tired. I couldn't believe he turned me down. I was ready to give myself to him, and he rejected me, saying it was for my own good. I don't know where we will go from here. Maybe he's not as attracted to me as I am to him.

"We should head back to town. Before it gets too late."

I nodded and stood up, helping him pack everything without saying a word. I felt so emotional right now, lost in thought and feeling, that I didn't know what to do.

I ignored his hand when he held it out to me and walked slightly behind him, as he knew the way and I didn't.

"I can feel your frustration, you know." He stopped by his Bentley and turned to me. "I know you're upset, but once we distance ourselves from this moment, you will see I did us a favor."

"I'm sure I won't." I scoffed as I slid into the passenger seat. My anger wavered, and I stopped the door from closing. I just had to know. "Just tell me one thing. Do you really feel something for me, or is this temporary to you?"

His shock was all I needed, but his words soothed my anger completely. "This will never be temporary to me. I'm yours completely."

"Okay. I'm sorry. I don't know what came over me." Maybe I was a little upset over nothing. My mind just plays tricks sometimes, and I wasn't done questioning him. I waited until he got in the car and started driving before I continued my questions. "I guess we should learn to trust each other first. How do you turn a vampire?"

"That's not a question I can answer."

"Why not?"

"It's a guarded secret. Only a few of the oldest vampires alive know it."

"Your parents didn't tell you?"

"No. Up until they turned Citino and Garcia, we believed they didn't know either."

"How long ago did that happen?"

"Citino was turned about eight months ago, and Garcia only a month before we left Lake Las Vegas."

"Wow. They must be learning how to adapt still."

"Not really. Vampires, born or turned, learn quickly. Most within days, others in a couple of weeks."

"So, there are no out-of-control vampires running around?"

He shook his head. "No, only the ones with bad intentions. Their personalities don't change when they are turned."

"Interesting," I said as I reached for his hand. "One more thing, before we reach town. What did that note say? The one signed with an O."

"Here," he said as he pulled his phone from his pocket. After a few buttons were pushed, he passed me the phone. On it was a picture of a small note, written on legal yellow paper, torn in all four corners.

Dear Leighs,

We know why you ran, and you won't get away with it. Your royalty status will not save you. The vampires are not here to cover for you anymore. Our ruler will find out about this and be called into action if you don't give us what we came for. Everyone you know will be the next to die. Follow in our footsteps, return what you stole, and maybe we will let you live. If not, you all will join your parents sooner than you think.

    O

"Swipe right and you will see a map." I did as he said, and from what I saw, it looked like an endless map, coded with numbers that seemed random but weren't. "Too bad it wasn't helpful. The numbers were coordinates, but they led to nothing but empty woods and back alleys. Nobody met with us, and we don't know what happened, where they are hiding, or how many are here."

I gave the phone back, uncertain what it meant. "You don't know what they want?"

"No clue. We believe our parents did or knew something, at least, but they are not around to tell us. Our parents apparently kept a lot from us. We have looked through every item they brought with them, and nothing stands out. As far as any of us know, we all just wanted a change. We didn't think our parents were running from anything."

"Well, you said you heard screaming, and when you got there, the five people were killed. That must be connected."

"It definitely is, but we don't know why. If they wanted something returned to them, why run before we get there and why dress the five humans up to look like us?"

"How were they killed?"

He looked at me sharply, and at first I thought I had said something wrong. "We actually didn't think about that." After a moment's pause, he whispered a curse before continuing, "We could tell they were killed one after the other and all had an organ removed, but not the same one. The killing led us to believe there are at least five vampires in town, but it didn't explain why they took a different organ from them." In a moment's pause, he huffed in disbelief before continuing. "A lot of curses are organ-based. Maybe a witch is in town, helping them. We need to search for her, not them, then."

The town slowly approached, and he turned to me. "I'm sorry, but do you mind if we cut this day short. I have to follow this lead. I know you wanted more answers."

I smiled and touched his arm. "I don't mind at all. I know this is important. I can wait. You will tell me later what you find, though?"

"I promise." He squeezed my hand gently. "As soon as I can. Thank you for understanding."

He drove me home, and I decided to question him. One question in particular was on my mind since reading that note from O. "So, you're royalty? How?"

He groaned and looked at me. "You had to pick up on that. Of all things in the note." I shrugged and waited. "Okay, so yes. Technically, we are, but we left that behind a hundred years before I was born. My family is from one of the four with very few humans turned vampires in our line."

"Why did your family leave that behind? What happened?"

"I'm not sure how much of the truth I have, but they just wanted out and never looked back."

"Okay. Do you and your siblings think you will go back?"

"No. Our family wanted out, and they got it. We all wanted the same. We all want to live our lives to the fullest, without royalty nonsense."

"Good to know. Who's the ruler? The vampire, the note mentioned. Will he, or she, actually come after you?"

"I can't say the name. It's punishable by death if an outsider learns about him. Until we make ourselves official, you are still an outsider in their eyes. I don't know if he will come, but I do doubt it. He's big on secrecy and wouldn't want to risk anything happening while he ruled."

I nodded and breathed in the air after rolling my window down a little. I couldn't believe I was in love with a vampire, and now I find out he's a royal one. Even if they gave up the fame and prospects that come with it, that fact would never change.

The rest of the day passed slowly, with Cinnia trying to distract me, but I couldn't stop worrying about Errol and his family. She knew something was going on, but I couldn't talk about it, not with my family. All I could think about was their safety. Did they find anything? Now there were witches and werewolves. What was I supposed to do in order to survive in their world? I was in such turmoil, I couldn't hide it. I tried hiding in my room, but Cinnia wouldn't let me be to deal with it alone.

"Hey, did you want to talk about it?" Cinnia pulled me, literally, from my thoughts as we sat on my bed.

I shook my head and signed before lying down and staring at the ceiling. "I don't know what to do. My mind is full of thoughts, and I can't talk to anybody about it."

"Since when can't you talk to me?"

"It's Errol. He left me today to deal with some family stuff, and I can't tell you because I promised to keep his secret."

"Is it serious?"

"Yes. And dangerous. More to those I care about, I think, than myself. I just need to know that he's okay."

"Girl, you lost me. Please, tell me. What's dangerous?"

"I can't tell you."

"Well, you need to talk to someone. We have walked upstairs, and you were so out of it, I bet you didn't even notice where you were until now."

"I have no one I…" I stopped as I rethought that issue. There was one person to whom I could talk. I have never been to her place before, but I knew she must have lived close to them. Would he be mad if I paid his aunt a visit? At least I will have someone to talk to if she is home.

"I have to go. I just realized I have somewhere to be." I ran downstairs and found Agento outside playing football with Adacio. I ran until I stood between them, about to tackle each other, and yelled stop. "Agento, I need you to drive me somewhere."

"Oh, really," he asked sarcastically. "I'm busy, as you can see."

I rolled my eyes, "No, you are playing around, killing time. I need a ride. It's way more serious than your silly game."

"Excuse me?"

"You heard me." I murmured as I got out my phone to text Mrs. Lacey for her address so I could come by to talk.

"What could possibly be so important that I would drop everything to drive you somewhere?"

"I can't tell you, but I know you love me, so you will drive me as it's important to me." Hearing the chime from my phone, I smiled and showed him the address. "This is where I need to go."

"You still didn't tell me why." He stood back and folded his arms.

I signed, unsure how to answer it without him asking too many questions. I couldn't tell him anything that was dangerous, and I wanted to make sure Errol was safe; he wouldn't let me go. Then I knew there was only one thing he wouldn't ask about. "It's a friend's house I need to go to because I'm broke and she has agreed to let me borrow some tampons for-"

He stopped me from going further, as I knew he would. "Let's go." He turned to Adacio. "Sorry, man. Maybe when I get back."

He had his hands up, warding me off as he replied. "No, I get it. Leave."

Agento tossed him the football as we walked to his new car, ready to back out. He paused, unsure if he would regret asking, but had to. "You're good now, right. Like you won't bleed on the seats."

"I'm good. I just have no more to use after now." I wasn't completely lying. I do have to go shopping this weekend before my period actually starts. Hopefully, he will forget about this by then.

"Great. Let's go."

Pulling up a long driveway, we saw the small black house, surrounded by a beautiful garden, being tended to by Mrs. Lacey as we stopped the truck. I stopped Agento from exiting. "Let me go. I'm sure you don't want to see me get the tampons."

His look of horror had me laughing, naturally, as I jumped out and ran over to Mrs. Lacey. Once she spotted me, she stopped tending to the flowers to give me a hug.

"What are you doing here? What did you need to talk about?"

Whispering in her ear as we hugged, I explained quickly. "I need to ask you about Errol, but I told my brother that I needed to borrow tampons from you so he wouldn't be suspicious." I pulled back, smiling.

She nodded and motioned to the door. "Of course, my dear. Let's go inside."

Her cottage was beautiful and serene. She had pictures of her family. There were plenty of Mrs. Lacey and who I assumed was her husband but I never met him. I wonder where her husband is. Nobody seems to mention him, and I haven't seen him at either of the family dinner invites I've gone to. He looks handsome, in the older way, with his dark looks, short haircut and strong build. The love was obvious even in the pictures between them. Knowing I didn't have time to chat when she returned, I quickly asked her how Errol was doing and if she knew anything from this morning.

She shook her head. "I know they are closer to figuring out what's going on, but I haven't heard anything for any of them yet."

"I guess I figured that, but I can't talk to anyone, and all I'm doing is worrying at home. I'm worrying my cousin as well."

"I know. It's hard with the people you love. I can guarantee you he is safe. He would never risk his life without reason, especially now. They are all equally strong. They have each other's backs and will never let someone come between them."

"Thank you." I turned to the door. "I guess I should go."

"Don't forget these." I looked back as she filled a bag with tampons and handed it to me. "Now you didn't lie." I smiled and hugged her goodbye. "Oh, and you can always call me. I will talk to you whenever you need me to. I could use the company as well."

"I will. Until next time. Thanks again."

Leaving Mrs. Lacey and walking back to the car, Agento was leaning on the door, waiting. "All set." I called over to him and got in.

"Good. No more errands, right?"

I shook my head and sat back, with the bag on the floorboard and serene myself in my thoughts as he drove. I wanted to ask her about her husband, but I knew I didn't have time. Agento would have come inside if I hadn't left when I did. Maybe the next time I see her, I will be able to ask. I hope it's not a touchy subject, one of heartbreak that I will be opening up about.

CHAPTER XVI

Arriving back home, Cinnia and I lay on my bed, staring at the ceiling and playing catch-up with each other. While I was waiting to hear something, anything, I decided not to let it ruin my day. We soon talked about boys, and while she was totally crushing on Marino, I still got nowhere with her. She wouldn't even tell me why. We did each other's nails and braided hair to keep our hands busy and minds from wandering.

We picked a family movie and ate popcorn until my stomach couldn't take it anymore. Before bed, I got my outfit ready and stood in front of my mirror. I pondered my thoughts as I watched my reaction, hoping to find peace, but only saw worry staring back at me. Now that I was alone, it all came up. I tried to quickly shut it down and lie in bed, once again staring at the ceiling, willing my phone to ring. Before I knew it, I fell asleep.

Looking at my phone the next morning, I saw Errol had texted me extremely late last night.

I signed, unsure if I wanted to go to school. It would be boring, but when Cinnia saw I was still in bed, she made it her duty to drag me to school. This was our last week. She wouldn't let my mood spoil school for her today, and she wouldn't let me lie in bed, moping and waiting for Errol to contact me. I was worried, and I couldn't stop thinking something bad, something horrible, was about to happen.

It was lunchtime that I found out why Cinnia was determined to have me attend school today. Marino sat down with us while Cinnia kept a grin on her face. The knowing glance I sent her made her bashful and uncertain. Marino noticed this as he stopped talking and asked her if everything was okay.

"It's great. I'm overjoyed."

"Yes, and nervous I won't like you," I commented, nudging Cinnia in the side. "Being her all-time favorite cousin, it's only right I find out all I can from you."

"I have no secrets. Ask anything." His hesitation and nerves went unnoticed by Cinnia, but not by me. What could he be hiding? Maybe I was overthinking and just being over-protective, so I let it go, for now, and for Cinnia's sake.

As Marino's attention was pulled to a friend sitting next to him, I leaned into her and whispered. "Tell me everything. How did this happen?"

She blushed but responded just as quietly. "After the mall, we started conversing in the halls. Then last week, he approached me and asked if he was the only one who wanted more. He asked me out in the end, and here we are." She hesitated before adding, "I know you told me it would happen, but I'm not used to this. It's all new. He's new."

"That's beautiful. How could you keep this from me?"

"Yes, in a weird way, you were right. And" she pointed at me, "you seemed distracted lately."

"One day, we will have to talk more about that. And I'm sorry if you felt I wasn't here for you."

"I know. I'm not ready, though, to dig into my past. Especially with Adacio or either of my parents."

"That calls for a girls' weekend. Did you want to invite some friends or just the two of us?"

"I could use a girls' night. But I already have plans for this weekend. Maybe next weekend in celebration of graduating."

"That's a deal. Where is he taking you?"

"I'm not sure. He's surprising me."

The bell rang, ending all conversations as we walked to class. Lunch was great as it kept me busy, but my classes left a lot of time to think. Errol still hasn't contacted me. I know it's important, but I still worry. Maybe I do need a hobby to help distract me.

Errol communicated through call and text most of the week, and I started taking up gymnastics at a place in Louisville to give me peace of mind as well as great flexibility. I kept going each day for an hour after school, and my mind has quieted. There was this girl who was amazing in my class, and we soon became friends and started warming up together every afternoon.

"Hey, did you want to hang out this weekend? I'll be in town all weekend, staying at my grandparents' place." Lona said as we started heading out of class. Looking at her hazel, almond-shaped eyes, I knew she was younger than I was, but only by a couple of years; she was pretty for her age, and a complete go-getter. She started unbraiding her long, light brown hair as we walked out the door.

"That would be great, but I have plans with my boyfriend. I haven't seen him in a few days, and we have stuff to work on, or I would like to see if you want to come over. Maybe next weekend. I have a girls' night planned and I can invite any of our friends, which includes you. We are celebrating graduation."

"I can try. My parents are extremely strict, so I don't get to hang out with others too often. I'll let you know tonight, okay."

"Sounds great. Text me anytime. See you Monday in class." I added as we parted ways.

The next afternoon, I received a text from Errol, wanting to hang out. I responded as I got up from my seat on the porch and got dressed. He was just pulling up when I headed outside to wait. He got out and stood by his Bentley, with his arms folded, waiting patiently for me as I walked over to him.

"Hey, I've missed you." We hugged and stayed close together, taking in the comfort we felt in each other's arms.

"I've missed you, too. It's been a difficult three days."

"What happened?"

"Not here. Let's go for a drive." He walked with me to the passenger side and held the door open, got into the Bentley and buckled before he drove down the driveway.

"Where did you want to go?"

"Our special place." His side-eyed glance had me hesitating, wondering if he, too, was thinking about the last time we were there. "We never did finish our conversation."

"No, we didn't." I smiled. I recalled why we parted so quickly that day. "Did you find the witch?"

"We did, but she wouldn't tell us anything. She was the one who wrote the note."

"What's her name?"

"Omella Acalia. She has it out for all born vampires. I doubt she's working with any. They must be turned vampires that she's helping. We may have found the witch, but without her talking, we still have nothing."

We pulled into a parking spot and got out, ready to walk the way to our secret place of peace and romance. The scenery was quiet today, no birds chirping. The wind was a little strong, and I pulled my long hair back into a high ponytail with the tie I brought just in case. I grabbed his hand as he led the way, and I continued my questioning.

"So, witches are real. Vampires are real. Werewolves are real. How many supernatural beings exist within our world?"

"Werewolves are out there, but rare. We, naturally, don't keep tabs on them. We don't have an exact number."

"Were the werewolves started the same way as vampires? By witches through a curse?"

"Yes. A different curse for a different reason, I'm sure. But witches are the common enemy among us, and the beginning of our existence."

"What was their curse?"

"I'm not sure. You would have to find them and ask them. Or you could ask witches, but they are often unreliable and closed-mouthed about their magic, especially curses."

"Shouldn't they be good and want to help?"

"There used to be all good witches, in the beginning, but now, I don't know exactly what happened. With humanity and the supernatural world, witches have become darker and more self-centered than ever before. It's difficult now to find a witch willing to help humans as opposed to decades ago. It's like their control over others, vampires, werewolves, and humans alike, has made they become twisted themselves."

"Times do change a lot." I whispered as we reached the clearing. Between the howling wind, the trees swaying, and the chill in the air, I doubt we would be here long. "No picnic basket this time?" I asked, sarcastically. I was secretly glad he didn't bring a basket. I wanted answers and no distractions, at least until my questions were answered.

"Sorry. I was in a rush. I've missed you and wanted to see you as soon as I could."

"I understand. We can enjoy the grass more as we sit on it and talk." I sat down cross-legged, waiting for him to join me. As he sat down, right next to me, I continued, "Have you all checked everything about your parents? To find this item, the killers are looking for?"

"Yes, but there are still a bunch of papers we need to finish looking at. They had packed every single paper we ever brought home from everywhere we went."

"What's your community like? Do you all even have a school?"

"Yes, we do. It was great there; there was a lot of space and nature all around, and growing up there, it was normally a peaceful day every day. If anything, it normally lacks adventure. Lately, it has changed. The vampire king was getting up there in age, and they had replaced him. Nobody likes the new rules set in place by the new king, so we left, as did others."

"You said there were only four born vampire families. Are you all related, or were they from different families?"

He smiled as he saw my hopeful expression. "The four original warriors were from different families, but some of their descendants have merged their lines. My line is not one of them, as we preferred, even then, to maintain a distance. We have the control and strength to rule, and other descendants have, I don't know what you prefer to call it. But they have polluted their lines by turning humans and using them to further their lines."

'Polluted' is not the word I would use, but I let it go as he did mention it. His ways are different from ours, but I love learning them and how we are seen in their ways. "How do they decide who rules? In which family?"

"There's a contest that two members of each family can enter if they desire to. My family prefers to stay hidden, so we are almost never in the contest. I believe a few of my family in my past have ruled, and a few more have entered the contest, but lately my family has grown even further distance from that crowd. The new king is actually the great-grandson of the previous king. He is not liked by most as he grew up with a selfish mother and didn't spend much time with his great-grandfather until recently."

I hesitated, unsure as to how he would take my question. It has been at the back of my mind since I found out, so I decided to go for it. "Would I have to become a turned vampire?"

"No," he said as he took my hand and faced me. "It's completely your choice. Besides that, I don't know how to do it. You might never become one, but" he paused, debating if he should continue or not, "if you really wanted to, we could find someone to help us."

"That's good to know." An awkward pause was created as they were both uncertain where they had gone from here. Did I want to turn? I know I didn't want to age if he wasn't, but then again, he did say they do age, so I have time to decide. Leaning to him and deciding, I continued, "I'm good waiting and seeing what happens, but I won't say no in the future."

The tension grew as he ran his fingers up the side of my face, into my hair. The kiss was so possible, but then I hesitated and pulled back, remembering our previous conversation. Upon seeing my hesitation, Errol pulled me with him to lie back and face each other. I pushed a strand of his hair back from his face and trailed my fingers down to his neck. The intense air surrounding us and knowing our bodies were only separated by a few inches, I knew all I had to do was lean in a little, and we would kiss, but I couldn't make myself. I don't know why, but I felt more connected with him by just being close and didn't want to push it. Maybe he was onto something after all.

"What are you feeling now? Through me." I added, curious to see what he felt and more of a test to see how much he was paying attention.

He smiled as he ran his fingers through my hair, pulling the tie off as he went. Pulling me even closer to him, he ran his fingers through my locks and spoke. "Everything. I feel you, your desire, your hesitation. I know you realize that I was onto something before. I feel my own feelings more intensely as they reflect yours. I feel your soft hair as it falls through my fingers. You truly are the only person I want. I'm glad we didn't. I don't know how I would have stopped."

"I want to know more, but I think it's better to experience it as we go. I guess I do want more with you."

"Whenever you have a question, just ask. I will never lie to you."

I had so many questions, but getting cold, I realized I needed to wrap them up for the day. "Am I going to see you tomorrow? It is our last two days before graduating."

"Yes. We can't do more until we find more."

"Time sure does go by fast."

"That it does. Makes you want to enjoy every day you get."

I turned to look at the blue sky as I listened to the wind. "This day is one we can enjoy."

He got comfortable and watched the few clouds in the sky go by. "One of the best." Soon, he pulled me over to lie against him as we watched the sky together. After I started shivering from the wind, we got up and headed back to town.

My last two days of school were better than any week ever, besides the week I met Errol, that is. Both days flew by with no homework, leaving me more time with my friend and family. I had finally gotten all of my questions answered, including some. The killer didn't go after anybody else, but Omella had escaped where they were holding her, much to their confusion.

Summer had begun, and I was still unsure how I felt about it. My parents had planned a vacation in the Caribbean Islands for us, but that was cancelled because of their deaths. Aunt Aida and Uncle Basil had offered to help pay for us to still go, but we didn't want them to go into debt for a week's vacation for us alone to enjoy. Agento and Adacio started looking for an apartment to share in town. Cinnia was ecstatic as she got to spend more time with Marino, and I would be spending time with Errol and his family. This summer should be fun and worry-free, but instead, I will be spending time helping the Leighs find this killer and stop the madness before someone else dies.

Graduation was exciting and flew right by. I didn't

remember the speech the valedictorian spoke as I sat with Errol, holding his hand. I wasn't surprised that even with their absences, all of the Leighs graduated as well.

I kept up in my gymnastics class with my classmates and became even closer friends with Lona. She was planning on visiting real soon. I was worried something would happen, especially because school was out. The Leighs were able to focus their full attention on the killer now, but I hope nobody else has to pay the price, especially Lona. I wondered if I could convince her to wait another week or two, but then again, maybe I was just being paranoid.

CHAPTER XVII

I sat down with Errol at Cravings Byanca for lunch, ready to celebrate graduation and discuss further plans. "Do you guys feel any closer?"

He hesitated, unsure whether now was the time to reveal the truth or not. No secrets is his policy, and he didn't like hiding things from her, so he figured, why not? "The Thursday before last, we had actually discovered something we had at first missed with our parents' papers."

"Wait, you knew this for over a week? Why did you say you found nothing when I asked twice since then?"

"I wanted to tell you, but my family thought it was best to wait and see. We were hoping for it to be over by now. We wanted answers and for you to stay safe."

"What did you find?" My dismissive tone was all he needed to know how upset I was.

He leaned over and grabbed my hand before explaining, "I only went along with it because I don't want anything to happen to you. I was hoping we could finally settle into our relationship and have a great summer together. I don't want this summer to be about vampires set out to kill us for no reason other than wanting whatever our parents stole."

I signed as I slowly calmed down and covered our hands with my other one. "I understand. But you should understand how hiding this was wrong. I should have been told."

"I know, and I did try, but my family outvoted me."

"What did you find?"

"All throughout our parents' paperwork, there are a few pages in between that don't belong. We started going through all of them and found a whole book's worth of paper among them. It's written in a dead language from the witches, so we are still unsure what they are. We contacted an old friend, and she is coming out this weekend to help us translate them. She's probably even the one who told our parents what they were in the first place. I'm telling you this because she's a witch, and it can cause issues if anything at all happens, especially to her. We need to find these vampires, but I don't believe we will in time."

"Just how powerful is she? Will she be a problem as well?"

"She is immensely powerful. She is the only descendant left in her generation of the first witch, the one who started the vampires' lineage. She has been helpful in the past, but like I said, she is not always trusted among all vampires."

"But you said she was an old friend?"

"Yes, but only to our parents, which is why she agreed to come out. Being the last of the witch lineage she has, she can't always side with us, though. Others expect her to find the solution to our existence. She is under a lot of pressure from everyone. They are hoping to end all the supernatural beings possible to begin anew with humans, but they are looking for a nonviolent solution first. They believe it will restore their good nature with the planet, which is why they are not using force as much right now. We haven't heard from her in years, but she has taken the time to come out, so we are hopeful; guarded but hopeful."

"Did her lineage trace to the werewolves as well?"

"Yes, but no. There were three original sister witches, and only two survived after the creations came into existence. We believe it was the second sister who created the werewolves, but it might have been the third. We only know it wasn't the same sister, as it was recently discovered, but without a werewolf or witch to share the knowledge, we are not sure what happened or who was behind them."

"Couldn't this witch friend tell you?"

"Yes, she could. But the witches won't, even her. They love their secrets, and they all work for the dark arts now. She is no exception."

"Is it even possible for the witches to turn back to good?"

"It is possible. The supernatural world and the human one alike would benefit from the good witches. But unhealthy habits are difficult to break, especially when it's been decades. They are trying, through our existence and their own. We are all on edge because we know we will all be caught in an endless war if they cannot find a peaceful solution to our existence."

We sat in silence for a few minutes, debating this latest information. "Do you know what happened with Omella? Where is her hideout?"

"No. She's still lost to us. We believe she left town, but without the time and resources, we can't hunt for her in every surrounding town."

"And the vampires? Has anyone else been killed?"

"We have found a few people they fed off of, but none were killed. They were not easy to find, and with only a few found, we are unsure if some had left town to feed or just fed more secretly."

"How many times do you feed?"

"Born vampires feed once a week. Turned vampires must feed every few days. So, we originally thought they were most likely turned, but maybe they were born. Omella's involvement makes it difficult to know. Why would she help born vampires against other born vampires? We are all hated the same to witches, especially Omella. She made sure we knew how she felt toward us while we questioned her, but we didn't know her from back home. We never associated with witches back home, even though they were close in Las Vegas. We really never left Lake Las Vegas unless it was dire."

We stood up and took care of our trash. We slowly walked around the crowded town today. Everybody was out to enjoy summer. Holding hands, I squeezed his to get his attention and whispered, so others wouldn't hear, but I knew he would. "It's all got to be connected somehow. Maybe once you find out what those papers are, the answers will be clear."

"We are hoping, but what are the chances of the papers explaining everything to us. We need to find the vampires, or at least one, but we don't know where to begin. They could be in different towns from each other but in contact and close by, or they could very well be blending in Crestwood."

"Now that school is out, we have more time to search for them."

"Who's we?"

"I'm not going to stand back and not help. I'm great at

reading people and getting them to open up. I can at least talk to them, and you can sense if they are vampires, right?"

"I don't want you involved. They have already made it clear they know who you are. Why risk it? Besides, I can continue searching the town to sense them like I have been doing since day one."

I moved to the inside of human traffic and stopped. I waited for him to stop as well. He turned to me with concern in his eyes. "You have been doing that for over two months now. It hasn't worked before. What makes you think it's different now?"

"I know eventually they will slip up. They can't make a move without coming into the open."

"What if they can?" I gasped as I thought it over in my head. "Remember, they kidnapped five people, killed them, and left the scene before you got there. What if Omella is doing something to keep them hidden? Is that possible?"

"It's very possible, one we thought of before. Our witch will be able to fight against Omella's magic, if she is, in fact, hiding them. Which is why we are waiting and only looking around town."

"But you said it yourself, you don't want to involve the witch. My way allows you to see and possibly talk to the vampires if we find them. Wouldn't that work faster than you running around town, hoping to run into one of them?"

His hesitation was all I needed to know. I hit the right spot. He knew he needed me, but it was his desire to keep me safe that he fought against. "I promised your brother nothing would happen to you. If we do this, I can guarantee he won't like it."

"That's only a promise you can keep by keeping me close,

and I'm sure he will understand. Once he knows the truth." I hinted as I was wondering myself when that would happen.

"I'm not so sure anymore." He signed and pulled me back into the human traffic. As we started walking, he thought it over. It was like watching him fight with the angel and devil on his shoulder. "Okay fine. You, Citino, and I will walk around town and talk to people."

"Great. Wait. Why Citino?"

"He is quick in a fight and used to be human. He's the best fighter in my family and understands how I feel around you. He has more understanding of how to behave than I do around others. Plus, I don't trust anyone else with you besides my family."

"Sounds good to me. When do we start?"

He chuckled a throaty, deep chuckle, one that shot right through me. "You are eager to start right now. How about we wait until tomorrow and enjoy the day together."

"Okay." I said, smiling. I will always choose a day out with Errol over anything else in the world.

We spent the rest of the day walking around town, going to the Gardens, and talking about non-threatening people. We ended the day at our clearing. The wildflowers were growing, so we sat more than lay down as the flowers were a foot tall, and nobody seemed to come out here. It was quiet, except for the birds constantly chirping and the bees gathering their pollen. I got to know more about Errol's childhood and what it was like when Clarebelle and Paio brought Citino and Garcia home.

Errol walked me home as the sun started setting. At the door, he promised to come by in the early morning with Citino so we could get started right away. We planned for the entire day and hoped that by this weekend, we would have found at least one of the vampires.

I dressed casually and with my running sneakers, knowing I would be walking all day. I headed downstairs for a quick breakfast before Errol and Citino showed up. But as I made my way down the stairs, someone knocked on the door. I was surprised when I opened the door and saw Marino instead of Errol and Citino. Looking behind him, though, I saw that Errol and Citino had just pulled into the driveway.

"Good morning, Gemma. I'm here to see Cinnia." Marino said, pulling my attention back to him.

I smiled and opened the door for him to enter, standing back. "Yes. I'm sorry. I will go get her. I didn't know you two were going anywhere today."

"It was last minute. I asked her which day she was free to spend with me, and she called me last night, saying she was free today."

"Please, make yourself comfortable. I will get her." I turned back to the entrance just as Errol and Citino were approaching the door. "Come in and sit down. I will be just a minute. This is Marino. Marino, this is Errol and Citino. Make yourselves comfortable."

I jogged back upstairs to tell Cinnia Marino was here. She was just finishing brushing her hair and looked upset. "What's wrong?"

"Nothing," she shook her head, then signed. "I will be down soon. Can you tell him I'm just running behind?"

"I will, but what's the problem. You look great."

"I still have to deal with my hair. I can't decide how I want it to look today, mainly because I don't know where we are going."

"Pull it into a ponytail. That way, no matter where you go, you will still look good. Walking around town, you don't want to leave your hair down, and you don't want to look too fancy either."

"You're so right. Thank you. Hmm, can you tell him I'll be right down?"

"I will tell him."

Heading into the living room, I heard no noise; they were sitting quietly, uncomfortable until I came in. "Hey Marino, Cinnia is finishing her hair now. She will be down soon."

He looked relieved. "Thank you."

Turning to Errol and Citino as they stood up, I stated, "I just have to grab something to eat before we leave. I'm running behind myself today."

"That's okay. We know we got here exceedingly early, and we didn't pick a precise time."

They followed me into the kitchen and waited quietly and patiently while I made a fruit bowl for a quick and easy breakfast to take with us. I occasionally saw a few glances shared as I was making the bowl, and after a bit, I couldn't take it anymore. I turned to them to ask them what was going on. "Why are you guys being so secretive?"

Errol shrugged, "Just waiting to leave, I guess."

"Well, we should discuss where we are going and what our strategy is for the day." As I spoke, I turned from them to finish putting away the fruit.

"Not here. We will head to town and talk on the way." Citino interjected. "Too many possible listeners here." He added, seeing my confused look.

"Okay, let's go. I can eat on the way." I said as I grabbed

the container and led the way to the door. Waving bye to Cinnia as she walked downstairs, I continued out the door.

"So, where are we going first?" I asked as I settled into the back seat of a genuinely nice BMW X5 and opened my container to start eating.

"We figured we can make two trips around town for the morning, take a break and make two trips after for the later walkers." Errol explained from the passenger seat.

"Sounds good." I hesitated, wondering if I should say anything or let it go. Knowing myself, I knew I couldn't stay quiet. "So, what happened in the living room with Marino? Why was it so quiet when I came downstairs? Do you not like him?"

The silent exchange between them was as noticeable as in the kitchen and made me more on edge by the time they finally spoke. "How much did you tell her?" Citino asked Errol.

"Everything. I mean, unless I forgot something, but I'm sure I didn't. She does know about them."

"What?" I couldn't take it. "Is he? Like you all?"

"No. He is not a vampire." Errol turned back to me and signed, but he hesitated for a minute before continuing. "He is supernatural, though."

"He's a witch? Or would he be a warlock?"

He shook his head. "Werewolf. A rogue."

CHAPTER XVIII

"What?"

"How long has he been here?" Citino asked.

"I do not know. Two months, maybe. I will have to ask Cinnia. I know she will know because she saw him around school before they started dating. I saw him for the first time at the mall over a month ago."

"That would be helpful if she could tell you more."

"You don't think he's involved, do you?"

"No," Errol interjected, "we don't. But, like I said before, werewolves are rare and we don't know much about them. Any information can be helpful, especially if it does turn out he is involved."

"But you don't think he is."

"No. Even rogue wolves tend to avoid us vampires. Witches are the only natural enemy we associate with."

"Is he safe for Cinnia to be around with?"

"He seems harmless."

Marino, a werewolf! Hard to believe. He is distanced from

others but has great manners. Cinnia told me he was a marine and only left them four years ago. I figured the distance was because of that. Maybe not so much, though. I hoped for her sake that he was harmless. She really likes him, and from what I saw today, I know he likes her.

As we reached town, I put my empty container aside and climbed out. Time to talk to everyone we see and hope we get some answers. The instant we started pulling people aside with more conversation than any good neighbor would, I started noticing just how different Errol was from Citino and me. Citino and I were talking our heads off as we met people while Errol was quiet, awkward, and unsure how to fit in. He seemed like an outsider, a loner, to the people we talked to, but I knew he was unsure what to say to them as he had to limit his speech to keep his secret. With a few people, we had to take over because Errol would say a little too much or act differently toward people as they questioned him right back.

I stopped at a small diner to speak to a few people I had previously made associations with, while Errol and Citino stood aside to talk to people themselves. Errol let Citino lead the conversation, but slowly spoke to them as well. This was our last stop till we had lunch, which I was sure I would be eating alone, but turns out I was wrong.

As I finished looking at the menu, they sat down and took it before the waiter could take it away. They only spend one minute looking at it before deciding and handing it to the waiter. Once our order was written, he walked away, promising to bring it out as soon as it was done. I sipped my water, wondering what made them order anything at all.

As if he sensed my curiosity, which, come to think about it, he did, Citino explained. "We need to. It would be weird for two guys to sit down at a diner and eat nothing. Besides, I don't mind eating normal food."

Falling for the dig, Errol responded, "I don't mind it either. I just don't see the point. I wasn't turned like you."

"Ouch, that hurts," Citino answered, and a quick, deep chuckle escaped his lips. "My brother-in-law, without a real good comeback. I will be teaching you yet."

"No thanks."

"What are you talking about? I'm already teaching you not to speak everything on your mind."

Errol shoved Citino at his comment, and I hid my smile behind my straw as I sipped my water again. It was so obvious they were siblings, even if it was because of marriage. "Nothing so far, but the day is only half over."

"We are all going to search for them in the town tonight as well. We plan on splitting into smaller groups to work faster. Hopefully, we'll find one of them by tomorrow morning."

After finishing lunch, which is the most I have seen them eat, we headed back outside. Errol, by now, had picked up on our cues and actions and became helpful in the afternoon when it came to talking to people. We were not finding anything out of the ordinary with the locals over the next few hours, so we found a bench to sit down on, next to Citino's BMW.

"We still have tonight, which is always more promising when it comes to our species."

"How many groups are you guys splitting into?"

"Just two. We don't want to split up too thin. That is a bad strategy. But we haven't decided which group is going where or who is going with whom yet. We have time, though."

"We have a lot of factors to think about to make it the safest all around and the most productive."

I nodded as I thought it over in my head. With Pagan, Citino, Clarebelle, Paio, Garcia, and Errol, both groups are still only three each. What if that's what the killers are waiting on, though? How can they be at their safest with only two other people watching their backs? Knowing my night is going to be restless again, I spoke up after a few quiet moments, "You will call me the moment you can, right?"

"Yes. It won't be until early morning unless we get lucky, but yes, I will call as soon as I can."

We sat there for a few minutes, thinking over the possibilities, before Citino got up. "You two stay here. I'm going for a run around the park." He left before we could respond.

"Why is he running?"

"He's a person of action. He can't stand sitting for long." He leaned back, placing his arm around my shoulders. "Besides, he's also giving us some privacy."

I looked around, uncertain how much privacy a public park would give us. But after seeing next to nobody around, I leaned into his arm and looked at him. "Not much privacy, but no kids are around." I whispered.

He smiled. "My thoughts exactly."

The tension thickened as he slowly leaned down, waiting for acceptance. I licked my lips in invitation before quickly closing the space between us. I wasn't sure how long we would have, but this moment was enough. The kiss started slow and gentle, but before long, he was pulling me closer for a deeper kiss. I gasped and opened my mouth when his tongue touched my bottom lip. I was nervous as I had never kissed before like this, but I only hesitated briefly, knowing I wanted to. I allowed him to enter, knowing I could trust him completely. The intensity around us made me light-headed as his tongue thrusted with mine. I forgot where we were and didn't care if somebody had seen us. I didn't want to stop, but soon reality had me pulling back. I was in his lap, and his hands were on my hips as I took in the scenery around us. The park had become busier, but people avoided this immediate area, knowing what was going on and not wanting their kids to see.

"Ahem, I guess you two took advantage while I was running."

I hid my face as embarrassment steeped in and quickly moved off Errol's lap. Smiling, Errol was at ease and just looked at his brother-in-law. "You were gone a while."

"Yes, and I made use of my time." Sitting on the other side of Errol, Citino pulled out his phone and showed Errol something.

I couldn't see it, but I used the time to calm my emotions and cool my face before asking, "What is it?"

"A clue. It looks like a boot print and a bloodstain around it."

Showing me the picture, Errol handed me the phone. It was the ground, a dirt path, with a faint boot print and dark stains surrounding it. "What does it mean?"

"It's vampire blood. I could barely smell it, but it was definitely strong enough for me to tell."

"Where was it? We should look closer."

"Follow me."

We got up and followed Citino into the forest. There were trails all around us, and I was glad to be with them. I knew I would never find my way back out without help. Listening to the birds chirp, watching the squirrels gather nuts, I followed them closely. It was about ten minutes before Citino stopped and pointed it out to Errol. He squatted down at the edge of the path and examined the boot print.

"It's without doubt a vampire, and it's fresh, which is how you were able to tell at all."

"I figured that out already. My smell isn't as potent as yours, and with others running this trail, it would have faded."

Errol looked up and sighed. "Why here, though?" He turned slowly in a complete circle before standing up. He moved to stand right over the print and turned again. He stopped suddenly, almost at the full circle, but not quite and walked a few steps into the forest. "That's why. Citino, come over here and look."

I was lost and stood just to the side of the trail to avoid anybody who might be running. I wondered if I should go over there, but I didn't want to interrupt. That could be the breakthrough they needed, and I didn't want to get in their way. They were pointing and whispering, looking around and mapping, in their heads and with their phones, whatever it was they saw.

After a few minutes of them whispering, I couldn't take it anymore. "What's going on?"

Citino looked over at me, then back to Errol, waving him to explain. "Your girl, your explanation."

Errol moved from his spot and came over to me to whisper in my ear. "We found the reason behind the blood. Someone attacked him."

"Are you concerned about that person still being out here? Is that why you are whispering?"

"Yes, because we don't know if they are. We should head back, though, just to be safe. First, I want more pictures."

Citino, after hearing this, started taking more quickly and

efficiently. We were soon leaving the forest behind, and I couldn't take it anymore. The sun was setting, so as we got into the car, I asked. "What did you see?"

"This is the best way to explain it all." Citino said as he passed back his phone to me.

I sat back and strolled through the pictures, shock setting in and disbelief at the horror scene. There were arrows embedded in tree trunks and in the ground. Blood stains throughout different areas of the trees. Spears were left behind, but hidden in the trees were more traps, bear traps. "How did I not see this?"

"It's hidden well. I am really great at focusing the camera on what I want. You are looking at the scene close up that goes a mile into the forest. There was a great battle there."

"Why only the one boot print, though?"

"The other was near it, just on the grass, so it wasn't as noticeable. We don't know for sure, but the one set of footprints must have been because he or she stopped there to let the healing start to work its magic. I don't know who was involved, but someone knows about us and set traps."

"Could it have been Omella? She might have thought it would trap you all and not her friends."

"No. The person who set the traps was there while the vampires were running through the forest. We couldn't smell him because of the two-mile distance shown in the pictures, but Omella wouldn't have done this. She would have used spells on them, not set traps like these."

Citino added, driving through town and heading to my place. "I'm wondering about Marino."

I gasped. "No, it couldn't be. Could it?"

"Yes."

The awkward pause had me handing back Citino's phone and awkwardly sitting in my seat, not looking at him or Errol. How could I tell Cinnia? Could Marino be killing vampires? Is he dangerous to just them or everyone?

Errol, breaking the awkward pause between us, spoke up. "Either way. We need to be sure. We need to talk to him."

I nodded and looked up. Citino focused on driving, unsure what to say, so I spoke up, quietly, knowing they would hear me. "I will ask Cinnia. I'm sure she can get him to talk to us. Maybe we can meet in town, in public, for safety. That way, everyone can calmly discuss this."

"That would be best."

Citino spoke up again as he drove down my driveway. "If it is him, we need to know if he's a threat to us all. If it isn't, we need to know who did this to ensure our own safety."

Errol walked me to the door, and after a brief but sweet kiss, he stayed close to whisper in my ear. "Please, be safe. Don't irritate him. Rogue wolves are unpredictable, and I can't live without you."

I smiled and leaned back to look into his eyes. "I promise. I'll see you tomorrow?"

He nodded. "I'll call you in the morning. Get a good night's sleep."

"I will."

He waited to walk back to the car until I walked inside. Closing the door, I leaned on it and let the day wash over me. The morning was great as I was shown the difference in Errol's and Citino's behavior while observing their sibling bond. Eating lunch and having a wonderful time with them was calm and relaxing, as if I had known them for years and not just a couple of months. The afternoon was different as Errol learned the proper way to speak with people as they went on with their daily routine. The kiss was the highlight of the day; I was still a little light-headed from just remembering it. The discovery in the horror scene of the forest, though, made my smile disappear as I started walking upstairs. Could I really ask Cinnia to set up a meeting with Marino? How much would I have to say in order for her to do it without many questions? Would he even agree to meet us?

Cinnia wasn't back yet from her day out. She must have been enjoying herself and lost track of time. Aunt Aida said she wanted us all back by sundown as she wanted us to spend the night together in celebration of graduation. Downstairs was quiet, so maybe she was out as well, getting stuff for tonight. As I made my way to my room, I heard the door downstairs open and close. I leaned over the railing to see who it was. Aunt Aida and Uncle Basil were carrying bags in. I went into my room and got dressed for bed before making my way back downstairs. As I walked past the door and went to enter the kitchen, Cinnia walked into the house with a huge, silly grin on her face. I knew 'that look' all too well.

"Hey," I stopped and walked to her. "I see today went great."

She signed and walked up the stairs. As we sat down on the bottom step, she answered. "It was perfect. I didn't want to come home. Marino is great, and we connected a lot today. We shared stories about our past and what we wanted in life."

"All of that sounds great. I'm glad you had such a fun time." And that gave me the perfect idea as well. "Hey, you know what would be even better?"

She looked at me, confused and hesitant. Not knowing where I was going with this. "What?"

"If Errol and Marino could get along as well. We should get them together so they can meet and bond. Then we can double date this summer."

She brightens at that. "That would be perfect. We should get together. When are you free?"

I smiled as I pretended to think it over. "How about tomorrow? Errol and I are supposed to go out, and you two can join us. That gives them time to get to know each other, and we can all hang out."

She hugged me. "I'll have to ask him, but I love that plan."

"I'll tell Errol about it in the morning when he calls. I'm sure he will be okay with it."

"Hey, are you two planning on blocking the stairs all night, or can we get by?"

We turned to see that Agento and Adacio were waiting behind us on the stairs. They had their own place, but set up the spare room, Adacio's old room, into a gaming room for them when they visited. "I guess we can move." I said as I helped Cinnia up. We rushed to the kitchen, ahead of them and smirked as we won. Agento nudged me from behind, but let it go as he walked over to help unpack the bags.

We laughed and enjoyed a night of family fun. We played new games, had new snacks, and watched new movies, all of which Aunt Aida and Uncle Basil bought tonight, well into the middle of the night. I started falling asleep, leaning my head on Uncle Basil beside me, when I was jerked awake by someone yelling a victory.

"I'm going to bed." I headed to bed, hoping I wouldn't miss Errol's call because I stayed up so late.

I had a wonderful dream, one of Errol and me traveling through the most famous romantic places throughout the world.

I woke up the next morning groggy, wondering what had interrupted my dream, when I heard my phone ringing. I found it on the floor as it had vibrated off my bedside table. I missed the call; I saw it was Errol's second attempt at calling me. I quickly called him back.

"Hey."

"I'm sorry. I was sleeping. I stayed up really late last night."

"It's not a problem. I'm sorry to wake you."

"So, what happened?" I listened to him as I sat up in bed and rubbed my eyes to fully wake up.

"We found a single trail that leads out of town. On the outskirts of town, we found their hideout. Although they haven't been back there for at least two days."

"How do you know that?"

"The scent is of one vampire, and it's faint. We don't know if they are hiding farther out or if only one stays there permanently. There might even just be one vampire out there."

"One vampire only? Are you sure?"

"No, but it does make a little sense that he hides from us so easily. Omella is helping him."

"One vampire took out two vampires and killed five people simultaneously. Isn't that weird?"

"Yes, my parents weren't pushovers. They had to have been taken by surprise, which makes sense based on what we saw when we found them. We are not at all sure what happened with those five people. It is possible, though, with Omella's help, that one vampire did it."

"I'm sorry about your parents." I blurred out without thought. Then I regretted it; maybe he didn't want to be reminded of that.

The silence was airy as he was lost in memory and pain. Changing the subject, he continued, "We need to know what Marino knows. He would have seen if it were one vampire or more that night of the attack. If, and that's a big if, he is the one who attacked them."

"I did talk to Cinnia last night. She agreed to meet us today with Marino. I'm just waiting to see if Marino agrees. We just have to pick a place and time. Just you, me, Cinnia, and Marino."

"That's fine. Where do you want to go today?"

I thought it over and thought of the perfect, crowded place. Safe. "The market?"

"That works. A bit crowded."

"Which we want. That way, a scene is less likely to happen."

"Right. I will be there in three hours."

"See you there."

CHAPTER XIX

After hanging up, I hurried to Cinnia's room to tell her the news. She texted Marino to meet us at the market's entrance, and we talked as we waited for a response.

"I'm glad he agreed on short notice to meet us."

"Yes, so am I. He is actually happy to spend time with you and Errol. Said he was looking forward to it." Hearing the chime, she looked at the text and smiled. "He will meet us there."

"Now we've got three hours to get ready. What are we wearing?"

After spending an hour in our closets, we decided on casual: adorable, noticeable, but casual outfits. We pulled each other's hair back into twists and decided we couldn't leave empty-handed. We headed downstairs to bake cookies to bring with us and clean the kitchen afterwards.

Running out the door with the two bags that held cookies in two containers, we speed walked into town. Our running sneakers were starting to wear out, but that just meant more shopping was in order. As we walked into town, we talked about the possibility of hanging out more with two great guys and enjoying this summer together. We got to the market before Marino and Errol, so we stood to the side and waited.

"I guess we shouldn't have walked so fast," Cinnia commented as we waited for a whole ten minutes before we saw Marino in the distance walking toward us. "I was just in a hurry."

"Me too."

"What's the rush?" We jumped as someone spoke behind us and turned to see it was Errol.

Smiling, I leaned in for a hug. "Just anxious for today. We plan on enjoying each and every day."

"I hope that happens." His pointed look said too much, but Cinnia missed it as Marino reached us.

"Hi, I'm Marino," he said as he reached out his hand for us to shake. Pulling out of the hug, we shook hands with him. "Cinnia's told me about you two."

Cinnia noticed the awkward pause this time as the guys shook hands. I wanted to interrupt, but there was no way to distract her from it. The air felt like a nuclear bomb was about to go off. The tension was undeniable and one that I understood, but she didn't.

"Do you two know each other?"

"No." They both answered quickly as Errol continued. "We do look forward to getting to know each other, though. Let's go sit over there, out of people's way." Noticing just how much attention we drew, we hurried over to the benches.

We found one slightly apart from other people sitting and sat down ourselves, unsure of what to say. Cinnia started talking animatedly, trying to find a topic that interested both

Errol and Marino. I stayed silent, wondering how they expected to talk with Cinnia here.

"Gemma, beautiful, I'm getting a little hungry. Would you mind going with Cinnia to find something for us to eat here?"

Looking at him, I took the hint and grabbed Cinnia's hand to lead her inside. "Come on. Let's give the guys a minute."

"Okay."

We walked down every aisle, hoping to buy them some time. I told Cinnia I wasn't sure what to buy, so we needed to keep looking until something grabbed my attention, and that Errol was a picky eater. She bought it because she knew he almost never ate at school, so we talked and walked.

"So, you have a nickname?"

I laughed as I saw her confusion. "Yes. I told him I hated love, so he sticks to beautiful."

She gasped and was awed before speaking. "That is wonderful. I'm so happy for you two. I wonder if Marino will be it for me."

"I'm sure he is, and if not, I know you will find someone better."

Looking in the door's direction, Cinnia wondered out loud. "I hope things are going well between them."

"I'm sure they are fine. Errol won't start anything, and I'm sure Marino will behave."

"He was in the Marines. I just hope his quiet nature doesn't come off as rude to Errol."

"No, he understands. Errol was quiet in the beginning as well. He wanted to talk to him alone. Mostly so they can get to know each other." I hated lying to her, but it couldn't be helped; she knew nothing about this world of supernatural beings. It would only endanger her if I told her.

Finally, walking down the second-to-last aisle, I 'found' something I told her he would eat, and she grabbed a similar sub for Marino. We headed to the registers. The lines were long, and we stood in one for nearly five minutes before we got outside.

Seeing them sitting on opposite ends of the bench, intensely in conversation, I stopped Cinnia. "Maybe we should give them a minute. They look like they are enjoying themselves."

"Don't you want to at least give Errol his sub?"

"Yes. We can go for a short walk after."

"I would love that."

"Here you go." I said loudly to Errol, as we approached, hoping to stop the conversation before Cinnia heard anything. I handed him the sub before continuing, "Cinnia and I are going for a short walk. We feel like stretching our legs. We will be back soon."

"Are you sure? We could all go for a walk together. It's safer that way." Marino questioned as he stood up to follow.

Cinnia waved him back down. "Girl talk. You two should talk and hang out. We will be fine. It's completely safe in this town."

"Okay." I shared a look with Errol before we left them. At least they seemed to be fine, considering what they were and how they felt about each other.

Cinnia and I walked for about ten minutes in complete silence, debating what to talk about; we are cousins and lived together. There's not a single topic we haven't already covered.

"What do you think about Marino?"

"I'm not sure yet. I barely talked to him."

"True, but you have always known who to hang out with

and who is dangerous. I've always liked that about you. You have the sixth sense I wish I had."

"He seems nice. I need more time with him, but I want Errol to get to know him first. That way, we can all hang out together, and I can get to know him then. I know I've been so busy with Errol lately, and it's difficult to separate my time."

"I know. I'm glad to have today with you." She hesitated and backtracked as she realized how it sounded. "I don't mind. I'm glad you found someone great like him. I guess I just realized I don't really know him either."

I laughed. "Yes, I know. We should hang out more for that very reason, but," I hesitated as I decided my words carefully, "he's just busy right now. His family is still dealing with the killer of their parents."

"Have they been contacted by the killer or the police?"

"Yes."

Unsure of which I was saying yes, she asked. "Are the police close to finding the person responsible?"

"No. They are close to calling it a cold case, but the family won't stop until they know what happened and why."

"I understand that. I know I would want to know as well. He's not in danger, is he?"

"In a way."

"What do you mean?"

"I can't tell you." I quickly added, "I don't know much."

Suddenly worried, she asked. "Are you?"

"No. I'm fairly sure I'm safe. Errol won't let anything happen to me. I'm safer with him than without."

"Does Agento know about this?"

"Yes, and he's not happy about it."

"As long as you're being safe, I won't push. But I do want to know what's going on."

"I know. Someday."

After a few minutes of silence, we decided to turn back to head to the market. "Well, I hope it all works out, sooner rather than later."

"So do I."

"By the way, Lona called. She said she can stop by in two weeks for a sleepover."

"That's good."

My lack of enthusiasm got her attention. "What's wrong? I thought you liked Lona."

"I do. I just don't think now is a great time for a visit."

"Why?"

"I don't know. I guess because someone crazy is in town, possibly killing someone else as we speak. You know, five people went missing as well."

"Yes, but that was weeks ago."

"You never know. It's been months since Errol's parents were killed. That guy is still out there."

"You have a point. But her parents never let her leave Wolf Creek, so I'm not going to tell Lona she can't come."

"I know. I won't either. I like hanging out with her. She's very spirited and always lifts my mood just being around her."

"Yes. I don't know where she gets it from."

We reached the bench where Errol and Marino stood as we approached. "We should go to the Gardens. We still have four hours before they close. It would be a great way to end the day."

Cinnia immediately agreed, and we headed toward the parking lot to Marino's car. He had a navy-blue jeep, and Errol climbed into the back before holding a hand out to help me while Cinnia sat in the passenger seat.

Marino and Cinnia fell into a comfortable silence, holding hands while Errol wrapped an arm around me and whispered in my ear, just random facts and questions, which I responded to. The comfort I got from leaning against him was new as I pondered why. I was falling for him quickly, and I knew what we had was real, but the reality of how fast it was happening was uncanny. Was this how all soulmates felt? Do Pagan and Daimon feel as comfortable as we do, or is it different for everyone? I silently hope Cinnia and Marino find the same comfort in each other. Even if he were a werewolf, the possibility was low for them.

The Botanical Gardens were crowded today, leaving a long line to the entrance, which we stood in. "Have you two been here before?" I asked Cinnia when we got to the end of the line.

"We came here on our first date."

"That's great. Did you want to walk together or meet up with us at the gift shop after?"

"Marino?"

"I would like to meet up after." He said as he pulled Cinnia close.

She smiled at him. "Great. Once inside, we will part ways for an hour or two before we meet up."

"Works for me." Being alone with Errol, I will take any day, but I wouldn't if Cinnia wanted to stay together.

Walking in the gardens holding hands, we walked in quietly through the crowd. The flowers were different as the season had changed from spring to summer, so I got a lot more pictures. As soon as we could talk privately, I planned on asking him about Marino, but with this crowd, no matter where we walked, I couldn't ask.

"This way," Errol said before grabbing my hand and leading me away from the third crowd and into the smaller path, away from them.

"Let's not get into trouble," I said as I realized we had walked past the do not enter signs and further into the trees.

"In this crowd, nobody will notice." As soon as we were hidden from all views, he explained the conversation in a quiet tone. "Marino is the one behind the attacks, and he knows we are not the ones he's after. He also saw only one vampire that night. He never picked up on another scent, and he's willing to help us, but only if we agree to his terms, which I told him we wouldn't, so we are on our own here."

"What were his terms?"

"That we leave town for good once this vampire is killed."

I gasped in disbelief. "That's crazy."

"He planned on making this his town, but he won't stay if we do."

I signed as I realized this meant he would leave. What would happen between him and Cinnia? "He won't stay. Even for Cinnia?"

"No. I don't blame him. We are enemies. It's not easy to live close to each other."

"But why? The witches should be the only enemies here."

"It doesn't work that way. And because we were here first, we have a claim, and he knows it."

"How did Omella help this one vampire kill five people and leave before you guys got there?"

"It's a powerful spell; one our friend wants to verify. Omella blocked the screams and made them sound out as one big one, one that sounded after the vampire had already left the warehouse."

"Why did I hear it that night and nobody else?"

"I don't know. You said you were having problems sleeping. Maybe that's all it was. Or she could have allowed you, specifically, to hear it."

"I was having nightmares. I can't remember what."

"If it really bothers you. I can try hypnosis on you and see if we can see what you saw."

I hesitated before responding, "No, I'm good. Let's save your powers for what they are intended for."

He smiled as he reached for my hand and pulled me closer. "Scared?"

"No-o," I stammered as my heart raced. The tension grew, and I wondered if we were going to kiss. I stopped and realized we had limited time to talk. "We should focus on the vampire and who he is. Did Marino at least give you a description?"

"No, he only saw shadows as the vampire used his speed to escape. He never got close enough."

"So, we wait until your witch friend comes."

"Yes, there's nothing else for us to do. We can't translate the papers."

"What's her name?"

"Verda Amparo. Her parents grew up with mine. Paio hung out with her younger brother Vero when they were younger, but we were never close. This distance is only helping us drive the wedge between our families even more."

"I thought she was the last of her line. Is her brother still alive?"

"Yes, but without magic, he cannot continue the line. The witch line must continue through her."

"Why doesn't he have magic?"

"When he was born, a sorcerer stole the magic from him while he slept and disappeared, forever changing his destiny."

"That's horrible."

"He doesn't think so. He blames magic for every wrong thing in life and left home when he turned sixteen."

"How long ago was that?"

"Three years ago. Verda is one year older than he."

"What made them lose touch with you guys?"

"We lost touch when we were still kids. I'm not sure what happened. Only Paio and our parents were close to them. You can ask Paio about it. I'm sure he will tell you, especially since she is coming."

"We should head back; we have much to still see."

"In a minute."

The intense look in his eyes, the warmth of his hand on the small of my back, and my racing heart all told me what to expect. I was so nervous about being caught; I couldn't relax. At the last second, I turned my head, and he kissed my cheek. I was never more comfortable being in his arms than anybody else's my whole life, but the fear kept me from enjoying it, or so I thought. Everything felt right in the world as he slowly moved to my neck, and I had no worries by the end of it.

Light kisses trailed to my ear, and he whispered, "We should go now." His eyes seemed to capture mine as I looked deeply into them. I felt I could see his soul the longer I looked. I watched as the desire dimmed in his eyes, and I broke eye contact.

I nodded and turned to walk back, but stopped as he grabbed my hand, holding me in place.

"I should go first."

I wasn't sure about that, but I wouldn't stop him. I know it was to ensure we wouldn't get caught. I followed a few feet behind him quietly and carefully out of the trees, making sure nobody was around before I walked out.

An hour had passed since we started walking, so we didn't stop in the café; we wanted to make the most of our time in the gardens. They were beautiful in the spring, but nothing beats summer. I was blinded by the colors, smells, and beauty around me by the time we walked back toward the entrance and gift shop. The sculptures were the best part as they brought life to the gardens. They were the true beauty as they were sculpted by famous artists and displayed to match the scenery around them.

I was exhausted by the time we reached the gift shop, but it seemed Cinnia had a wonderful time.

"I just love the flowers every time I come here."

"I do as well. I love the sculptures."

"They are great too."

I laughed and we walked into the small, cute gift shop. I noticed Errol and Marino standing outside the doorway while we shopped and found a few items each: a couple that were unique to the shop, one for ourselves, and something we hoped the guys would like. I didn't know for sure when I would give him the gift. I still had the other gift to give him. Maybe for his birthday, I knew it was at the end of summer. Or maybe when we can finally relax and enjoy the summer.

The rest of the day passed by as we spent time hanging out around the park and small town stores and eating dinner together before Marino dropped us off at home. Errol parted ways and took his own way home.

CHAPTER XX

The rest of the week passed uneventfully: no sleepovers, killings, appearances, or drama. I prepared for the weekend ahead: both Lona and Verda were coming in on the same day. I was more nervous than excited to meet Verda this weekend. A lot could happen in a day.

Because Lona was coming out this afternoon, I got picked up by Errol early in the morning. Verda got there at about three in the morning, so she had already settled in and was getting to the papers by the time we arrived.

"You will find them in the library. Verda got started translating the papers right away this morning. She is convinced she will have it all done by tomorrow morning." Palma greeted us as we walked in.

"Thank you, Aunt Palma."

She smiled and waved him on. "Go on. I will make breakfast for everyone. I'm sure Gemma and Verda will at least eat."

I smiled as I thanked her and followed Errol upstairs and down the charcoal hallway. This was the first time I made it upstairs, and it just added to my already nervousness. The hallway was huge, fitted three people easily walking side by side, and the walls were charcoal gray with hardwood floors. No pictures hung on the walls, giving the walls an endless feeling to them. There was a total of eight rooms on this floor, and Errol led me to the last one on the right side: the library.

Pagan, Clarebelle, Citino, and the witch were the only ones here, all sitting in a circle close to a fireplace. The walls were lined with bookcases, floor to ceiling and had a podium in the middle of the room, currently empty as they used the chairs and coffee table to sit around the fireplace.

They all looked up as we entered. The power was evident in the room, coming from Verda herself. Verda was petite in form, but the power that radiated from her made her seem like a giant in size. She looked at me through crystal blue eyes for a few minutes before dismissing us all and turning back to the pages in her hands and all around her. Her curly blonde hair fell down her back, and a few strands fell over her shoulder as she wrote in the notebook lying on the table in front of her.

"Verda, it's been a while. This is Gemma, my soulmate."

"A human." She commented without looking up.

"Yes."

"Nice to meet you. I'm just busy right now. I want this to be finished. It has so much information. This will take my complete concentration."

"Do you know what it's about?"

"Yes. I knew the moment I saw the pages."

"What-"

"Errol, we can talk over there. She really needs to focus." Pagan commanded as she stood up and motioned for everyone to move to the opposite side of the room. We stood together in a small circle and spoke quietly, trying not to disturb Verda.

"What is it about?"

"What everybody wants. This is the book that explains everything vampires, witches, and even werewolves would kill for. It's the secrets that have been held tightly by the rulers for centuries. It details the Nexus, the beginning and end of everything."

"What?" he exclaimed and quieted his voice before continuing, "How did our parents get it?"

"We don't know, but it certainly explains why they were killed."

"It would explain a lot. Our heritage, secrets, how to turn someone, and so much more. Let alone what it holds for witches and werewolves."

"I know."

"This is not something we are going to hand over, right?" Citino asked. "I will fight to death to keep this hidden."

"Right. We don't know who is after it, but the ruling class wouldn't have sent someone like this to us. They would have used the direct approach, so this is someone else who is after it." Pagan explained. "Something big happened, and our parents must have taken it to keep it from this person. But why they would hide it from us and not use caution when we got here is a mystery. One, I plan on finding out."

"We all will use more caution now." Errol rubbed his hand up and down my back. "This is huge."

"It is." Clarebelle said as she looked over to Verda. "Which is why we don't want to interrupt Verda right now. We need the translation as soon as possible."

"She's able to understand it perfectly?"

"Yes. It's ancient, but with her bloodline, it's perfectly clear to her. It was made by her ancestor and the other sister after the death of their third sister. It's how they grieved and swore vengeance by."

"We need to discuss where we go from here. What are we going to do with the killer? How do we find him?"

"A werewolf's sense of smell is greater than ours. Too bad we don't know any."

I gasped and looked up at Errol. The silent exchange grabbed Clarebelle's attention. "What is it?"

"You should explain it to them." I whispered.

He signed and nodded. Looking to his siblings, he continued, "We found out about a werewolf that lives in town. He's the one who set the traps in the woods for this vampire."

"You talked to him?" Citino asked.

"Yes."

"Wait," Clarebelle said as she looked from Errol to Citino. "You knew about a possible werewolf and didn't say anything to me."

"I wasn't sure. Errol had to verify. I didn't want to say anything if it wasn't true."

"Okay, so it is. Can you get him to help us?"

"No. I can't. He's stubborn and will only help if we all agree to leave the town forever. He wants to stay but won't if we do."

There was a moment of silence as everyone debated this. I held my breath. Would they agree to move away? Would I lose Errol because of such unnecessary hatred? Would Cinnia lose Marino?

"I'm fine leaving," Pagan finally answered.

"Of course you are. Daimon is a vampire, so he will follow

you easily." Errol responded. "Not everyone wants to leave town."

"Not my problem."

"Pagan," Clarebelle commanded, putting her hand on her sister's shoulder. "Our brother's happiness is most definitely your problem. We don't leave family behind."

"Okay fine, but how do we find this vampire when a witch is hiding him from us?"

"Maybe we can with Verda. Nobody can be stronger than her."

"Unless it's from the other bloodline."

"Right. We will find a way. And I know Omella isn't from that bloodline, not directly at least. We wouldn't have held her so easily if she were."

"Marino, the werewolf, is Cinnia's boyfriend." I commented after they went silent. "I don't see this ending happily for everyone. If it comes down to it, you should use Marino. I don't mind leaving town. I only came here because my parents died."

Errol pulled me close. "We will not leave town. You and I both have made a home here."

I signed as I leaned into him and stared directly into his eyes. "True, but what about Cinnia. I don't want my cousin to be unhappy."

"We will figure it out. Right now, we want to focus on the vampire at hand. Even if we move, it's not going to be because I made a deal with a werewolf."

"Okay."

We made our way back to Verda and saw she had made progress; three pages of progress. She was quick and efficient.

We sat down quietly for a few minutes before I couldn't take it anymore.

"I'm sorry, but can we go somewhere else. I dislike the quiet."

"No problem. Let's go downstairs."

I followed Errol downstairs and we hung out with Palma while she finished making breakfast. She left us to bring Verda a plate and told us to help ourselves. Errol made two plates and sat back down at the table before sliding mine to me. We ate, well, I ate. Errol picked at his food while we talked about easy topics, and neither one of us wanted to discuss leaving town just yet, which left the awkward discussion for later.

I stayed at his place over an hour before leaving, wanting to get a few items in town to prepare for Lona's visit. I made him drop me off and leave, as I haven't had exercise all week and could use the walk home. I shopped alone, wanting the space to think about all I learned today. There was much to talk about, but we avoided them out of fear of the unknown future.

As I started turning down the third aisle, I felt someone watching me. My anxiety spiked, but I couldn't see anyone out of the ordinary, and no one was suspicious. This feeling didn't leave me, though. I quickly walked to the checkout, wishing Errol had shopped with me. At the very least, I would have someone to talk to. I wouldn't be anxious with him here. Maybe I was imagining things, but I could have sworn I wasn't.

By the time I walked out of the store with my four bags of items, the feeling disappeared. I slowly relaxed as I walked home and regretted not asking Errol for a ride. My arms felt like spaghetti by the time I got home. I only wanted a few items, so I thought I would only have one bag, maybe two. I should have known better.

I headed straight to my room once I got home. I knew I only had a couple of hours before Lona showed up, and I wanted everything in place before then. Cinnia helped set up the room for the sleepover, and we made appetizers, and Aunt Aida had baked cookies earlier for the night. Aunt Aida helped with the movies in the living room.

The knock at the door sent me sprinting through the hall to open it. Lona stood there with her backpack and luggage in tow, waiting with a smile. She was wearing sweats and a skin-tight long-sleeved shirt; all dressed for the night.

"I'm so glad we have this weekend together." I said as I watched the car drive away, her parents, I assumed. I wondered why we haven't met yet. They have always waited for Lona in the car.

"I am, too. It's great to get away from my parents. They are too protective of me. My brother has more freedom than I do."

I laughed. "Come on and let's get you settled." We walked upstairs to leave her bags by the bed and headed down to the kitchen for a snack.

"What is on the agenda today?"

"The usual. Games, dance, movies, and talk about boys."

"Sounds great. What's first?"

"First, we find Cinnia and go outside for games. Before it gets too late. Agento and Adacio are visiting so they can play as well. They should be here any minute."

"Even better."

We left the kitchen after finishing our snack. I had a feeling I would find everyone outside, as it was too quiet inside. Aunt Aida was outside, sitting on their swing, knitting. She smiled and waved as we passed by and found everyone in the gym, looking through the game choices.

"Hey, shouldn't Lona choose first. She is the guest."

Cinnia ran over as the guys ignored me and continued looking through their choices. "Hey, it's been a while." She said as she hugged Lona.

"Just a month." She said, returning the hug.

"Five weeks."

"Hey, I'm just glad I got here."

"Yes. One day, and soon, we must meet your parents. Maybe then they will let you visit more often."

"I will ask them, but they are very busy."

"What do they do for work?"

"Um, I can't say. They don't like us talking about their jobs." Changing the subject, she continued. "We should go over and pick something before the guys do."

"Weird." Cinnia commented after Lona walked away. My thoughts exactly. We shortly followed, only to wonder more about Lona and her family. They sure did have a lot of secrets. We argued for a good ten minutes before Aunt Aida came in and allowed Lona to pick first.

We played soccer, and Lona and I won against Adacio and Agento with Cinnia playing as the referee. Lona was dominating the field, making me sure she was a star athlete. As soon as Uncle Basil got home, he and Aunt Aida joined in the games, making Uncle Basil the referee. We played a total of four games by the time we all headed inside to eat dinner, previously made by Aunt Aida to sit in the crock pot until we were ready to eat. Agento and Adacio soon left after dinner, and the rest of us made a sitting area on the floor for movie night. Aunt Aida and Uncle Basil watched from the couch, and we settled on the floor in our pajamas with popcorn; each one of us picked a movie, starting with the one Aunt Aida and Uncle Basil picked.

Once their movie finished, they headed upstairs for bed, leaving us to watch our movies. All of which didn't happen as we sat in a circle to talk about boys.

"So, Lona, anybody keep your eye yet?"

She blushed and looked down at her hands, hesitating, before smiling and looking back at us. "As it so happens, yes." Our shared gasps sent Lona giggling. "Before you get any ideas. No, we have not started dating. I don't even think he knows I exist, outside of my family anyway."

"What do you mean?"

"He's a friend of my family, so I know on some level, he knows I exist. But I don't talk to him, and when we see each other, he doesn't do more than say hello to me."

"Sometimes the first step is on you."

"Yes, make a move. See what happens."

She quickly shook her head. "I can't. What if I embarrass my family?"

"You won't."

"I can't. Maybe he will, someday."

Deciding not to push her, I changed the subject to Errol. Soon after Cinnia and I shared our boyfriend stories, Lona started relaxing again. I worried about her. Why was she so intense when it came to her family? Who was this guy she liked? I wanted to ask her more, but I didn't want her to become guarded and upset. Once she was ready, I knew she would come to us if that's what she wanted to do.

"So, are we going to dance?"

I looked at Cinnia, and she signed, understanding perfectly

what to do and got up to leave the room. "Her favorite part," I said, smiling at Lona.

She smiled back as she realized Cinnia had to go make sure her parents were, in fact, asleep. I got up to change the movie to a karaoke CD we had recorded for these nights. I heard Cinnia walking back downstairs as I had finished setting up the karaoke for the three of us.

"We are good to go."

The night passed with so much fun, neither of us noticed anything outside of the living room. Lona soon loosened up, and we danced and sang the night away. I slept peacefully and only got five hours of sleep before the police came knocking on our door.

Uncle Basil got to the door as we all woke up and gathered the bedding off the floor. Who would be here so early? Uncle Basil was just on his way out for work. Aunt Aida wandered into the hallway just as we did, waiting to see who was there.

CHAPTER XXI

"Good morning. Sorry for the early visit. I am Detective Casale and this is Officer Dupuis. Can we come in?"

Uncle Basil stepped back and waved them in. "What's this about?"

Detective Casale spoke in a grave voice. "We are sorry to have stopped by, but Agento Sheard and Adacio Claude were attacked this morning and were immediately brought to the hospital."

"What happened?" Lona asked as we were all too shocked to say anything. Tears started down my face as Lona pulled me to her. Cinnia was leaning into her mother, and Uncle Basil stood too, in shock to move. This couldn't be happening.

"It appears they were attacked outside the club in town and had fought off their attacker, but there were no injuries. They both had cuts on their arms, neck, and scratches on their backs. We are looking into it and will find this person responsible. We were heading to talk to them now and thought you would want to know."

"Thank you. We will head right over there." Lona pulled us all out of our frozen states in order to rush us to the hospital. Aunt Aida and Uncle Basil were in good graces with the locals, so we followed the police and made it there in record time.

I couldn't believe what happened. Nothing bad has ever happened in this town, at least not in the ordinary. I wanted so bad to call Errol as I waited, but until I knew more, I didn't want to assume anything. This was too much of a coincidence not to be connected. We made it to Norton Brownsboro Hospital in no time, and the emergency room was quiet this early in the morning. We rushed through to the waiting room that the police told us to go to and followed behind.

They talked to the nurse there and shortly came over to give us the two room numbers. They asked us to wait until they talked to them first. They weren't crucial, so I sat down, unsure if I could wait. If it weren't for Lona, we don't know what we would have done. This just didn't happen, and I was sitting, tapping my hands on my knees, anxious to see for myself that my brother was fine. Cinnia and Aunt Aida were silently crying while Uncle Basil tried to be strong and comfort them.

Lona got us food and some water from the vending machine and stayed with us until the police came back out. She stayed there in the waiting room after we started heading back, not wanting to overcrowd Agento and Adacio's rooms. I followed my family down the hall, unsure where to go. I was grateful to have Lona there. She got us here, and I don't know what would have happened had she not been there.

Aunt Aida and Cinnia went to Adacio's room while Uncle Basil went with me to Agento. The rooms were across the hall from each other. He was bandaged and hooked to multiple machines, and a nurse was checking his vitals when we entered. We waited until she finished before moving next to the bed. He looked tired and only barely aware of us.

"Hey," he said quietly.

"Hey. How are you feeling?" My voice shook as I spoke.

"I'm okay. Tired. Police had stopped by."

"We know. We followed them here."

"What happened?" Uncle Basil asked, sitting down in the chair after pulling it close.

"It's all fuzzy." He paused before continuing, "Adacio and I were leaving the club when this guy came out of nowhere. He attacked us and we defended ourselves. It seemed we were no match for him." He took a deep breath before finishing, "If that person didn't leave the club at that time, I don't know what would have happened."

"There was a witness?"

"Yes, I heard someone yelling out for help before I passed out. Next thing I knew, I was here."

"I'll ask the police if they have a lead later today. Right now, we want you to focus on recovering."

I remained quiet, unsure if I could talk without crying. This was just too much. What if that person didn't come out when he did? I could have lost my only brother. After a few minutes of quiet, Agento fell asleep with my hand in his. Soon after, Uncle Basil went to check on Adacio. He pulled the chair closer to me and made me sit before he left to see his son. I sat down for an exceedingly long time, just watching him sleep and looking closely at his bandages. His neck was wrapped, his forearms had bandages here and there, and his stomach and back were wrapped all around with a huge bandage, leaving much to my imagination as to how bad it really was.

The door opened, and Cinnia walked in. "Hey, how's he doing?"

"Okay, I guess. He's been sleeping for a while. How's Adacio?"

"Sleeping as well, but okay. They will both be good as new before we know it. How are you doing?"

I signed and leaned into her as she came behind me. "I don't know. I keep thinking it's worse than it is."

"But you know it's not. Your mind is just playing tricks on you." She pulled another chair over and sat next to me.

"I know. But at the same time, how do I know it's not worse? I can't see his injuries, and I don't know why this even happened."

"The doctors say they are not in serious condition. He's going to recover completely. And, knowing why this happened won't help you right now. You should only be thinking about the good news of his recovery and not what could have happened."

"I know, I just can't help it. This year hasn't been kind to my family."

"I know." We sat in silence for a few minutes, watching him sleep in silence for a few moments. After my own eyes started falling closed, she asked, "Have you told Errol?"

I jerked awake. "No. It just happened."

"He would want to be here for you, you know. I've seen how close you two are. Besides, maybe he is what you need right now. Someone who is close to you but not family."

"I'll call him later." I resigned.

"No." She stood up and grabbed my purse before returning to her seat. "Now. You will only keep torturing yourself other-wise." She handed it to me and wouldn't back down.

"You're so bossy." Dialing his number, I called, murmuring to her. "Did you call Marino for support?"

"Yes, I did. He will be here in two hours once he gets off work." Her so there look made my eyes narrow at her.

After the happy greeting I got, I choked up, but I told Errol about what happened and with his support, I did feel better when I ended the call. He was on his way and would be here within the hour. "He's coming. Happy now."

"Yes."

We sat quietly as we waited. We were unaccustomed to this happening. Crestwood was normally a safe place. What are the odds of this happening to my brother? It had to be connected, right? Why go after Agento in the first place? Why not me? As I sat there, holding his hand in both of mine, I couldn't help but blame myself. Would this have happened if I had stayed away from Errol like Agento wanted?

My phone soon chimed with a text from Errol asking which room. I replied and spoke. "He's here."

She patted the back of my hand. "Good. I wanted to go back to Adacio and see if he woke up, but I'm not leaving you alone."

"Cinnia," I hesitated, "do you think it's related to the five people that went missing and are presumed dead?"

"What? No way."

"Then why. This doesn't just happen. Why did they get attacked?"

"I don't know. They are not missing or dead. Gemma, don't make this into something that it's not. Crazy shit this like just happens."

"Okay." At the knock, I looked up. Errol entered the room

and headed straight toward me as he took in the room. "You're here fast."

"Yes, well. I had nothing I was doing at the time, so I headed straight here. Do you two need anything? I will go get it."

"No, thank you." Cinnia stood up. "I will go get something for you two. I was leaving anyway to head to my brother's room. What did you want to drink?"

"I'm fine."

"Just water." Errol interjected as he sat down.

"Okay. I'll be back soon."

We waited a whole minute after she left before he pulled me close. My hand left my brother's, and my eyes were stunned. "How are you really?"

"Shaken."

"What happened?" He whispered as he ran his hands down my back, the best he could with the arms of the chairs in the way.

I replayed every detail Agento gave us, and we quietly sat while watching Agento sleep. Was he thinking what I was? After Cinnia brought the water, Errol made me drink; she promised to check on me again soon before heading across the hall to see her brother and parents.

I couldn't take the quiet any longer. I had to know. "Was it him?"

"I don't know for sure, but the signs would point to it being yes. I will need to look closely at his injuries and the scene. Preferably sooner rather than later."

"Why?"

Errol knew what I meant. "This could be his way of saying he knows about you."

"Why wouldn't he come after me?"

"Maybe you weren't as easy to get to. Or maybe he didn't feel the message would be the same. What were you doing last night?"

"Girls' night. Cinnia, Lona, and I. It's not like we would have put up a fight." Oh, that reminded me. Errol hasn't met Lona yet. Now wasn't the time to discuss that, though. Maybe next time she's in town.

"I don't know why, then. Maybe your brother and cousin were closer to him. I will find out, though."

"I know you will."

"I need to call my family. Will you be okay if I step out for a minute?" But as he pulled out his phone, Agento started to wake, and he stopped.

"Hey," He murmured. "Where did you come from?"

"I came to see how you were doing."

"Good." He looked from Errol to me. "Hey, you should go home. You've been here long enough. I'm fine."

I smiled and shook my head. He always was the concerned brother, first and foremost. I was glad he was awake, but I still wasn't comfortable leaving just yet. "I'm not leaving until everyone is ready to leave. It really hasn't been that long. You should rest."

"I will after you leave." Turning back to Errol, he continued, "You should take her home."

"I would if she would let me. We are both here, concerned for you."

"Nonsense."

"Are you thirsty? The nurse left water for you." Standing up, I brought the water to his mouth without waiting for a response.

"I got it." He said as he took it from me and drank the water through the straw. He flinched a little and shakily put the water back on the tray nearby. "See. I'm good."

"Stop being the brave brother for once. I'm not going until you are really good. I don't have anything better to do."

Before he could protest, Errol interrupted. "I agree with Gemma. Right now, it's best she stays here, safe, with you."

Agento's confused look reflected my own. Was he going to tell Agento what really caused this? Here wasn't the time for that conversation. "What are you talking about?"

"I told you before I would keep your sister safe. Right now, here is the safest place for her."

"Are you saying my attacker is your parents' killer?"

"I'm not saying yes or no. I am saying it could be, though."

"Shit, man. You better find out."

"I am. I was just going to call my family when you woke up."

"Go do that. We are not going anywhere today."

Errol nodded and turned to walk out of the room. I sat silently, unsure of what to say and what not to say until his return.

Agento, on the other hand, didn't feel like being silent. "Just how much do you know about this?"

"I don't know what you mean."

He knew I was lying when I couldn't look him in the eye. "Don't play dumb with me. You know I know you know something about this. You wouldn't risk your life otherwise."

Resigned, I looked up. "I can't tell you about what I know, but I believe it is strongly connected to your attack."

"Why?"

"Because the killer knows I'm involved with Errol. I guess he attacked you to let us know he knows."

"That's crazy. How involved are you with this?"

"I'm not involved at all. I'm only involved with Errol."

"Why is this person attacking others? What does he want?"

"I don't know."

"You know something, though. Something huge that you're not telling me. Why are you hiding it?"

"I can't tell you. I want to, but it's not something easy to believe. Right now, you should just focus on healing."

"I'm healed enough."

"Yes, to have a conversation. Not to discuss something that will change your view on the world."

"What crazy shit are you talking about? What shit does he have you believing?"

"I can't tell you, but one day soon I promise we will."

"If some guy is out there, hunting this family, then I want you to end this relationship. It's obviously not safe for you."

"No."

"You promised me that if it went too far, you would."

"I promised if I were in direct danger, I would, which I'm not. We don't even know if this was connected. You were attacked, not me." Okay, so I was grasping at straws, but I was also hoping that it was all a coincidence. Would I be next? Would this be the final straw Errol needed to find this person?

Before our conversation continued, Errol walked back in. "So, I have my family heading to that club in town. They will look around and call me once they know something."

"Good. So, we just wait."

"Yes."

"If you wanted to go, you can. We will be fine here."

"No, it's okay. They got it handled. I'll just hold them up as they are closer than I am." Sitting back down, putting an arm around the back of my chair, he continued. "So, do you recall any more details?"

"No, I don't." Agento pushed the button on the side of his head and sat in a more seated position. "I told the police everything I remember, and I'm sure Gemma told you what I said."

"True, but with more rest, people normally distance themselves from the scene and recall details they didn't before."

"That's true, but I'm still recovering and only slept for a few hours since then."

"More like four." I said, not being heard as they stared at each other. Speaking louder, I drew their attention. "Agento, do you remember anything more?"

He looked at me and signed before looking out the window. "Not really. I do know I can recall greater detail about what I remember, but not much has changed. It's all there but not."

"Do you know what the attacker was doing or saying?"

"I don't recall him saying anything."

"Can you describe him?"

"No. He was like a shadow. All black. A blur, really."

The look we exchanged got Agento's attention, but Errol interjected before he could question us. "How do you know it's a man and not a woman?"

"He was extraordinarily strong and fast, but his shape was huge. Not petite like a woman."

"Okay. What exactly did he do?"

"We had just walked outside the club, and he was like, right there, from nowhere it seemed. He pushed Adacio into the wall and turned to attack me. I defended myself as best as I could without knowing what was going on. It was so fast, and I acted on instinct, but it wasn't enough. The next thing I knew, I was on the ground with him over me. I think he had a knife; I don't know, it was something that cut me. He cut my neck before Adacio came up behind him. He hit him with something, probably a two-by-four, I don't know. You will have to ask Adacio. The guy, he…" he paused and squinted his eyes before continuing, "it sounded like a hiss, maybe. He turned and attacked Adacio. That's when someone came out and started screaming for help."

"You remembered more than you thought."

"Yes, well. The doctor said it would help to talk about it."

"My family should be calling soon, but I do believe this is connected."

"Well, then, my sister shouldn't be involved with you."

"That's not my choice. I've told her already, and she won't listen."

"Hey, I'm right here." I pushed Errol's arm away from me. "I'm not breaking up with you because of a crazy person."

"You know it's more than that." Errol's pointed look kept me quiet. I did know this was serious, but I wouldn't let some crazy person, vampire or not, run my life.

"Hey, my sister may know, but I don't."

"This isn't the place."

"Where is the place?"

Errol signed and exchanged a look with me. I nodded and looked at Agento, wondering how he would react. "Okay. When you're recovered, Gemma and you can plan a visit to my place, and we can explain everything. This requires a great deal of privacy, and you must promise to keep the secret."

"Okay. Well, I'll be out of here by tonight or early morning."

"Morning," I interjected quietly as Agento continued, "then we can talk about when. As soon as possible would be best since I won't be thinking about anything else until then."

"Understandable. Gemma and you plan the day, and we will talk."

CHAPTER XXII

rrol stayed with us for another hour before his family called, and he stepped out to answer it. Agento and I talked about random family topics while breaking out the cards and started playing War.

Errol soon returned, only with news that he had to leave. "I have to go. I am sorry, but my family needs me at home."

"That is okay. Go. We will be fine."

After a quick kiss on my forehead, he left with a promise to return when he could. Agento signed and looked at me after Errol walked out.

"I guess I see why you won't leave him."

I looked away from him. "What do you mean?"

"Oh, please. Anybody who just saw that would know. You are completely in love with him. He is, too. I can't believe I didn't see it before."

"We haven't been dating that long."

"Who do you think you're talking to? I know you better than anybody. I know it hasn't been long, but with that look

232

and deep care you two obviously have for each other, it's a no-brainer."

When I didn't answer, he continued. "I won't stand in your way. I do want you to be safe, but I know you deserve to be with someone like that. Someone who cares enough about you to fight for you."

"I am safe with him."

"Then I will give him the benefit of the doubt."

I was soon watching the scenery outside, while Agento decided to play solitaire. I wondered what would happen once Agento knew the truth. At least now he knew how I felt and wouldn't tell me to end my relationship.

Aunt Aida was the next one to enter, after Agento fell asleep again. Aunt Aida sat down next to me, pulling out a puzzle book for me and knitting for herself. We sat quietly, both engrossed with our projects.

Before we knew it, dinner came around, and Uncle Basil brought us food from Shady Lane Café takeout. I got a mixed greens with grilled chicken salad and a cold club sandwich. The sandwich was piled high with ham, turkey, bacon, lettuce, tomato, and cheddar cheese, which I gave most to Agento after the nurse left the room. He murmured thanks after trying to force the hospital food down. I was grateful that he had his appetite. Shady Lane Café was great and filling with their servings. I loved giving them a great review.

We all headed home for the night soon after. I said good-night to Adacio on my way out and apologized for not visiting sooner. He cut me off, understanding why, and wouldn't let me feel guilty about it. His injuries weren't as severe as Agento's were, but his left arm was in a sling and his back was bandaged.

Lona had left the hospital when her parents came for her, and I felt bad about leaving her alone in the waiting room for the few hours it took for her parents to come. She reassured me that it was okay. She wished the best for Agento and Adacio. She understood and would let me know when she could come by for another visit later in the week, at our class in Louisville.

I texted Errol as we were driving home.

> Hey, I'm heading home. Agento is doing great. You don't need to come back to the hospital. He will be released early in the morning.

After a short wait, he responded.

> Are you sure? I can come and meet you in the morning.

> Thanks, but no. I hate hospitals and have had my share enough. Tomorrow morning will be quick in and out.

> Can I meet up with you after?

> Yes. I will text you when I'm free.

> Great. Sweet dreams.

> You, too.

I had nightmares that night. All different scenarios of what could have happened. I was beyond exhausted, waking up early and having us all head back to the hospital. I was glad summer was here, so I could take a nap later if needed. Aunt Aida drove us to get Agento and Adacio, as Uncle Basil couldn't take another day off work. They were more aware of their surroundings this morning and acting more like themselves. We walked to the rooms and could hear the arguing from the halls. They were arguing with the nurses' orders of rest and non-stressful activities for a week.

"They are back to normal." Cinnia chuckled, and I agreed.

"Yes, but they need to realize it's a recovery week." Aunt Aida said as Agento and Adacio were led from their rooms by the nurses and pushed to the entrance doors, with us following.

"A recovery week doesn't have to mean a week of doing absolutely nothing," Adacio commented, hearing his mother's warning.

"Yes, it does."

"We will see."

"It's going to be a long week." She huffed and smiled her thanks to the nurses.

Cinnia and I laughed as we pictured it already. We knew our brothers would give Aunt Aida a hard time. They were too active to just do nothing. We both assisted in getting them into the car, much to their disbelief, as the nurses headed back inside.

We stopped and grabbed takeout for breakfast before driving home. Once Agento and Adacio were settled back in their respective, temporary rooms, under the watchful eye of Aunt Aida, I texted Errol that we were home. My day was open, and I was more than ready to learn what Verda found out and to see him.

I got a response from Errol five minutes later.

How is he today?

Great. Upset at the nurses for the bed rest,
they have him and Adacio on for this week.

I get that. When did you want to come over?

Give me an hour. I want to make sure they
are settled before I leave. I also want to
shower and change.

Perfect. Verda leaves this afternoon.

Getting ready and being reassured that everything would be fine if I left, I headed downstairs to wait for Errol. Cinnia was there as well. Marino had stopped by and was trying to get her to leave the house as well.

"I'm sure he will be fine if we go out for an hour."

"I just got home. My mom needs help getting them settled."

Not wanting to interrupt, but at the same time, Cinnia did need to get out. I jumped in to help Marino, "Cinnia, I just talked to your mother. She is all set and wants us to go out."

She gave me a traitor's look before signing and looking back at Marino. "Okay. Fine. But only an hour."

"Okay." He smiled and nodded thanks to me.

I nodded back before I opened the door at the sudden knock. "Hey, let's go." I pulled the door shut quickly. I wanted to leave now before I changed my mind.

Errol drove us to his place while holding my hand. "What did your family find?"

"A lot. I will let them explain it."

"Okay. It's a 100% sure it's the vampire, right?"

236

"Yes, we believe so. Did you see your brother's wounds?"

"No, I didn't ask to."

"I understand. We do have enough to know it was the vampire, but we might have been able to get a scent from the wounds on your brother. Depending on how fresh it was."

"Maybe you can, when you drop me off later."

"We will see. I should have looked while I was in the hospital, but I didn't want to push it. He's been through a lot. As have you."

After entering his house, Pagan met us instantly. "Hey, I'm heading out. Need anything?"

"No, I'm good. Where are you going?"

"Date." She sang as she edged by us and out the door.

"Well, that must be going well."

"Yes, it appears to be." He murmured before grabbing my hand and leading me to the library upstairs. Much like before, everyone stood around Verda as she was explaining something. She stopped instantly when she noticed us entering, and everyone turned to see.

"Hey," I whispered nervously.

"Welcome." Garcia said as she stepped forward to hug me. "We are so sorry for what happened to your brother. How is he?"

"Better. Arguing like normal. He's not happy about being on bed rest for a week."

"I know I wouldn't like it either. If there's anything we can do, just ask."

"Thanks." Wanting to change the subject, I asked, "Did Verda finish translating the book?"

"Yes, she had finished yesterday but needed a break. She was just explaining it to us. Come."

We followed her over and stood next to everyone. Verda soon continued her explanation, recapping it from the beginning for Errol and me. "Okay, it's like I told you before." She took a breath before continuing, "This book is essentially the book on all things supernatural."

"You mean, everything is in that book." Errol exclaimed.

"Precisely. Dating from the very first to now." She turned the translated version toward everyone so they could see. "These details are the beginning of witches, vampires, and werewolves. It has the biggest curses in it, the most powerful, forgotten spells, and the ruling classes in every species. It holds the ability to turn vampires, werewolves, and people into witches. This book is essential for anybody who rules in their respective species. There were supposed to be three separate books in existence." She paused and looked at everyone before continuing. "This book is a combination of all three."

"How?" Paio asked. "If they were separate books and hidden so well by their elders. How is this a combination of all three?"

She shook her head as she turned the book back to her. "I don't know. As far as I know, each ruling class has its respective books. Nothing was reported. It's like someone copied them and put them all together for an easy reference. But that doesn't make sense because all species would have disagreed to have this done, and none of them would allow some random person to see their book. Not even the next in line can see them until it's their time and is respectively passed to them."

"Someone in secret must have done this. But how did our parents get it? I can't see them doing it themselves." Clarebelle asked. She was so unsure of what this meant.

"I agree. Your parents respected the laws. They wouldn't

have done this. They must have found someone who did and stole it from them. It would explain everything. The only question to be answered is who."

"And why they would do it."

Citino sat forward and asked what they all were thinking. "What if complete control over all species is what he's after? Could this book mean that to someone in possession of it?"

Verda looked at him and acknowledged the seriousness behind this discovery. "Yes. It has everything. The strengths, weaknesses, and more."

"Total domination. That explains a lot."

"What do you guys do now?" I asked after a few moments of silence.

Everyone looked around before Paio spoke. "I don't know. I do know we are not giving him this book, though. Not after everything."

Garcia stated in a low voice. "We do need to get together and figure out the best thing to do. We can't find him. Omella is a bigger threat right now. She's blocking him from us."

We all looked at Verda. She looked back and sighed. "I'm sorry. I wish I could stay and help. This book does change things, but I'm needed back in Las Vegas. My grams won't let me stay here any longer."

"We understand that. But is there anything you can do before you leave?"

She hesitated as she thought it over. "Yes. I can put a temporary hold on magic in the area. This town is small enough that for 24 hours, I can block all magic from happening. But, only for 24 hours. After that, you will be on your own."

"That's great. That's all we need in order to find him."

"I will start it after I get home. I can't be here or it won't work. The user can't block themselves, so they cannot be nearby."

"Understandable. We will make do in the meantime."

"I will call the moment it's done, so be ready to go. Twenty-four hours go by quicker than you realize. Especially with no magic."

"We will be ready." Clarebelle answered. "We've been waiting for a long time now. We are grateful for your help."

"It wasn't just for you. I learned much as well. This book should go back with me, and I would definitely take it if I thought for a second you couldn't be trusted with it. I promise not to let others know unless it becomes absolutely necessary."

"Thank you."

"Keep it safe. And hidden. I wouldn't even tell Pagan since she thought her date was more important than this."

"I understand. We will talk to her after it's resolved."

"I'm going to rest now. I haven't slept much, and I do need some sleep before my flight this afternoon."

We will watch as she walked away, leaving the book and the translated copy on the coffee table. We all stared at it, unsure of what to do.

"This is huge," Garcia said to no one in particular. "What do we do with the books?"

"We hide them." Clarebelle said as she stood up. She grabbed both copies and held them before turning to everyone. "I will hide them. Only I will know where they are. This will ensure their safety."

We all agreed and left the room to give her space. Walking throughout the house, we all would turn our backs whenever we saw Clarebelle with the books. We knew she wouldn't keep them in the library. We made sure not to pay attention to her for the next hour.

Errol and I left to walk the gardens out back. "So, how is he really doing?"

"Truly, I believe he knows he has a way to go. Overall, he is coming to this reality and will be fine. He lost a lot of blood from his neck, he has a concussion, scratches on his arms, and a bruised back and ribs."

"He's lucky."

"Yes. They both are. What did your family find?"

"The vampire is definitely a male vamp. The witness confirmed she saw enough to know he was built and too muscular for a female to be. It was the vampire without a doubt. There was a faint scent, one caught by Citino. He's hoping to find a lead or be able to follow it somewhere. He's going back tonight with Paio and me to look."

"Why are you waiting so long to go?"

"Because the police have the place surrounded right now. I was hoping to visit your brother as well before we left. If Citino sees him, he might have better luck with Agento than at the club."

"Why?"

"Because he bit your brother. That scent lingers a lot longer than a smell at a location."

"Okay. You and Citino can drop me off and ask to visit as a concerned friend."

"That's a great idea. Probably the only one we will get without Marino's help."

"I'm sorry about that."

"Not your fault."

"But it is. You would have considered leaving if it weren't for us."

"No." He quickly stopped and grabbed my arm to keep me from walking on. "I will admit I want to stay close for you, but you already said you would leave if needed. You know, we chose this place; our parents picked it. We don't want to leave. And we won't unless we have no other choice. This isn't your fault. This is between us and Marino, and if we can come to a peaceful agreement or not."

"Okay."

We walked all throughout the gardens in silence, just enjoying each other's company. We came to the entrance and stopped.

"When will Verda get home?"

"It depends on her flight and if it's delayed or not. She should be there tonight either way. Her flight's at 3, so it's a four-hour flight. She should be there no later than 9 tonight."

"Will the scent last long enough for you guys to follow it after hours in between?"

"Yes. Once Citino has a strong enough scent, he can follow it for hours at a time, a day if needed. It's just getting the scent that's been the issue."

"Good. We should head out. I want to make sure you do get it before it gets too late."

"I'll go get Citino. Meet you in the car."

The ride was quiet as we were all lost in our own thoughts. I was glad their parents weren't thieves, but someone else was and had the means to make their lives miserable. How could Pagan choose a date over finding out this discovery? It was huge and affected her as well. Was Errol choosing time with me over his family as well? How much did he not know?

I breathed a sigh of relief, seeing that Agento was not asleep when we arrived. He was just getting out of the shower and stepped into his room as we got upstairs. Aunt Aida offered to bring them food, but I told her I could make it and bring it up myself. I knew she was working twice as hard with my brother and cousin. This gave Errol and Citino some time to explain what they needed from Agento, whatever that was exactly. After making some sandwiches, only a few as I knew Citino and Errol wouldn't eat them, I headed up with a tray of them, a bag of chips, and two 20-oz waters.

I silently knocked on the door and waited for Errol to open it for me. He took the bag and the water from me and helped me set everything up by the bed. Agento and Citino were talking in low voices; Agento was trying to understand what Citino was explaining that they needed.

CHAPTER XXIII

"I just don't understand why you want to sniff me."

Citino signed and explained the best he could for the fourth time. "Like I said before. I can't explain it right now. Time is of the essence, and I need this in order to find your attacker."

"Why? Are you going to sniff him out? What are you, a werewolf?"

"No, and I thank god for that."

"Is that a joke?"

Unsure how to answer, Citino signed and turned to me. I could tell Agento was getting on his nerves, but he contained himself so well I would barely see it if I didn't know him so well. I knew Agento didn't understand what was going on. I decided to intervene before things escalated.

"Agento, Citino just needs to do this. Please, I will explain what I can when I can."

"Right now, we need this. It's essential." Errol explained, sitting next to Citino in the spare chair.

This left me standing, but it gave me the opportunity to serve Agento food and water. "Here, Agento. Aunt Aida said you need to eat."

"Gladly. Now, explain why you brought these two to smell me right now. I don't care to wait for an explanation."

"It's complicated. But they are here for a reason. Please, just go with it. Once we talk about it later, this will all make sense to you."

"Why not explain it now? You are both here."

"We can't. There are too many people here, and anybody could walk in. Citino is a great tracker and knows what he's doing."

He signed, realizing we weren't giving in. "Fine. But do it quickly. This is weird. You'd better explain it in great detail later."

"We will."

"You can close your eyes if you feel uncomfortable about it." Citino said as he stood up and leaned down.

"You bet your ass I will."

I sat down on Errol's lap as Citino leaned down and sniffed as closely as he could to the bite mark under the bandage. Agento had his eyes closed tightly until he knew for sure Citino was nowhere near him anymore.

Citino was a few feet away before he replied. "I have it. We can leave. When Verda is ready, I will be too."

"I should go," Errol whispered, and I reluctantly moved so they could leave. It's not every day that we get to sit and enjoy ourselves. That was always something between us.

Before they got out the door, Agento shouted to them. "Hey, this weekend, after I'm off bed rest. Your place and explanation had better happen. And not a minute later."

"Count on it." Errol nodded back before following Citino.

I sat smiling. I couldn't believe it. Soon, Agento would know the truth, and I would have someone to talk to. Hopefully, by tomorrow, everything will go back to normal, as normal as having a vampire for a boyfriend could be. At the very least, we would have a break from the drama and get in some much-needed alone time.

I hung out with Agento until he finished his lunch. I ate one sandwich, and we watched TV for a couple of hours in silence. He didn't ask me about that scene with Errol and Citino, as he knew I wouldn't tell him anything. Soon enough, he would know everything, though, and I couldn't wait. Cinnia and I went outside later for much-needed air. The rest of the afternoon was spent cleaning.

Errol texted me when they dropped Verda off at the airport, and we talked on the phone before bed; we were just missing our quiet afternoons together. Summer was turning out to be incredibly stressful, but hopefully, it will all end tomorrow for the better.

The next morning, I didn't try to contact Errol. I knew he would be busy tracking down the vampire. I spent my whole day with my family. Adacio and Agento were allowed a few walks around the house for a few days. We laughed, cried, argued, and joked around as normal. It wasn't until late into the evening that I realized Errol didn't text or call me. I started to worry and wanted to talk to him, but what if he was close to this vampire? I had to wait.

The moment I woke up the following day, I checked my phone. Still nothing. I started dialing without thinking twice. I just had to hear his voice. He answered on the third ring.

"Good morning."

My irritation flared. "'Good morning.' That's what I get after a whole day of silence."

"Look, I'm sorry. We ran into a problem."

My temper dimmed. "What happened?"

"It's Verda. Once she landed in Las Vegas, she had an accident." He signed and took a breath before continuing. "Someone ran into her car. She will be all right, but she's hospitalized for a week, recovering."

"That's horrible."

"Yes, it is."

"Do you think Omella?"

"We do. The timing is just too close for it not to be. But we can't be sure. How Omella knew Verda was here is beyond us."

"It is weird. She didn't leave your place at all?"

"No. Nobody saw her except us."

"What happens now? Can Citino still track him?"

"No, he can't. But the scent is still with him. If he crosses the vampire in town, he will know."

"I really hope you will consider Marino's offer."

"We won't. It's not that dire."

"How isn't it?"

"Clarebelle is getting hold of Verda's family again today. Maybe one of them can help us."

"Do you think they will? What if they think you are to blame?"

"That's a risk, but she can convince them if anybody could. She has the book hidden after all, and she will use the knowledge of it if needed."

"I'm sorry. I didn't want Verda to get hurt."

"Neither did we." I heard someone in the background

before Errol came back on. "Look, I have to go. We need to figure this out. I'll call you once we know something."

"Okay."

"If anything happens, know this. I love you."

"I love you, too." A sob started as I hung up. It was heart-warming to have said it finally, but it also felt more like a goodbye. Was it a good or bad omen?

Cinnia knew something was wrong and made me leave the house. We decided to walk around town for exercise as she tried to get my spirits up. I really wanted to talk to her, but I couldn't. She wouldn't believe me even if I did. How would she even react?

I missed Errol. I was sad for Verda. I was angry at this unknown vampire and Omella. I wanted the summer to have one happy moment that nothing could break. I was worried about Agento and his reaction to Errol's secret. Would I ever get to talk to Cinnia about this? Would she understand? Would my happiness end hers? This thing between vampires and werewolves could end her relationship, or I would have to move and never see Cinnia again.

I couldn't stop these thoughts as I walked with Cinnia. We walked, shopped, ate, and talked about nothing. I tried to enjoy myself, but every hour I would stare at my phone, hoping for it to chime. The day dragged on until finally I got a text from Errol.

Clarebelle got a family member to do the spell. Tomorrow the hunt starts. I will be busy all day. Hopefully, we have this weekend to ourselves, without worrying about this anymore.

That's great. Let me know the moment you are free.

Will do. Be safe.

My spirits lifted. My night was great. I will have a worry-free summer the day after tomorrow. But you know what they say: the best laid plans are always the worst ones.

I decided not to let anything ruin my day. Aunt Aida, Cinnia, and I all headed for the mall. Uncle Basil stayed home to make sure the guys stayed in bed until we got back. I bet Cinnia they would wait all of five minutes before they were up and outside doing something they shouldn't be doing.

"As long as they don't push it, Aunt Aida will never know." I whispered as we walked the mall. Aunt Aida walked with us between the stores but shopped away from us in each store, to give us space. No teenager wants to shop with their parents, or in my case, their legal guardian, and she respected that.

"Right. I'm sure they will, and she will be so mad."

"I hope not, though I know how unlikely that is. Agento and I have plans with Errol this weekend. He cannot push himself today."

"How's it going between you two?"

"Great." I looked around for eavesdroppers before continuing, "We actually said 'I love you' to each other. Over the phone, and I can't wait to see him to say it in person."

She gasped. "Oh my gosh. That's terrific. I'm so happy for you."

"Where are you and Marino at?"

She signed as she picked up something to look at. She seemed reluctant to answer. "I don't know. One day we are close, then the next he's distant like he doesn't want to be with me."

I didn't know what to say. Hopefully, he explains everything to her, but I wasn't going to get in the middle. Well, maybe I should? I know she would have if it were the reverse. I'll have to talk to him when I see him next.

"I'm sure it's nothing. Remember the first time with Errol and me. I thought he was hiding something, and when I did find out, it just brought us closer."

"Wait," She turned to me. "You think he's hiding something from me?"

"Well, I mean, isn't everyone in the beginning?"

She didn't know what to say, and we finished looking in the store to move on to the next one with Aunt Aida. Cinnia wasn't into talking all that after that first store, but after five or six, she started to chill out again, and we found lighter topics to discuss.

We sat down with pizza for lunch and ate in silence until Aunt Aida finished and started in on us. "Let's hear it. I haven't heard one word from either of you in weeks about your boyfriends. Tell me something. I want to know how it's going."

"Gemma's in love." Cinnia said as she shot me a look. I rolled my eyes, knowing she meant well but wasn't ready to share her news.

"Yes. Things are great between Errol and me."

"Well then, he should come over for dinner one night. Errol

seems like a great guy. We want to get to know him as well. Especially since you two are closer than I thought." Even though Aunt Aida was surprised, she didn't question me or how I felt. She was generally curious.

"I will ask him." Smiling at Cinnia, I decided to return the favor. "Cinnia is falling hard for Marino as well." Her look of horror was all I needed to know, and I hit the mark. Maybe her mother could talk sense into her.

"Cinnia, is that true?"

"Yes." She murmured and grabbed a slice of pizza, knowing she wasn't hungry but needed something to do.

"Well, tell me about him. Why hasn't he been over for dinner? I swear, you girls nowadays."

"He's private. And while I do like him, I haven't told him 'I love him,' not like Gemma has."

"I want to meet him soon. I have a feeling it won't be long before you do say it."

"I'll ask him."

"Great. Now let's head out. I'm sure Basil hasn't kept those boys in bed like he should have."

We had a fun day with Aunt Aida, except for lunch. Now we had to discuss a family dinner with Errol and Marino, and end up getting grilled by our family. We ended up piling the trunk full of bags, with a few up front with us. Uncle Basil helped Aunt Aida bring the bags in, and Cinnia and I organized which bags went where and to whom. Agento and Adacio sat in the living room, looking innocent, but I wasn't fooled.

After putting all the bags in the correct rooms, I sat down in the middle of them and confronted them. "So, just how far did you guys go today?"

"I don't know what you're talking about." Adacio tried.

"Oh, please. Like, I don't know the moment we left, you all didn't go outside for fun."

He looked guilty and couldn't deny it when Cinnia started in on him as well. "Okay, Okay. We went outside, played games, and helped Dad with work. But we didn't push ourselves. Once we felt the pain in our muscles, we came inside to rest. Per Dad's orders."

"Agento, is that true?" I asked, looking at him.

"Yes."

"Okay, then. At least you know how to listen to your body. They are still healing."

"They are mostly done healing. Barely got a scratch showing."

"True, but the muscles take longer, and you and I have plans tomorrow, remember?"

"How could I forget?"

"You better not forget."

He chuckled, and I left the room. I spent the rest of my day organizing my bags, from gifts to personal items. I turned the radio on to have something playing in the background as I moved about my room, distracting me from the time.

I was just getting ready for bed when the grave news came through a call from Errol. I picked up the phone as soon as I noticed my phone vibrating, nearly off the stand. I forgot I had the volume down as I sat on my bed, dressed in my pajamas, and got comfortable before answering.

"Hey, how did it go?"

His voice was grave and quiet. "Not good. I have terrible news."

My heart sank. "What happened?"

"Pagan," his voice broke, and he took another breath before saying, "She was killed a couple of hours ago."

"What?" I said in disbelief. This couldn't be happening. Not again. "H-how?" I couldn't get a sentence out.

"Daimon. He's the vampire. She was with him, and he used her to make his escape before we got there."

"Oh my god. That's terrible. I'm so sorry."

He signed and hesitated before answering, probably getting control of himself. I can't believe it. "We just got home, but I don't think we should have you or your brother over tomorrow. A lot's about to happen. Maybe if we do this next weekend or the weekend after."

"Can I come over? I want to be there for you. You shouldn't be alone. I know what death does to a person."

"I can pick you up tomorrow late in the morning. Early morning, we are feeding." His hesitation told me everything. He really wasn't himself.

"I understand. Again, I'm sorry. Pagan was great and will be missed." I really wish I knew her better.

"That she will."

I hung up, unsure what to do. I ended up crying myself to sleep that night. I can't believe the answer was right there the whole time. And Pagan paid the price. I guess they weren't soulmates after all. Daimon fooled not just Pagan but all of them.

CHAPTER XXIV

I sat up in bed the next morning without wanting to move. Last night was horrible, and as badly as I wanted it to be a dream, I knew it wasn't. Pagan was gone, the family had more grieving to do, and I wanted to be there for them. I had to wait so they could feed. I got out of bed, realizing I needed to talk to Agento about changing the dinner plans.

"No, you two promised you would explain, and now that day is here. Now you want to push it off."

I signed and looked away as I explained. "Something bad happened. This couldn't be helped."

"It doesn't change the fact."

"It does. They lost someone last night. They want time alone. I'm only going to support my boyfriend, not grill him about who he is."

"What do you mean? What happened?"

As I explained, there was a catch in my throat. "Pagan, the oldest sister, was killed last night."

He sat up, and when I looked at him, all I saw was disbelief on his face. "That's horrible. I'm sorry. I mean, I didn't know her, but I wouldn't wish death on anybody."

"I know. I'm going today only to be there for them."

"I'm going."

"Agento-"

"No, stop. If you're going to show support, then I am too. I know what it's like to lose someone, and I know they have it worse than we did."

"I will have to ask Errol if it's okay. They weren't all that happy about me going. They have a lot to deal with."

"That's fine. Just let them know I want to help. And that I'm sorry."

"Okay."

After a moment of silence, he said. "I know I only met them once, but I know how close you are to them. Pagan was nice and will be missed."

"Thanks."

He pulled me into a hug and signed into my hair. "I'm sorry you are dealing with this as well. It's been a year of loss for us, and the year's only half over." I just hoped we wouldn't lose anybody else. I don't know what I would do if we did.

"I know. I hope it's over. I don't want to lose another person. Especially to this person."

"Does the police have any leads?"

"I don't know. I only found out right before I went to bed."

"Jesus, you slept with this in your head?"

"Yes."

"I'm surprised you could sleep at all."

"I cried myself to sleep." I confessed.

"You should have come to me. We could have talked about it."

"You were most likely already asleep."

"You make me sound old." I choked out a laugh. After a good laugh, we calmed down and stared at each other. "You know I'm here for you."

"Yes. I know."

"Good. Now I'm hungry. Let's go downstairs and wait for your boyfriend's call." He got up, and I followed him out the door.

"I'll be down after I change and text him."

"Okay." After another quick hug of comfort, Agento made his way downstairs as I headed for my room.

Errol agreed to Agento coming, but only so I would have support as well. I hoped the day would go by with ease as I waited downstairs with Agento after he changed and got ready. The family had to deal with their parents by themselves, and I didn't want that to happen with their sister. I would show my support for as long as they wanted, and so would Agento. I wondered when the funeral would be or if they even did funerals.

Errol called and said that he was outside waiting for us. We headed for the door, only to be stopped by Aunt Aida with her casserole, pie, and some beverages. We had to tell her as she noticed the grave expressions on our faces and the anxiety while we waited.

"Take this with you. You can't go empty-handed, and we want them to know we are all here for them. They should have something to eat today that they didn't have to cook themselves."

"Thanks. We will be back later."

"Take your time."

Agento carried the casserole and pie while I carried the

beverages. Errol sat in the car without getting out. Agento sat in the back, letting me sit up front with the food and drinks sitting next to him on the back seat.

Seeing his expression at the food and drinks, I explained. "This is from our family. They wanted you all to not worry about cooking but to eat something today."

"That's exceedingly kind of your family. Thanks." But I knew they wouldn't eat the food or drinks. Drinking was the one thing I noticed they didn't do; occasionally, they ate something, but drank, no.

We sat in silence on the drive to his place. We didn't know what to say, how to comfort him, when our own emotions were everywhere. Palma's vehicle was in the driveway as well when we arrived. We walked in with our arms full. Palma hurried over and helped us place everything in the kitchen before we walked into the parlor, where everyone else sat or stood in various positions. The only similar aspect they all shared was the grief of loss, the pain Agento and I understood.

We walked around, greeting and saying words of comfort to each and every one of them. By the time I got back to Errol, I was lost for words. What more could I do? I wasn't that well put together myself.

We stayed in the parlor, without saying much of anything, just being there in comfort was enough. It was late afternoon when Agento suggested they all go into the kitchen and eat something. Palma seconded it, and we will walk into the kitchen and sit down. Not much was eaten, but enough to satisfy Palma and Agento from being too suspicious. We stayed after that as I pulled Errol aside, needing much to talk. I knew today would be difficult, but it needed to be figured out.

"I know now isn't the time, and I'm sorry for mentioning it, but what is your plan? You have to think you all not being out there is what he's counting on."

"I don't know. We haven't talked about it."

"And I get that. But it's something that needs to be done. Maybe Palma can help you all pull it together."

"Maybe."

I really wanted to comfort him, but at the same time, I didn't want the same thing to happen to him as it did to Pagan. "Look. I get it's hard. But I can't help thinking it's going to keep happening unless you pull out of this and go after him. I can help you grieve after."

"You don't get it. Your parents' death was an accident. Ours and Pagan's were killed because of a book. Because one vampire thinks he can rule the entire world."

"Okay. But I know if you don't go after him, he will be coming after you. You will be blindsided, and someone else will pay the price. Again."

He looked away, knowing I was right but unable to see past his grief. I knew I shouldn't push the issue, but I was afraid of this happening again because nobody did anything.

"I'm sorry. I really am. Today shouldn't be about going after him. Look," I touched his arm and waited until he would look at me. "I just don't want anything to happen to you, or to anybody else in your family."

"I know. I just can't right now." He leaned into me, and I held him close as he regained his composure.

"Shh, it's okay to grieve. Just don't let it consume you."

"I hate to interrupt, but we should talk." Agento said from the end of the hallway. We walked back to the parlor where everyone else had sat down and waited.

Errol started as he stood between Agento and me. "I

know I agreed today would not be the day, but," he looked to me and back to his family, "we can't let Daimon ruin us or our plans. Agento needs to know in order for us to move forward, which we need to do if we hope to avenge our sister, and we will. There will be time later to grieve for her."

"Wait, are you serious?" I asked in disbelief.

"Yes. Agento," he continued, looking to Agento. "Our family has a huge secret. One we wish to share with you today, if you can promise to keep it no matter what happens. Nobody in town but your sister knows this."

He looked around the room, unsure how real this was, before looking at me and seeing how serious and hopeful I was. He nodded and turned to Errol. "Okay. I promise, no matter what, your secret is safe with me."

"Here's the thing. It works best by showing you, but I will only do so if it's necessary." He took a deep breath and watched Agento closely as he explained, "My family and I, among others, not Aunt Palma, are vampires."

"I'm sorry. What?"

"We were born vampires. Our whole community in Lake Las Vegas is made up of vampires, with a few witches there. The killer behind our family is also a vampire wanting to rule the supernatural world, in which our parents, and now we, are trying to stop."

"I'm sorry, but are you crazy?" I felt so bad for him, I knew exactly how this sounded and how I felt hearing it the first time.

"No, I'm not." We watched as his face changed, exactly as I remembered it. I turned from Errol to see Agento and how he reacted. Agento stared in disbelief at Errol, wanting to look away, but couldn't as he saw the impossible becoming possible. "As I said, showing is better."

"T-this isn't real." Agento stammered and backed away.

"It is, Agento." I said calmly, hoping to help him see what was in front of him. "The supernatural world does exist."

"How?"

"Witches."

"We can explain everything in depth now. We have nothing to hide." Errol said as his features quickly returned to normal. "We have much to discuss, though."

"How long have you known?" Agento asked me.

"Since the last time we came here."

"Why didn't I know then?"

"We weren't sure about you then." Errol interrupted. "But now we are. Your sister is not to blame."

"We are sure you have many questions, so why don't we just start talking. In the end, if we don't cover something, you can ask us, and we will clarify." Clarebelle explained.

"Okay," Agento said as I led him to a seat.

Sitting down next to him with Errol on my other side, Clarebelle started the conversation. On occasion, someone else would explain their part, but mostly Clarebelle explained all the details of vampirism and who was who. When it got to werewolves, Errol took over, explaining to Marino as well.

"So, Palma is human because she is your mother's sister."

"Correct. And our last human family."

"This is crazy. But" looking around Agento continued, "somehow I believe you. It's too detailed not to be, and I know what I saw. It also explains some of the weird shit I've seen with your family. Wait, you all haven't explained what happened recently."

"True. We thought to let it sink in with you before adding more." Paio said, deciding it was his turn to explain.

"Why is this Daimon after you? Why did he attack me?"

"He's the one we just discovered yesterday who wants the book we have hidden so he can dominate the entire supernatural world. He attacked you as his way of saying he knows about Gemma and Errol's relationship and isn't above using it to get what he wants."

"So, you are in danger?" He said, looking at me.

I huffed. "That is beside the point right now."

"No, not after what you promised me."

"Can we talk about this later? There is more to be said."

Errol continued as if we didn't have that side conversation. "Citino is our best tracker. He got the scent from you, but a witch has been helping Daimon. We didn't find him until yesterday evening, right after he killed Pagan to stop us from continuing after him."

"He used your sister to stop you. That's cold."

"She was with him, convinced they were soulmates. He had us all fooled. He probably planned this as a backup if needed. Our witch got us within reach of him, and he got desperate enough to do it."

"That's terrible. Who thinks they can rule a whole world? That's like crazy serial killer thinking."

"Yes, it is."

"Can your witch help you locate him again?"

Garcia spoke up for the first time since the explanations. "No. Witches don't like vampires, even though they created them. This was a one-time thing and only because it was a vendetta for Verda, our witch friend. We don't know why Omella is helping Daimon."

"The witch," I whispered to him before he could ask.

"Oh," he whispered back. To them, he continued, "So, what happens now?"

"We don't know. We have to figure that out. We can't let this go. He must pay for Antico, Maya, and Pagan."

Still reeling, Agento sat back and signed. "Well, I must say. I did not expect this secret. I really only came to support you all, but I'm glad I know. Weirded out, but glad."

"We have debated it for some time."

"Any way that I can help, just ask."

"We will keep that in mind, but as a human being, there is truly little you can do. Believe me, I know."

"I get that I'm not as strong or fast as you. But, as a human being, I have intel that you don't have. And I know the people in town, I bet better than you. Especially since you have never been here before."

Clarebelle interjected. "That's true. But Aunt Palma is better yet, as she grew up here."

"Now, now. A new pair of eyes, especially younger ones, is always greatly appreciated." Palma commented.

While we talked about vampires, witches, werewolves, and what to do about Daimon, I kept a close eye on Agento to see how he really was doing. His expression stayed blank the whole time, and I was left feeling unsure. We had to find Daimon. He was not getting away with what he did. Citino was sure he could now find him since he had his scent and knew who he was looking for. He plans on walking around town with Agento and Errol tomorrow to see what they find. Hopefully, a lead. I plan on helping others strategize a plan on how to stop him.

I was so happy I had Agento to talk to now. The only thing

that would make this day better would be if Cinnia found out, at least about Marino. He couldn't just up and leave without some plan, right? He didn't seem the type to do that to Cinnia. She would be by herself, wondering what she did when it had nothing to do with her.

The next day turned into a week-long search and strategizing. Daimon seemed to disappear from town. Nobody had seen or heard of anybody with his description, no further attacks happened, and without finding him, we couldn't decide what to do. Clarebelle was by herself, torn as to whom to turn to. Verda had recovered from her accident but was not answering her phone. Their so-called family in Lake Las Vegas wouldn't help them. Their sister was the only one who got close to Daimon, possibly enough to know where he hid. That didn't end well for her.

Truth be told, I don't think they wanted to find him. They weren't going out unless they were made to by each other, mostly by Palma. They were too depressed, and I wanted to help them, but how? I kind of understood what they were going through, and being vampires, they felt everything more intensely than we humans do. But their situation was different from mine, and I was unsure where to go from here.

Lona asked if I could visit her hometown, but I put her off. I wanted to, but I didn't want to leave Errol and his family right now. Who knew what would happen? I definitely didn't want them to worry about me either. I hope that once this is over, Lona and I can stay great friends. This summer was one huge disaster. One I wish I could wake up from, and one I could use a good friend for in the end.

Cinnia and Marino seemed closer recently. They spent more time together, never questioning their future. This made me suspicious. Surely he wasn't trying to be nicer only to leave later, right? I planned on confronting him, but he kept his distance from me, only making me worry more about it. I wouldn't be the one who interferes with a happy relationship, but I wanted to make sure my cousin wasn't wasting her time and ended up getting hurt. I spent all the time I could with Cinnia as I wanted her to know I wasn't choosing Errol over her. She knew, like my whole family, that I was helping Errol get through this difficult time.

Agento and Adacio were more than happy to return to their bachelor's pad. Agento wished me luck whenever we talked on the phone. He kept a distance, though, one that made me think all wasn't good between him and the Leighs. I know it's a lot to take in, and he is trying, but I wish he wouldn't distance himself from me. Adacio and I still have a cousin bond, despite the distance, but loving. It's hard, but I know he's there for me whenever I need him, and that's enough for me right now.

Aunt Aida and Uncle Basil spent their whole weekend together, leaving town for something new to do. They started dating night up again now that everything was back to normal with Adacio and Agento. Everyone but me seemed to be enjoying themselves. Why couldn't I catch a break?

CHAPTER XXV

A second week has started, and I have had it. Still no change, and I knew Errol and his siblings were not trying to find Daimon. I couldn't let them let him go, and knew they had to step up and do something. The time to grieve was put on hold until he was caught. I wanted a good summer, at least what was left of it.

I called Errol first and asked him to come over and get me. He tried disagreeing, but I stayed persistent this time and changed his mind. He knew we needed to do something, and I knew I had waited long enough.

Waiting for him to arrive, I paced the living room, thinking about what we knew, what needed to happen, and the possibilities of how to get it to happen. Pagan was the key; one they didn't want to think about. She had to have known something that could help us now with Daimon. Hopefully, she kept a diary or journal, something. I would even be happy if she had a map, and even if she were still here to tell us. She was in love with Daimon, so somewhere it had to show.

The knock at the door sent me jogging to answer it. I grabbed my lightweight vest before pulling open the door.

"Hi," I smiled as Errol stood back to let me out. "Look, I'm sorry if I pushed-"

He stopped me. "No. You were right. We have been pushing it off."

"And I understand why."

"We should go. Everyone is waiting."

"Errol," I hesitated as he drove through town. "I'm sorry if you don't want to hear this but," I paused, deciding fast was the only way. "Pagan will be missed, but she needs you guys to pull it together to find Daimon and avenge her, and your parents."

"I know."

The silence was so tense, I stayed quiet for the rest of the ride. I was sure I had pushed my limit and didn't want a fight.

"I can't believe it's been almost two weeks." Errol whispered softly after parking the car and looked at the outside of his house. Sitting, I turned to him, unsure if he meant for me to hear him or not. "I keep looking for her, waiting for her in the morning to walk downstairs. She has always been there. I have known her from day one, and we were close, not too close, but it's what makes this hard. I don't know how to move on." He finally turned to me.

I could see he was barely holding it together and wanted to comfort him, but at the same time, I didn't want to interrupt wherever he was going, so I stayed unmoved and waited. His guilt was emanating from the distance he had from Pagan. He wasn't alone: a lot of siblings have rivalry and some distance between them. Thinking this reminded me of Agento and me. Was any sibling truly really close?

He reached out for me, pulling me awkwardly toward him. Unbuckling to settle closer and uncomfortably with the buckle on my side, I leaned into him. "I'm sorry if I'm not the best company today. I'm trying for Pagan. I am glad you are here."

"Me too."

"Let's go inside. Everyone's waiting to see what we can find today. It hasn't been a productive week."

Walking side by side with his arm around my back, I kept close to bring comfort and reassurance to him. His whole family was there, and it felt like I had walked into a fresh funeral.

"Let's see if anybody can bring something new into the light." Palma said as soon as we entered.

"I know something," I said, looking around the room. "Did anybody check Pagan's room for clues? Did she keep a diary or journal?"

I was met with heads shaking no. "We haven't really done anything, other than talk." Garcia said.

"She was in love with Daimon. She had to have some clue as to his hideouts. With any luck, his favorite spots and home location."

"That's right. We should check." Garcia stood up and pulled Clarebelle with her. "Let's go. We girls, and Aunt Palma, can look in Pagan's room. Citino, why don't you, Paio, and Errol take a special look at the places in town we know she's been with him?"

Errol left with the guys after a quick goodbye hug to me. I slowly followed the girls and Palma upstairs, wondering if sending them out was really a good idea. Their minds weren't in the right place right now, but Garcia probably knew what she was doing.

After looking through the room for an hour, I got tired and sat on the floor in the closet. Nothing. She had a deep purple theme, which seemed, at first glance, to be dark and moody. But after spending an hour here, I noticed the purple colors blended into a calm, relaxing atmosphere, like a love nest.

I looked around to see how everyone else was faring. Clarebelle was looking under the bed, getting frustrated. Garcia was crawling around on the floor, hoping for a secret panel. Palma searched through the desk, again coming up empty.

I leaned my head back, wondering. What did we miss? The lack of information was something, right? There had to be something. Banging my head against the wall, I noticed a hollow sound. I gasped and turned quickly. Tapping it with my hand, I called out to the others.

They rushed over, and together, Garcia and Clarebelle managed to open the tiny panel, only big enough to be a hand-sized hole. Just enough for a small book and pen.

"This is it." Garcia exclaimed.

"Yes. I knew it." I whispered. I had just given up hope. "Let's take it downstairs and see what's in it."

The cover was worn, a lavender purple with a matching pen. I wonder how long she's been writing in it. We all headed downstairs, a pep in our steps as we finally got a break.

The first date in the journal was from fifteen years ago. "She's had this since she was a child. Do you know when she got it?"

"Yes. I actually got it for her on her one-year birthday. I was too young to think much of it. I didn't think she liked it much less kept it all these years." Clarebelle explained. As she got emotional, we sat back and waited for her to regain control.

"I know this must be painful for you." I whispered and put my hand over hers.

"Thank you. I just never realized how close she and I were until now. Death takes a toll on everybody, but this should help us."

"I'm sure she knew and was very proud of you."

"Let's start at the end."

It was in code, one even Clarebelle wasn't sure about. We understood enough to know she was writing about Daimon, but when it got to their favorite places, she started writing in a different language.

"I don't understand why she did this."

"Me either. It makes no sense." Garcia said.

"Maybe she was hiding more than you knew." Palma said, trying to find the reason.

"But why? We were in this together."

"I don't know, but she was hiding this diary. From everyone, we see she's hiding more inside the hidden diary. There is something huge here. Why else hide it?"

"I didn't even know she wrote. Much less in a diary from childhood. What made her hide something that was already hidden in something?"

"That's the mystery." Palma sat forward and grabbed Clarebelle's arm. "Look. You knew Pagan more than anybody. If someone can figure this out, it's you. You need to focus on this."

"I don't know where to begin."

"Maybe if you read every entry. Front to back. Maybe the code is in there somewhere. Only you will know. Just remember your time together."

She started shaking her head. "I don't know. We grew apart."

"True, but it's your childhood that goes by too. You had been with her for three years before Paio was born. Maybe it's from then, maybe later on when you gave her the book. You need to think back and read your sister's diary. Only then can you know the truth if it's there at all."

"Okay. I'll go do that right now."

We watched her get up and leave. I turned back to Palma and Garcia. "Isn't that a long shot? Three years. They could barely walk, let alone have a secret code made up."

Palma laughed for a good minute wholeheartedly. "Thank you for that. I needed that."

I turned to Garcia, confused, only to see Garcia hiding her own laugh behind her hand. "What?"

"I'm sorry. I forget how new this is to you. You just fit right in."

Garcia touched my hand, and I looked at her. "Pagan, Clarebelle, Paio, and Errol are born vampires. All born vampires' abilities are enhanced. You understand that, right?"

I nodded. "Yes, but-"

She shook her head. "This started from birth. They were talking in complete sentences by age one."

"Wait, seriously?"

"Yes. I'm afraid so."

"Yes. Two years of perfect language. Those two girls had plenty of time to create a secret code. Even if Clarebelle doesn't realize it now." Palma explained. "Even with enhanced abilities, we, and they, tend to forget the young times."

I sat in silence, reminiscing about what that meant. Errol was eighteen, four years younger than Paio. Did that distance them at all as kids? I know now that it didn't. Paio and Errol were as close as any siblings, including their sisters. I tried to remember my first few years, but I couldn't. Pictures helped, but they weren't the same as remembering.

We sat there until we heard the guys walking in. They seemed in high spirits, and we rushed to the hallway. They were happy and celebrating something.

"Out with it." Palma demanded.

"Well, we found a possible location. At least one we know for sure he's used." Citino said.

"Really? Where is it?"

Paio stepped forward, more than ready to explain. "Don't get too much excited. He hasn't been back there in over a week, but we know he used it last week. He might go back, and if he doesn't." He paused and pulled out a map. "We have a map to find him by. Our sister was smart, though she was in love with him."

"Bad taste. But resourceful." Citino said.

"Let's see."

"Where's Clarebelle?"

"Upstairs. She's busy with another kind of map. Pagan's coded diary." Garcia said, smiling as she wrapped her arm around Paio's.

"I'll go get her. Don't start without us."

"He might be a bit. She has a lot to remember and sort out."

We walked back to the kitchen and sat down around the counter. Paio laid out the map and pointed out the spots they found that Pagan and Daimon hung out at. Errol was marking them all with a Sharpie when Clarebelle and Citino returned.

"Citino filled me in. So, you found his hideout. Are we setting a trap or lying in wait?"

"Trap, sister. It's already set." Paio explained. "Citino had it done before we knew what he was doing."

"Great. What is it?"

"A bomb. One not to kill, but it is very painful, and no magic will block that noise."

"Great. I only got through ten pages. I'm not sure, but there might be something there. Something is telling me to look closer, but I don't recall what my childhood with Pagan could be telling me."

"It will come to you. I'm sure of it." Garcia said as she pulled her close. "Right now, let's see what the guys mapped out."

I stayed in the shadows, or tried to, but Errol kept pulling me closer. I loved seeing this family in action. They were so close; kept as a family, strong as friends, and loved to no end. I almost felt bad for Daimon. That is, if he hadn't killed their parents and sister. I was happy to be involved with this family and Errol. I knew I was safe, no matter what.

We spent two hours looking over the map. At the places they visited, shopped, stayed overnight, and possible locations of more hideouts. They were possibilities as they were estimated by distance to all these hangout places Daimon had been to. Besides the one hideout, they couldn't be 100% sure if Daimon's hideouts included those they found, but their instincts were dead on, and I didn't question them.

I was so tired by the time Errol called it quits. He pulled me aside into the hall before whispering in my ear. "Gemma, beautiful, you don't have to stay. Go home and get some rest. You look so tired."

"No. I'm not going anywhere. I want to help."

"You have helped enough. You got us working on this to help bring peace to our family. The rest is up to us now."

I stubbornly shook my head. He looked deeply into my eyes and sighed. Pulling me tighter, into a hug, he resigned. He knew it wouldn't be easy to convince me.

"I'm sorry about Pagan."

"I know you are. Please, let me take you home. I will call you first thing in the morning."

"I'm not ready to leave you yet."

After a few moments, lost in our thoughts, Errol finally said what I had been waiting to hear. "I love you. I'm sorry I didn't get to say it in person the first time."

I smiled and looked up at him, staying as close as I could. "I love you, too. That's okay. At least we were talking and not texting. That would have been horrible."

He chuckled before leaning back to see me more clearly. "You always find the right thing to say."

"I never would have believed it if you texted it. Not the first time anyway."

"That would have been cowardly if I had."

"You know," I whispered, so low I hoped he heard me. I really didn't want his family to hear me. "I've been thinking. It's been quite a while since we've been to our clearing."

He raised his eyebrow before leaning into me and whispering in my ear. "That's true. I would say it's way overdue. How about we leave now?"

"Yes." I shivered as he moved a strand of hair behind my ear.

"Wait for me in my car."

I grabbed my vest before heading out the door, hoping he wouldn't be long. Our clearing was special, and I very much wanted some time alone with Errol. Even in this dark time, maybe because it was so gloomy, the clearing was all about good memories.

I waited no more than five minutes before the next thing; I knew Errol was next to me and putting the car in gear. "What did you tell them?"

"That we were going out. My family doesn't need details when it comes to my dating life. As I don't need, or want, to know theirs."

"I just thought they would be concerned. Daimon is still out there."

"That would be true, but he doesn't know about our clearing, and I know how to fight."

"Errol. I'm sure Pagan did too."

"True, but she was blindsided."

"And you won't be?"

"We are not being followed, not by him. If it makes you feel better. I know this for a fact because Citino and Clarebelle are following us. Until we get through the forest."

"What?" I looked outside but saw nothing.

"They know where to turn back. They won't follow us to our hidden spot. Just long enough to make sure he won't be following either."

"Okay. That makes sense."

I relaxed and enjoyed the ride, knowing we were completely safe. We passed the town's outskirts, and he pulled over to the edge, hidden in the trees, before he stopped. I got out and followed him, carrying a basket that he had in the back. We were completely alone, free to be together. Not to think about the disaster around us.

The scenery was as beautiful as ever. The sun was just over

the horizon, setting behind the trees and casting shadows among the trees. Normally, I would worry about the shadows, but I always felt safe here, and Errol made sure we would be. I'm surprised nobody else has noticed the hidden pull-off before. The path was barely there and easy to miss, but if I lived here my whole life, there's no way I wouldn't have found it and missed out on this beautiful scenery.

After unrolling the blanket and helping each other get comfortable, we lay down facing each other. I don't know how long it was before one of us moved or spoke. We always lost track of time here. I just loved spending time with him and watching his facial reactions.

"So, where were we?" I asked after my arm started feeling asleep.

"I believe we have discussed the basics of the supernatural world. What else did you want to know?"

I thought for a moment, recalling my questions, but they were answered, and now I wasn't sure. "Right now, I have no questions. You answered them all. Do you have any for me?"

"No. You've been more open than any average human teenager. I feel like I have known you my whole life."

"Okay then. What did you bring?" I sat up and looked at the basket.

He pulled out four different containers. "I wasn't sure what you would have preferred, so I brought a variety of food."

"It all looks great. Are you eating as well?"

"No. I ate this morning."

I hesitated, unsure how I felt about hearing him talk so calmly about blood. I guess it is normal for him. I slowly ate picnic food and talked idly with him while I finished.

We soon packed the food, but before he could get up, I

stopped him. I wasn't ready to leave yet. I wanted to watch the sun set before we returned to reality. And hopefully, for another kiss.

"This isn't a good idea." He commented as I straddled him.

"I know, but I'm not ready to leave yet."

"You can't watch the sun from here." He whispered as his hands ran up and down my back. "The trees are blocking it."

"We have a little bit of time before then." I thought it over for a moment. But realizing the time now, I leaned back and signed. We really had a little bit of time, but we needed that to get to someplace where we could watch it. "Alright. I guess we can watch it from your car."

"Let's go. I know a great spot to see the sunset."

"Of course you do."

He laughed as I got off him, and together we got the blanket rolled and packed on top of the food. We headed to the car and drove to his spot, which turned out to be the park.

CHAPTER XXVI

"There are trees here as well." I commented as I got out.

"True, but not where the sun sets." He pointed out as we made our way to the spot. We soon were not alone as his family sat around us, surprising me as I didn't hear them or know why they were here. I was glad to share a nice sunset with his family. They needed the break more than I did.

"Sorry for intruding, but the park is one of the location possibilities. We didn't want you two here alone."

"Besides. A sunset is beautiful and not something you want to miss. Even if it's every evening, something about it is different each day."

I just listened as the family whispered among us. I didn't mind the added people, and we were in a possible spot. Safety in numbers. I didn't even think about it, but Errol must have when he called them and told them where we were going.

We all watched until the last of the rays left the sky, and I used Errol to find my way to his car. The darkness would have frightened me if I were by myself. We made sure nobody left the parking lot by themselves. We drove in a tight line, watching everything until we needed to go our separate ways. Even then, one vehicle followed Errol, and I relaxed into the seat.

"Sorry about the family outing."

"Stop that. I don't mind. I know it's safer right now."

He reached over and squeezed my hand. "You're amazing, you know. Not everybody would be okay with what just happened."

"You guys have dealt with more than anybody should have to. I don't need an explanation for it. We will have more outings by ourselves once Daimon is found and taken care of." I hinted and relaxed into the seat, listening to the quiet night air.

"I hope it's over this week. He can't hide for long, even with Omella helping him."

"You have the map, Pagan's diary, once Clarebelle understands it, and you know who is behind it. I bet by this weekend you will find him. Maybe even before the weekend."

"I hope." He turned to me as he stopped the car. We stared into each other's eyes for a few minutes before he signed and turned away. "You should go. It's late."

"Right." I said, disappointed. On some level, I had hoped he would ask me to stay with him. I knew this wasn't a normal relationship, but sometimes I wish it were.

The next day passed with a shopping spree with Cinnia and our friends in town. Errol had called and said Clarebelle was trying to understand her sister's secret code. She said she was getting closer, and until then, they were waiting for Daimon's next strike. They were walking around town, searching, while waiting. I tried to push it to the back of my mind as I spent more needed time with my cousin and friends.

Christabel bought a lot of college brochures over the summer, and we all sat down at Gustavo's Mexican Grill to help her decide. We were flipping through them while eating our shared shrimp nachos in the outside seating area, waiting for our order to be ready.

"So, I'm weighing on these two." Christabel said, handing them to us and stacking the others in a pile.

Looking at the two, I'm impressed. She wants a liberal arts college, but I didn't think she would aim high. "Go big or go home, huh?" I looked up and saw a deep blush on her. "Nothing wrong with it. These two are the best choices for you."

"Thanks."

"So, what's the difference, and how important are they to you?" Medea asked, approving the choices.

Leaning forward, she pointed to the first. "Berea College is the best in academics, diversity, and value." Pointing to brochure two, she continued. "Centre College has better professors and safety protocols."

"So," Cinnia said, after finishing the last of the nachos. "Why not go to both? You can apply to both, take the tours, and then you can see how different these aspects are and which one better suits you."

"I think Berea College is better." I murmured. I had no idea what I wanted to do in life. "Both are great, but you want a variety of courses so you can try out different ones. It'll help you decide what you want in life, and the value is important as well. Centre does better with their safety protocols for students and would benefit in life."

She signed and started piling them back in her bag as the food arrived. "I know. It is great to have options. Thanks. You have reassured me that both are great."

"You still have time to decide." Medea said as she started eating.

"Not much time, but yes. My parents just want a definite answer. It's their way of coping. I have to have one answer by the end of this week, or they will use that against me to get me to go to their choice."

"They should be happy you have two you like."

"Not with theirs being their option."

"So, they haven't given up on that yet? What about what Reverend Adamus said?"

"They are listening to his advice, but they just can't help themselves, sometimes." She said sadly. She kept her head down as she ate, not noticing the looks we exchanged. I was glad I didn't have to worry about it. Aunt Aida and Uncle Basil were low-key about us and college: it's our choice completely where we go and if we go at all. I just hope Christabel gets to the one she really wants to go to.

Lunch passed to lighter topics, shopping, boys, and sleep-overs, while we finished lunch. We split the bill and left to shop for some more. We ended up weighed down with bags of food, clothes, and gifts. Luckily, we got a car today. Adacio was waiting for us at the end of our shopping trip to bring us home. After dropping Christabel and Medea off, we headed home. He helped us unload the car before he left for the night.

I was exhausted by dinner, but hopeful when I got a call from Errol. "Hey, good or bad news?"

"It's good news. While we are still waiting on Clarebelle,

we have found a few places for sure Daimon's been at. We set traps and are waiting for him to return to them."

"Are you sure he will?"

"Pretty sure. His scent was new. We even found blood stains in one place. We are thinking he fell for the other trap because it was tripped."

"That's great. So, you're closer."

"Yes. Now we just need to keep getting closer. These traps are non-lethal, much to Citino's dismay, but he understands why."

We talked nonstop for over an hour. This was such great news, not much, but they are closer to finishing this. I wonder what life will be like after we don't have to look over our shoulders, deal with the death of a loved one, and just get to relax. We talked until my eyes burned and I had to say good-night. We planned on going out to Lexington for more possible dates. We wanted to see more in Kentucky and heard a lot of great things about Lexington.

This week progressed slowly, and I am waiting on Clarebelle to translate the diary and Daimon to come out of hiding. He knew they were on to him. He had returned to one place, but he managed to get in and out before Errol and them got there. They found a secret exit he used, and now he's quiet.

Lona contacted me to go visit her, as her parents finally gave her permission. Cinnia and I planned a trip together to Wolf Creek in two weeks. I needed a break, and we were still hopeful that this would end this weekend. He couldn't hide forever, even with Omella. Agento was being protective but reasonable, given the reality around the Leigh family. Every day, I got a call from him, verifying I was still alive. He would ask about Daimon and the progress Errol and his family had made, and then he would soon hang up to go to work. I wanted to spend more time with him, but I was so stretched with Cinnia, Errol, our friends, and Lona, I didn't know when I could hang out with him again. He understood, but we were hopeful for next week.

Clarebelle finally made a breakthrough on Thursday afternoon. She got it all translated for us by Friday morning. Garcia showed up to take me over as the guys were hunting, for both blood and Daimon. We stopped and grabbed Palma on our way.

She came out with a package and a grave expression.

"What's wrong?" Garcia asked as Palma sat in the front seat.

"Got a package in the mail. Let's go. I can't say anything without the others." She buckled and looked out the window after setting the package on the seat next to her, leaving Garcia and me exchanging a glance of worry. What could it possibly be?

The ride was short, but that didn't help with the tension in the air. Palma refused to speak again until she was inside the house and surrounded by everyone. We had to wait until the guys arrived, watching anxiously for the package. Luckily, they got there within fifteen minutes.

"So, I went outside this house to the garden, like always, and found this next to my pear tree I started growing." She slowly opened it and showed it to everyone before continuing. "This is disturbing as these belonged to your parents and sister. The note adjusts me and me only."

I gasped as I saw the most beautiful set of gloves, a hair clip with a triangle at the center, and a watch. Looking closer at each item, I noticed the same crest on each, showing a wand, wolf howling, and fangs dripping blood, all connected by a link pointing to the center of a triangle. The fangs were at the top and enhanced to overshadow the others.

"What does it mean? Your family?"

"All vampires, really. But yes, these belonged to my parents and sister." Errol leaned forward and grabbed the watch, turning it to show it in the light. "The crest is not specific for a family. They were created as a means to identify each supernatural being to one another. The witches call it the nexus; the point is the center that serves to join together groups, always connected. The supernatural world is the hidden nexus of the world you live in."

"So, you all have something that has this on it."

"Yes. In which we always wear or carry with us." He leaned back and pulled out his wallet. There it was, plain as day, the symbol dead center. "It's best to keep hidden when needed." He explained before putting it back in his pocket.

Trying to figure it all out, I asked. "So, if you were a werewolf, the wolf would be centered at the top?"

"Yes, and the wand for witches and sorcerers for them. It stays in order by counter-clockwise."

"What does the note say?" Garcia asked.

Palma read it out loud.

Dear Leighs,

Spying on my hideouts will not get me to run away. I will start hunting again soon, and this time I will not hold back. Your precious human friends and family are next. Enough stalling. Bring me what I want, and I will leave town.

*P.S. You have until this weekend before I start with
your family.*
Daimon

She stopped reading and looked at everyone. "He's serious. He knows where I live, which is why he sent it to me. He knows about Gemma as well. What are we going to do?"

"You know we won't let anything happen to you, Aunt Palma, or Gemma." Clarebelle declared.

"I know, dear child. But that doesn't change the outcome."

As everyone debated among themselves, I turned the issue over in my head. I wondered. "Hey, what if we do give him what he wants?" At everyone's look of disbelief, I quickly added. "At least what he thinks he wants. If we can copy a fake book to give him. It will get you all to him. He won't know that it's a fake at first when you hand it to him, and then you can end this."

"That's a great idea." Paio agreed. "If it's possible to do. We only have today to do it by. He purposely didn't give us much time."

"Are you artsy enough to do it?" Palma asked, looking only at me.

"Wait. What? Why me?"

"Because it was your idea, and I know my nieces and nephews have not been in an art class before."

I hesitated, wondering if my limited time recently would be good enough. I wasn't known to be an artist, but I know the basics, and some of my doodles have been good. "I might, but I don't know your ancient language. I don't know if I could copy it."

"I can help you with that." We all turned and gasped as we

saw who the new voice belonged to. Verda was standing in the doorway. She had just taken off a raincoat as we all took her in. "Where can I hang this? The rain outside is pouring. It came out of nowhere."

"Allow me." Palma said, taking on the role of responsibility without conscious awareness. I wondered about the rain as we could hear it, but the weather was calm when we arrived. "Please make yourself comfortable. We are so happy you came."

"I am as well." Sitting in front of us, in the empty chair in which Palma faced, she continued. "I know you all weren't expecting me. I wanted to surprise you. Our families were once close, and this issue affects everybody in the supernatural world. I want to stay and help."

"What does your family say to this?" Clarebelle asked.

"They know everything. They are backing me up from Las Vegas, should we need extra help, and I reassured them I would be fine. You all have my back, and I will use extra caution."

"Well, that's great. I'm glad to know we can look past the past." The uncertainty between the two had emanated as they stared at each other. I wondered why Verda had been so quiet since she left, and if this issue was being communicated between them as we sat quietly for a few minutes.

"I as well." Taking a breath before Verda continued. "So, catch me up. I heard only that we are faking this book. How much time do we have?"

As we caught Verda up, Palma made a quick, small appetizer for everyone. It would be an exceedingly long day. Verda agreed to work with me while Citino, Paio, Errol, and Garcia left to plant some cameras around the added hideouts Clarebelle told us about. Pagan's diary was extremely helpful, and while I wanted to stay and hear more, I knew I had limited time.

Verda and I headed upstairs to start our project at once. The time was spent quietly as we focused on what we needed to do. The beginning and a few pages here and there would be exact, just in case Daimon wanted to look at it from a distance. We had to make him believe it was the real thing. After all, it was not like he would keep the book. He would soon die afterwards for what he'd done and wanted to do with it.

I ended up staying so late that I called home to ask if I could stay overnight. Uncle Basil would swing by with some clothes and toiletries that Cinnia packs for me before he heads to pick up dinner for tomorrow. We were only halfway through the difficult language writing, and the artwork to make it look authentic. We took breaks here and there and talked a little. Garcia and Clarebelle came in to help a few times as well. Verda was nice enough, but I felt a distance with her. We didn't know each other enough to be comfortable. I wondered if her heritage had something to do with her distance. I hoped that after this was over, maybe we could talk, and she would stay in the Leighs' lives; they needed people they could count on. She was friendly, well-organized, and well-mannered for a witch, at least compared to the ones I've watched on TV.

Palma stayed the night as well for her own safety and brought me my bag once it was delivered, saying Uncle Basil was nice but in a hurry. There were a few extra rooms, just enough for all three of us to stay. After finishing the book, thanks to Garcia and Clarebelle's help, I headed downstairs to find someone to help me find my room for the night. Verda went straight to a room she had used before, but I did not want to play pick a room, not knowing which one was empty and which ones were not. Walking around downstairs, I found nobody. I was about to give up when I heard whispers and giggling coming from the backroom, the back entrance. I hesitated, wondering who could be out there. I didn't think anybody would have left, not this close to Daimon's threat, and the more time I took to walk over there, the more nervous I got. I had seen too many horrible films and vowed never to watch them again.

My head fought with itself as I approached the door. Should I open it or go upstairs? Should I find a weapon? Was I being paranoid or not? The voices were in and out, and then I heard noises as they sauntered to the door. I decided to be brave and open the door, but as I tried, the handle wouldn't turn. I stepped back and waited, hoping the people were trying to open it themselves, and it wasn't locked. When it was opened, I breathed out a sigh of relief. It was just Clarebelle and Citino.

"Gemma, what are you doing up?"

"I was heading to bed, but I wasn't sure which one to use. So, I was looking for someone to help me."

"Oh, I'm sorry. I thought someone had shown you. Follow me." Turning to Citino, she said. "Wait here, I'll be back."

"I'll be waiting." The smoldering glance was not meant for me to see, and I turned away.

Walking upstairs with her, I couldn't stay quiet. I wanted my mind to relax for the night. "What were you two doing? I mean, if you don't mind my asking."

She laughed. "I don't mind. We were just getting back from a hunt."

"Oh." I hesitated and recalled how little I had talked to her. Maybe I could use this time wisely. "How did you two meet?

Errol told me your town was vampires only, well, with a few witches." I really did not mean to pry, but I was curious.

"That's true. I met him when I left town for a breather. I felt suffocated with every person being a vampire. I was curious and used that day to shop at the malls that humans love so much." She saw my look of confusion and laughed. "I wasn't looking where I was going, leaving the mall and walking the streets. I had just put my bags in my car and decided to walk around, you know, see what the appeal was all about." She signed as memory took her back, I almost thought she was lost in thought before she continued. "I was taking a turn around a corner and ran into him. It's a really long story; one I hope to continue, but we ran out of time. Here's your room."

I shrugged. "Thanks. I do want to know more about your story. When we have time."

"I look forward to it. I was very distracted by Citino when we first started. Heck, we are still very much distracted. I know you must be curious about your situation as well." She hesitated before she decided to say it. "You know we are recently married, right?"

"Yes. And Garcia and Paio, a few months before you and Citino."

"We never got time alone. The move here put everything on hold. We were hoping for a summer vacation, but that got put on hold as well."

"Oh, like a summer honeymoon."

"If that's what you call it. I'm still learning your ways. Citino has called it a honeymoon before, but I still see it as a quiet retreat from everyone. The chance for us to connect more."

"That's basically what a honeymoon is. Well, outside of the

bedroom. I hope you two do get away. Go someplace warm and beautiful."

"Thank you. I'm glad Errol found you. He's been so lonely since we all started finding each other."

Nodding and turning so she didn't see my face, I motioned to the door. "Well, I should get to bed. Thanks for helping me."

"You're welcome. Good night, Gemma."

"Night, Clarebelle."

CHAPTER XXVII

I woke up to a phone ringing: my phone. I sat up groggy and unaware of my surroundings. Where was my phone? I found it sitting on the floor. Huh, it must have vibrated right off the bedside table. I picked it up as the call ended and waited. If it were important, they would call right back. Sure enough, it started again. Agento was calling.

"Hey," I answered.

He sounded anxious. "Hey, where are you? I came over to see if you wanted to hang out today."

I was confused. "I'm at Errol's. I stayed the night helping them with something. Aunt Aida didn't tell you?"

"Aunt Aida is shopping. I didn't see her, and Cinnia didn't know or wouldn't tell me. I don't know."

"Sorry. I was busy and haven't talked to Cinnia yet. I guessed Aunt Aida would have told her."

His anxiety quickly turned to anger. "What are you doing there that made you stay overnight?"

"Umm," I hesitated, should I tell him? He did know the secret but didn't know how close we were to finding Daimon.

"Don't tell me I have to come over and kick his ass. You didn't-"

"No! I'm helping his family stop Daimon."

"What? I don't want you near that crazy vampire."

"I'm not. I just had to help them with a plan so they can stop him for good. It's ending this weekend, hopefully today."

"Good. Just don't do anything stupid." He slowly calmed down, although I knew he wouldn't be happy. At the same time, I didn't know he would want to hang out today.

"I'm not. I'm glad you called. I wanted to warn you about today."

"About what exactly?"

"Daimon sent them, through Palma, a threatening note. He is threatening everyone in their life this whole weekend. Please, be careful today and don't let anybody you don't know near you."

"I will. You be careful as well. I don't want anything to happen to you." He paused and continued. "What about Cinnia? Does she know about this? How do we tell her?"

"We don't. She can't know. Not right now."

"But she could be a target as well. What should we tell her?"

"Hang on. I have an idea." Pulling the phone from my ear, I texted Cinnia asking her what she had planned this weekend.

After a few moments, she responded.

I'm getting ready to go out now with Marino. Tomorrow, I plan on hanging around the house, you know, cleaning and whatnot. What about you? You stayed at Errol's? What happened? I want details, girl.

I stayed at Errol's to help him and his family with something. I'm still here. I wanted to see what you were doing, and maybe we can hang out tomorrow. And FYI, nothing happened.

Bummer. I look forward to spending the day with you tomorrow. I have to finish getting ready for my day with Marino. He will be here any time.

Wait. When he gets there, can you please tell him to call me? I don't have his number. I want to talk to him before you leave the house.

Sure, no problem.

"All set. Cinnia will not be in danger today or tomorrow." I told Agento. This was just my lucky day, and it was just beginning. Hopefully, it will last all day.

"What do you mean?"

"I will talk to Marino before they leave the house. She's completely safe with him."

"Does that mean what I think it means? Is he a vampire as well?"

"No. Werewolf. And completely safe."

"Okay. For now, but I have questions. Starting with Marino

and ending with Errol. Is there anything else I need to know about? Is anybody else in our lives a supernatural being?"

"No, to both. All is good, and I promise once this is over, we will talk. I understand about having questions, Agento, I was there too."

Within the hour, Marino called me on Cinnia's phone. I had just finished showering, and I was brushing my hair when I grabbed my phone. I explained to him quickly as Cinnia waited in the background. He understood and promised that nothing would happen; he would stay with her all day and keep a look-out. I knew I could count on him, even though he wanted the vampires to leave town. I hoped, for Cinnia's sake, that he would decide to stay. He was good for her, and I wanted to get to know him better as well.

Heading downstairs, I found everyone ready to go. "What's the plan? How do you contact him?"

"He contacted us." Paio explained. "We already set up a meeting place with him. We are to hand over the book, and he promises to leave town without killing anybody."

"Great. What time?"

"In a couple of hours." Citino explained. "Verda will stay here with you and Aunt Palma. We should be back in an hour, maybe two."

I knew I would stay behind. I never wanted to be involved, not that closely, but I did want to make sure nothing bad happened to anybody else. They have lost too much already. I am glad I wouldn't be waiting alone, and I knew everyone I love would be safe today. If Daimon had just left town without meeting them, all would be better. I know he wouldn't, though. He really wanted that book.

"As soon as you all leave, I plan on putting up a protection spell around the house. Just in case." Verda exclaimed. "Make sure you call me on your way back so I have time to disarm it."

"No problem. We are glad you are here. If you need anything in the future, just ask."

"Thanks. I will." The grave expression shared between Verda and Clarebelle made me believe she would be calling them soon enough. I wonder what's going on with her. Hopefully, it won't be something huge, something that will bring more death to this family.

We all sat around the dining table looking over their plan and debating the better ways to go about it. They were prepared for different overcomes and flexibility with whatever Daimon and Omella could possibly throw at them by the time they had to leave. Verda gave them charms to wear to protect them from Omella's magic, as much as she could. I knew it would be difficult with magic involved, but they were hoping to, but not counting on, eliminate Omella early on.

Errol had pulled me outside for some privacy before they left. "I know this must be difficult for you. It is for me as well, but I feel much better with you here with Verda as protection. She's one of the best."

"I know. Just be careful."

"I will. I have my siblings with me. I wish Pagan would be there, but we are doing this for her."

The sadness in his voice made me pull him into a hug. "She is watching, I'm sure."

"Thanks." Pulling back to look into my eyes, he continued. "When this is over, can we go somewhere. There's a place I found just outside of town that I want to show you."

"That sounds great."

"For the weekend?"

I hesitated, unsure what he meant and didn't want to assume.

"We don't have to do anything you don't want to." He quickly said, seeing my hesitation. "I just want to spend more time with you and without family butting in. And we still have the Lexington trip to plan."

"Okay. I would love to go. After this trip, we can discuss Lexington more in-depth. And this weekend."

"We can-"

"Hey, lovebirds. Errol, you need to leave, and Gemma, you need to get inside. I'm setting up the spell now."

"Verda, worst timing ever."

"Love you too. Get going. Show Daimon and Omella why they should fear you and avenge your sister and parents."

"Gladly."

Walking inside, I found Palma in the kitchen, getting stuff out to bake and humming quietly. "Hey, they left."

"Yes. And they will be back, so no worrying is allowed. Come help me make this cake."

I walked over and saw the recipe for a cake. "We are celebrating?"

"Yes. I know they won't eat it, but we will."

"And it will go straight to our hips and butt."

We laughed in harmony, and she passed me the bowl to start mixing. "True, but that's okay. A little fat never hurts anybody."

Together, we mixed the cake mixture from scratch, as Palma had taught me. Verda was just coming in as we turned from putting the cake in the oven. Palma started the timer, and we sat down at the table. For a few minutes, nobody said a word. We all just stared at the plans that lay before us and waited.

"This won't get us anywhere." I said, tired of the quiet and worrying.

"No, and I did say no worrying was allowed. I'm open to suggestions. What did you have in mind?" Palma asked.

"I don't know. I mean, I've never waited on news from people out on a justice mission. We could watch TV, play games, or talk about our lives."

"Good ideas. Verda, sweetie, which one do you want to do?"

"Umm, I guess we could play games. It would pass the time the quickest and keep us busy."

"Wonderful. I'll get the board games, and I will pick the one to play first." She headed to the TV stand and started pulling out games.

We cleaned the table off as she looked through the game choices. Maybe today wouldn't be so bad after all. We played game after game, alternating the person's choice next. In between the games, we pulled the cake out, frosted, and decorated it before setting it in the refrigerator and returning to our games. We laughed, joked around, and felt like long-lost friends coming together again. Verda had loosened up quite a bit, and I never knew how competitive Palma was. Added in my own competitive streak, we were loud and unaware of the noise outside until it pushed through the door with a loud bang.

We all jumped, and Palma pushed me down behind her as Verda stood in front of us, ready to face whoever it was. Omella walked in with a knife in hand and strolled forward until she came up against what seemed like an invisible wall. She smirked.

Verda edged us closer to the stairs as she faced Omella head-on. "Nice try. I don't know how you got in, but you're not getting closer."

Omella laughed as she held up the knife. This is weird. Why would a witch have a knife? What could a knife possibly do against a witch's forcefield? "I think I can if I try hard enough. I do have this and I plan on using it." Showing the knife to Verda, she continued. "You won't be able to stop me. Gemma will die, and so will you, and their precious aunt."

Omella took aim and threw the knife at Verda. Deflecting it easily, Verda turned her attention back to Omella. "That's all you got? You don't realize who you're up against."

"Oh, I knew you would deflect it. But you see, I also knew you just took down your shield."

As she stepped closer, she didn't stop, making Verda stare in shock. "How?"

"You see, dear, that knife is charmed. You broke your nearby magic when you deflected it."

Realizing the mistake, Verda turned to Palma, "Run. I've got this."

She took my hand and pulled me with her as we ran upstairs, leaving Verda to deal with Omella. "Wait," I breathed out breathlessly, "We can't just leave her."

"Yes, we can. You forget she's here to protect us. She's also not a pushover, and Omella doesn't know her full extent of power. She got lucky with that knife, and Verda won't let her get lucky again. Trust me. We need to hide now."

Following Palma through the hall, to the far end, she turned before the door, staring at the wall. "It's here somewhere. It's been so long since I've used it." Palma murmured.

I gasped as I realized she was looking for a secret room.

"Wait, there's a secret room here? How? Didn't they just move here?"

"Yes, but I used to live here and wanted a smaller place, so I moved and offered this place to my sister when she called me to tell me she was coming, that they all were."

"Wow. I didn't know that."

"It's not common knowledge. I didn't even tell my nieces and nephews about it."

"Why?"

She grabbed my hand and huffed. "No time. Help me search. There should be a slight bump on the wall. If you find it, just push to open it. And hurry. We need to hide."

I helped Palma search along the wall, trying to hurry and not worry about Verda. How will I live with myself if something happens? I soon heard Palma call me and rush over. She found it and pulled me in.

It was a small, dark room, fitted with only one chair and an end table. I could barely move around and had only one lamp, darkened by the shade on the lamp but well lit. Palma sat down and watched me as I took it all in. There was no window in here, but the air felt clean. I didn't see a vent, but maybe I overlooked it; it was still dark with the light on. I tried not to jump at every noise I heard from downstairs. I instead focused on the room and what little I saw before turning to Palma.

CHAPTER XXVIII

"So, why did you say earlier that Omella didn't know the full extent of Verda's power? I thought Verda was particularly important in the supernatural world. Wouldn't all witches know it, considering how famous she is?"

"Normally, yes, but I looked into Omella's background. She's a rogue witch and doesn't take too kindly toward the royals. She is a nuisance and stubborn. She may know of Verda, but everyone outside of the royals underestimates their true power. They keep it well hidden and protected. Witches are not known for their goodwill nowadays."

"But Errol said they used to be?"

"Yes."

"What happened?"

"I don't know. I'm not a supernatural being. I'm sure if you ask Verda, she will tell you."

"I'm worried."

"I know, dear. But that won't do you any good."

I sat down on the floor, crisscrossed, as the room only

allowed a little movement. We quietly listened, waiting for the noise to stop.

"I have been wondering, if you don't mind, and it's not a sensitive subject." I hesitated, but couldn't stand hearing the noise of breaking furniture and not doing anything about it. Talking was a great distraction. "I've seen pictures of your husband. Where is he?"

"Recouping. He was in the army but needed time to recover. I haven't seen him in over a year, but he should be home in the next three months. He had a spine injury."

"That's horrible. I mean, I'm glad he's doing well and coming home soon."

"Yes. It's been difficult, but I will be happy to have him home."

"I can't wait to meet him. Can we have a family dinner when he's back and is ready for visitors?"

"I would love that."

After a few more bangs, furniture breaking, and cursing, finally, dead silence came. I held my breath, unsure if I should be happy or worried. I waited to see what Palma would do.

"Give her a minute."

I nodded and stood up, anxiety setting in. At least with the noise, we knew Verda was okay and still fighting. This silence was deadly, and the outcome is unknown to us. Talking was great as I was distracted, but now, I couldn't stop the panic from rising in my throat. I held my breath as we soon heard footsteps coming up the stairs. Palma stood up and pushed me back, but by then the footsteps stopped in front of the door. Palma reached out, ready to open it and waited, holding her breath.

"Palma, it's me." My own breath released as I sat down and waited for Palma to let Verda in. "Thank God I found you."

"Wait, what?" Palma asked and shut Verda in with us.

"She told me she had someone helping, a human. I was worried that person would find you two, and I would be too late. I should have ended it faster, but I really didn't want another person's death on my hands."

"That's not good that she got a human to help her. Did you find anybody out there?"

"I have not, but I also haven't looked much. I need to, but I had to make sure you two were okay first. She will not be a problem anymore, but she did have help, and this fight may not be over just yet."

"Go. We are safe here." Palma interjected.

"Good. I'll be back. Hopefully, Daimon is taken care of as well, and the others will be on their way home."

I let Palma sit in the chair and paced in this small room. The house was huge, so I knew we would be here for a while. I wish we had something else to do. I was no longer worried. I knew a human, if he or she was in fact still here, would be no match for Verda. I never thought I would be claustrophobic, but pacing a few steps only in one direction made me think it was possible. There was no fear, just the need for space.

About ten minutes later, the door suddenly opened, revealing Verda, exhausted from running around the house searching. "Nobody. Are there any other hiding spaces like this one?"

"No. I only built this room for safety. I don't think my nieces and nephews have built any."

"Great. Well, the human helping Omella is not here, so it's safe to come out. You two should go to your guest rooms while

I go downstairs to clean up." She turned and left us with no chance to argue with her.

We walked to our guest rooms and parted ways. I was feeling better knowing nobody was hiding in any closets. I did wonder which human would help an evil witch. Is the town really safe after all? Did I still have to watch my back? Would it be best to just leave town? I really wanted Errol to walk through the door. He would know what's best. Maybe Marino will get his wish after all. Cinnia would be happy, and I know they would make a great couple.

I sat down on my bed, wanting desperately to call Errol, but I knew I couldn't. So, I settled on texting Cinnia to see how her date was going.

> Marino is great. I originally thought that the date was over, but he just found something else to do. I'm not complaining, though. I love spending time with him. I just hope I don't become clingy after today.

> Where has he taken you? It's only been a few hours.

> We ate at the Botanical Gardens and walked the grounds. That is where it was supposed to end, but he said he wanted to see more. We went to the train museum. Now we are heading to the town's historical museum. I wonder what's next? Where else could he possibly want to go?

> I don't know, but I'm glad you are enjoying yourself. Marino is a great guy, and you didn't have other plans for today, right?

No plans, and I am having a great time. I just hope it's not a flute.

I'm sure it's not.

What are you doing today?

Errol went out with his family; something essential for them to do today. I'm hanging out with his aunt and a family friend from out of town until they get back.

Wow. What are they like?

They are a little quiet, but we had fun playing board games. Right now, I'm in the room I slept in.

I want to hear more when we get home tonight. Right now, I have to go. We just arrived.

Go. Have fun today.

I soon heard noises, like a door and voices, coming from downstairs, a few minutes later. Maybe Palma went to help Verda clean up. I walked out of the room and listened closely as I inched my way toward the stairs. I knew I should wait until Verda came and got me, but I was curious, and if Palma got out of her room, why couldn't I? As I neared the stairs, I could hear the different tones in voices and ran up the stairs. I knew those voices. They were finally back. Which meant only one thing: Daimon is out of our lives for good! I couldn't wait to hear the news and to see Errol again.

"-buried now. One less thing for you to worry about." Citino was saying as I reached the bottom of the stairs.

"See. That's where you're wrong, but I appreciate the sentiment." Verda replied as she finished sweeping the room. She noticed me on the stairs and smiled. "All is good. Errol and Paio are taking out the trash as we speak. Clarebelle and Garcia are helping inside."

I released my held breath, unknowingly that I had been holding. "I can help as well."

She shook her head. "No, it's already done. They got back right as I was halfway through." My look of confusion made her laugh. "Vampires are faster than witches at all things, including cleaning."

"Right." I knew that. I guess it took time to remember. They just seemed so normal that I don't think about their abilities all that much.

Suddenly, the two blurs came to a stop. Paio and Errol walked in from the front door, and Errol stood by me. Now, everyone was standing around me, excluding Palma. "Where's Palma?"

"Kitchen. Where else? It's her way of coping with everything." Clarebelle explained. "We are glad you're okay."

"It got interesting for a bit, but Verda handled it smoothly. I didn't know she had such great hidden power."

"Yes. She's badass." Paio said, glancing at Verda and standing next to Garcia with his arm around her back.

She looked away, uncertain of what to do. "Well, umm. Now that it's over, I guess I'll be heading out. It was great to see you all again."

"Don't be a stranger. I know it's been years, but our parents would have wanted us to reconnect." Clarebelle said as she pulled Verda into a hug. Looking her in the eyes after, she continued. "For them and for Pagan, thank you for all your help."

"You're welcome, Clarebelle. I do look forward to seeing you again. Maybe you and Citino can come visit me next time."

"We would love to. Just name the time." Citino said as he walked over and wrapped both arms around Clarebelle.

"You will hear from me." She nodded to the others before stepping away from Clarebelle. "Pagan will be missed. So will Antico and Maya. When I return home, I will give them a proper funeral. The works, just for them."

The family said their goodbyes to Verda, and she soon left. "She left fast." I commented.

"Yes, witches are anxious around vampires, and with our personal history, I'm glad we saw her at all." Paio explained.

"What happened?"

"Right now, I just want to celebrate." Errol whispered to me. Turning to his family, he continued, "Daimon is gone. Antico, Maya, and Pagan will all remain in our hearts. Now is the time to celebrate Daimon's demise. Tomorrow starts the mourning for our lost."

"I couldn't have said it better." Garcia said before she turned away from everyone. Palma finally came out of the kitchen with the cake as Garcia turned the TV on for pop music to fill the parlor.

Errol quickly pulled me from the parlor to talk privately in the kitchen. "If we whisper, they won't hear us over that music."

I laughed at his disgust at the music. "Not a fan?" I whispered.

"No."

Turning serious, I asked what I had been dying to since I saw him. "Nobody was hurt, right? You all seem okay."

"No. Daimon was too easy to kill. It only took Clarebelle to take him down. Not that she's a pushover. She's feisty."

"Wait, she alone killed him?"

"Yes," he smiled, and his love for his sister was clear enough. "She is a fighter. It's why Citino can keep up with her."

"And here I thought it was the other way around."

"Oh, they are perfect for each other. It's why I didn't mind him being human, like Paio at first did."

"Really? Paio had a problem with Citino."

"Yes. At first, they couldn't stand each other. But then we got to know him, and Paio calmed down."

"Wow. Who would have known?"

He chuckled and stepped closer. "I do need to ask you." Pulling on a strand of my hair, he leaned in. "We do have the book, and I was wondering." His hesitation piqued my interest. "Would you consider turning? I wouldn't expect you to now, but in the future, would you?"

I thought it over for a few moments. Weighing the pros and cons. I have thought about it before, but once Errol told me it wasn't possible, I stopped wondering. Now it is, and I had the chance to stay with Errol forever. It turned out to be a no-brainer.

"Yes. In the future, I would love to turn." The expression on Errol's face reminded me of a five-year-old getting every-thing he wanted for Christmas, and I giggled. "How could you think I wouldn't? You know we are soulmates. I want all I can get to be with you."

"I didn't want to force the issue. If you change your mind at any point, I won't mind. I just want you, however you are." He hesitated and stepped back a foot. "But I am glad you chose this option as it gives us a lot more time together."

I stepped up to him and pulled him close, keeping my arms around his neck. I decided to fess up. "I have wanted to from the beginning. The moment I found out. But then you said it wasn't possible, and I stopped thinking about it. There is no doubt in my mind."

"We should return to the celebration. If not, I can't be held responsible for what comes next."

"I don't want it any other way."

The second our lips were touching, someone pushed open the door. We moved apart and saw Palma entering. "I'm sorry, but I have to feed the family. They actually want to eat that cake Gemma and I made from scratch, and we are waiting on you two."

"We will help you with whatever you need. Did you make anything besides the cake?" Errol asked as we watched Palma grab the plates and silverware.

"Yes. Bottom shelf." She nodded to the refrigerator.

With arms full of cups, silverware, plates, and drinks and food, we all headed to the dining table to set it all up around the cake. Clarebelle came over to help us while Garcia danced in the parlor, enjoying the pop music, much to Errol's dismay but to Paio's joy.

We joined in the celebration, ate food, and laughed as a family. Antico, Maya, and Pagan were, hopefully, looking down at us and celebrating for themselves. We never got our kiss that night until he dropped me off at home. But that was okay, as I knew we had a lot more coming in our future. I had hoped for a peaceful summer, but this one was better. I got a new family, a hopeful future with my soulmate, and a new reality of life.

A couple of weeks after I returned home from my weekend getaway with Errol, I got the best news of all. Marino had found a place a few towns away to call home. Cinnia found out his secret and was overjoyed, leading to Errol agreeing to tell her everything about him and his family. And best of all, no stress from a vampire serial killer.

The weekend away was wonderful, and I looked forward to repeating it someday soon. But coming home was just as great, seeing everyone again and talking to Cinnia about everything. Agento was even hanging out with me and the Leighs family. Even the visit to Wolf Creek was the best ever, although something was off with Lona. Neither Cinnia nor I could get her to open up about it. Wolf Creek seemed to have eyes everywhere, watching you like a hawk. The atmosphere was intense, and Lona said she would visit us from then on, as her family didn't like outsiders. Cinnia and I didn't push the issue as we weren't sure what was going on, but the feeling we got there was that we were happy not to visit again anytime soon.

I got a call from Clarebelle the following Friday, saying she wanted to talk to Errol and me about something of utmost importance. He picked me up on his return from hunting, and we walked into a noisy household. Everyone seemed to be talking over each other, and nobody noticed us until Errol hit the play button on the radio and brass music blared out.

"What's going on?"

"Finally, you're here." Clarebelle stated as she walked over to hug us. Turning back to the others, she motioned to Citino, where we saw him standing with two suitcases. "Citino and I are leaving. Garcia is not happy."

"No, because we all should be going. It's clearly dangerous."

"I was asked to only come with Citino. You know how important this is. How frantic she must be to even ask me."

"Wait, hold on. What's going on? Where are you going and who asked you to go?" Errol asked, stepping in between them. I was as curious as he was to know, but I bit my tongue in hopes of learning the truth.

Clarebelle took a breath and turned to look at Errol. "Verda. She needs help, so she asked us to go. Garcia has been arguing with us all morning. She thinks we all should go for safety concerns."

"I see her point. Clarebelle, whatever is happening must be huge."

"I know. I'm not going back on my word. I'm going and so is Citino. If, and that's a big if, we need you guys, we will call. It has taken a lot for Verda to even ask for my help."

He slowly nodded as he thought it over and turned to see everyone's face before turning to me. "What do you think?"

I was surprised but somehow knew why he asked me. I was the neutral party here. "I hate to say it, but Clarebelle is right. With witches and vampires, what you have told me, it must be huge for Verda to ask. But" I continued, looking to Garcia, "having everyone show up will only add to her pressure. You have also told me how she wants to help, but she has a lot riding on her shoulders. Clarebelle and Citino can handle it, I'm sure."

"We will see you off then. And that's the end of it. Garcia, I see your point, but you know this is the right way to go about it. For now."

Suddenly, everyone nodded and started hugging Clarebelle and Citino before we all walked them out. I had a bad feeling, but hopefully, whatever is going on, they don't have the need for backup.

ABOUT THE AUTHOR

Rosalie has her BA in Creative Writing with a focus on fiction through a variety of genres. This passion of hers started in sixth grade through short stories, songs, and screenplays. She has published a short story on Booksie and Wattpad, which she plans on turning into a novel soon. The Nexus trilogy was inspired by her cousin years ago. She enjoys spending her free time reading, drawing, playing with her two cats, and horseback riding. She loves to travel and photograph for inspiration in writing.